W8- BWB- 417

"A taut, nifty exe . . . sey runs the gamut, A to Z, for she's the gutsiest, grittiest female operative going."

—*Daily News*, New York

"One of the better mysteries to come along this year. . . . A sly and delicious mystery concoction. Grafton's sleuth is plucky and funny, not too blusteringly hard-boiled, resourceful without being comic-book heroic, and cynical without lapsing into tired gumshoe disillusionment."

—*Milwaukee Journal*

"With this complex mystery and her ever-deeper glimpses into its heroine, Grafton's series promises to hold readers all the way to Z."

—*Publishers Weekly*

"Raymond Chandler probably wouldn't hesitate to give the Good Crime-Solving Seal of Approval to any of the six investigations into the simple art of murder by Sue Grafton's private eye creation, Kinsey Millhone."

—*The New York Times Book Review*

"Kinsey's face—which is makeup-less, she tells us—is a refreshing one in the world of detective fiction. Grafton's writing is clean and straight up."

—*Boston Herald*

Bantam Crime Line Books offer the finest in classic and modern American mysteries.

Ask your bookseller for the books you have missed.

### Rex Stout

The Black Mountain
Broken Vase
Death of a Dude
Death Times Three
Fer-de-Lance
The Final Deduction
Gambit
Plot It Yourself
The Rubber Band
Some Buried Caesar
Three for the Chair
Too Many Cooks

### Max Allan Collins

The Dark City
Bullet Proof
*coming soon:* Neon Mirage

### Loren Estleman

Peeper

### V. S. Anderson

Blood Lies
King of the Roses

### William Murray

When the Fat Man Sings
The King of the Nightcap

### Eugene Izzi

King of the Hustlers
The Prime Roll
*coming soon:* Invasions

### Gloria Dank

Friends Till the End
Going Out in Style

### Jeffery Deaver

Manhattan Is My Beat
*coming soon:* Death of a Blue
Movie Star

### Robert Goldsborough

Murder in E Minor
Death on Deadline
The Bloodied Ivy
The Last Coincidence

### Sue Grafton

"A" Is for Alibi
"B" Is for Burglar
"C" Is for Corpse
"D" Is for Deadbeat
"E" Is for Evidence
"F" Is for Fugitive

### David Lindsey

In the Lake of the Moon

### Carolyn G. Hart

Design for Murder
Death on Demand
Something Wicked
Honeymoon with Murder
A Little Class on Murder

### Annette Meyers

The Big Killing
*coming soon:* Tender Death

### Rob Kantner

Dirty Work
The Back-Door Man
Hell's Only Half Full
Made in Detroit

### Robert Crais

The Monkey's Raincoat
Stalking the Angel

### Keith Peterson

The Trapdoor
There Fell a Shadow
The Rain
Rough Justice

### David Handler

The Man Who Died Laughing
The Man Who Lived by Night

### Jerry Oster

Club Dead
Internal Affairs

### Benjamin Schutz

Embrace the Wolf
The Things We Do for Love

For Pat Case—

# "F"
# Is for
# Fugitive

## Sue Grafton

*Waverly*

*Sue Grafton*

**BANTAM BOOKS**
NEW YORK · TORONTO · LONDON · SYDNEY · AUCKLAND

This edition contains the complete text
of the original hardcover edition.
NOT ONE WORD HAS BEEN OMITTED.

"F" IS FOR FUGITIVE

A Bantam Book / published by arrangement with
Henry Holt and Company, Inc.

PRINTING HISTORY

Holt edition published May 1989

Bantam edition / May 1990

ISBN 0-553-28478-9

Published simultaneously in the United States and Canada

Bantam Books are published by Bantam Books, a division of Bantam Doubleday Dell Publishing Group, Inc. Its trademark, consist-
ing of the words "Bantam Books" and the portrayal of a rooster, is
Registered in U.S. Patent and Trademark Office and in other
countries. Marca Registrada. Bantam Books, 666 Fifth Avenue,
New York, New York 10103.

PRINTED IN THE UNITED STATES OF AMERICA

OPM     0  9  8  7  6  5  4  3  2  1

*For Marian Wood*
*whose faith keeps me afloat*

The author wishes to acknowledge the invaluable assistance of the following people: Steven Humphrey; Deputy District Attorney Robert P. Samoian, County of Los Angeles; Patricia Barnwell, M.D.; Alan S. Gewant, Pharm.D., and Barbara Long, La Cumbre Pharmacy; Jail Commander Pat Hedges, San Luis Obispo County Jail; Officer Eben Howard, Santa Barbara Police Department; John T. Castle, Castle Forensic Laboratories, Dallas, Texas; Vice President Peter Wisner and Financial Consultant Michael Karry, Merrill Lynch, Pierce, Fenner & Smith Inc.; Lieutenant and Mrs. Tony Baker, Santa Barbara County Sheriff's Department; Anne Reid; Florence Clark; Brent and Sue Anderson; Carter Blackmar; William Pasich and Barbara Knox; and Jerome T. Kay, M.D.

# 1

The Ocean Street Motel in Floral Beach, California, is located, oddly enough, on Ocean Street, a stone's throw from the sea wall that slants ten feet down toward the Pacific. The beach is a wide band of beige trampled with footprints that are smoothed away by the high tide every day. Public access is afforded by a set of concrete stairs with a metal rail. A wooden fishing pier, built out into the water, is anchored at the near end by the office of the Port Harbor Authority, which is painted a virulent blue.

Seventeen years ago, Jean Timberlake's body had been found at the foot of the sea wall, but the spot wasn't visible from where I stood. At the time, Bailey Fowler, an ex-boyfriend of hers, pleaded guilty to voluntary manslaughter. Now he'd changed his tune. Every violent death represents the climax of one story and an introduction to its sequel. My job was to figure out how to write the proper ending to the tale, not easy after so much time had elapsed.

Floral Beach has a population so modest the
number isn't even posted on a sign anywhere. The
town is six streets long and three streets deep, all
bunched up against a steep hill largely covered
with weeds. There may be as many as ten businesses along Ocean: three restaurants, a gift shop,
a pool hall, a grocery store, a T-shirt shop that
rents boogie boards, a Frostee-Freeze, and an art
gallery. Around the corner on Palm, there's a pizza
parlor and a Laundromat. Everything closes down
after five o'clock except the restaurants. Most of
the cottages are one-story board-and-batten, painted
pale green or white, built in the thirties by the
look of them. The lots are small and fenced, many
with power boats moored in the side yards. Sometimes the boats are in better condition than the
properties on which they sit. There are several
boxy stucco apartment buildings with names like
the Sea View, the Tides, and the Surf 'n' Sand.
The whole town resembles the backside of some
other town, but it has a vaguely familiar feel to it,
like a shabby resort where you might have spent a
summer as a kid.

The motel itself is three stories high, painted
lime green, with a length of sidewalk in front that
peters out into patchy grass. I'd been given a room
on the second floor with a balcony that allowed me
to look left as far as the oil refinery (surrounded by
chain-link fence and posted with warning signs)
and to my right as far as Port Harbor Road, a
quarter of a mile away. A big resort hotel with a
golf course is tucked up along the hill, but the

kind of people who stay there would never come down here, despite the cheaper rates.

It was late afternoon and the February sun was setting so rapidly it appeared to be defying the laws of nature. The surf thundered dully, waves washing toward the sea wall like successive buckets of soapy water being sloshed up on the sand. The wind was picking up, but it made no sound, probably because Floral Beach has so few trees. The sea gulls had assembled for supper, settling on the curb to peck at foodstuffs spilling out of the trashcans. Since it was a Tuesday, there weren't many tourists, and the few hardy souls who had walked the beach earlier had fled when the temperature began to drop.

I left the sliding glass door ajar and went back to the table where I was typing up a preliminary report.

My name is Kinsey Millhone. I'm a private investigator, licensed by the state of California, operating ordinarily in the town of Santa Teresa, ninety-five miles north of Los Angeles. Floral Beach is another hour and a half farther up the coast. I'm thirty-two years old, twice married, no kids, currently unattached and likely to remain so given my disposition, which is cautious at best. At the moment, I didn't even have a legitimate address. I'd been living with my landlord, Henry Pitts, while my garage apartment was being rebuilt. My stay at the Ocean Street Motel was being underwritten by Bailey Fowler's father, who had hired me the day before.

I had just moved back into my office, newly refurbished by California Fidelity, the insurance company that accords me space in exchange for my services. The walls had been painted a fresh white. The carpeting was slate blue, a short-pile wool shag that cost twenty-five bucks a yard (exclusive of padding and installation, folks). I know this because I peeked at the invoice the day the carpet was laid. My file cabinet was in place, my desk arranged near the French doors as usual, a new Sparklett's water cooler plugged in and ready to provide both hot and cold trickling water, depending on which button I pushed. This was classy stuff and I was feeling pretty good, almost recovered from the injuries I'd sustained on the last case I worked. Since I'm self-employed, I pay my disability insurance before I even pay my rent.

My first impression of Royce Fowler was of a once-robust man whose aging processes had accelerated suddenly. I guessed him to be in his seventies, somewhat shrunken from an impressive six foot four. It was clear from the way his clothing hung that he'd recently dropped maybe thirty pounds. He looked like a farmer, a cowboy, or a roustabout, someone accustomed to grappling with the elements. His white hair was thinning, combed straight back, with ginger strands still visible along his ears. His eyes were ice blue, brows and lashes sparse, his pale skin mottled with broken capillaries. He used a cane, but the big hands he kept folded together on the crook of it were as steady as stone and speckled with liver spots. He'd been helped into the chair by a woman I thought might be a nurse or a paid companion. He didn't see well enough to drive himself around.

"I'm Royce Fowler," he said. His voice was gravelly and strong. "This is my daughter, Ann. My wife would have driven down with us, but she's a sick woman and I told her to stay at home. We live in Floral Beach."

I introduced myself and shook hands with them both. There was no family resemblance that I could see. His facial features were oversized —big nose, high cheekbones, strong chin—while hers were apologetic. She had dark hair and a slight overbite that should have been corrected when she was a kid.

The quick mental flash I had of Floral Beach was of summer cottages gone to seed and wide, empty streets lined with pickup trucks. "You drove down for the day?"

"I had an appointment at the clinic," he rumbled. "What I got, they can't treat, but they take my money anyway. I thought we should talk to you, as long as we're in town."

His daughter stirred, but said nothing. I pegged her at forty-some and wondered if she still lived at home. So far, she'd avoided making eye contact with me.

I don't do well at small talk, so I shifted down a gear into business mode. "What can I do for you, Mr. Fowler?"

His smile was bitter. "I take it the name doesn't mean much to you."

"Rings a dim bell," I said. "Can you fill me in?"

"My son, Bailey, was arrested in Downey three weeks ago by mistake. They figured out pretty quick they had the wrong man, so they released him within a day. Then I guess they turned around and ran a check on him, and his prints came up a match. He was rearrested night before last."

I nearly said, "A match with what?" but then my memory gave a lurch. I'd seen an article in the local paper. "Ah, yes," I said. "He escaped from San Luis sixteen years ago, didn't he?"

"That's right. I never heard from him after the escape and finally decided he was dead. The boy nearly broke my heart and I guess he's not done yet."

The California Men's Colony near San Luis Obispo is a two-part institution; a minimum-security unit for old men, and a medium-security facility divided into four six-hundred-man sections. Bailey Fowler had apparently walked away from a work detail and hopped on the freight train that rumbled past the prison twice a day back then.

"How'd he get tripped up?"

"There was a warrant out on a fellow named Peter Lambert, the name he was using. He says he was booked, fingerprinted, and in the can before they realized they had the wrong man. As I understand it, some hot-shoe detective got a bug up his butt and ran Bailey's prints through some fancy-pants new computer system they got down there. That's how they picked up on the fugitive warrant. By a damn fluke."

"Bum deal for him," I said. "What's he going to do?"

"I hired him a lawyer. Now he's back, I want him cleared."

"You're appealing the conviction?"

Ann seemed on the verge of a response, but the old man plowed right over her.

"Bailey never went to trial. He made a deal. Pleaded guilty to voluntary manslaughter on the advice of this court-appointed PD, the worthless son of a bitch."

"Really," I said, wondering why Mr. Fowler hadn't hired a lawyer for him at the time. I also wondered what kind of evidence the prosecution had. Usually, the DA won't make a deal unless he knows his case is weak. "What's the new attorney telling you so far?"

"He won't commit himself until he sees the files, but I want to make sure he has all the help he can get. There's no such thing as a private detective up in Floral Beach, which is why we came to you. We need someone to go to work, dig in and see if there's anything left. Couple witnesses died and some have moved away. The whole thing's a damn mess and I want it straightened out."

"How soon would you need me?"

Royce shifted in his chair. "Let's talk money first."

"Fine with me," I said. I pulled out a standard contract and passed it across the desk to him. "Thirty dollars an hour, plus expenses. I'd want an advance."

"I bet you would," he said tartly, but the look in his eyes indicated no offense. "What do I get?"

"I don't know yet. I can't work miracles. I guess it depends on how cooperative the county sheriff's department is."

"I wouldn't count on them. Sheriff's department doesn't like Bailey. They never liked him much, and his escape didn't warm any hearts. Made all those people look like idiots."

"Where's he being held?"

"L.A. County Jail. He's being moved up to San Luis tomorrow is what we heard."

"Have you talked to him?"

"Just briefly yesterday."

"Must have been a shock."

"I thought I was hearing things. Thought I'd had a stroke."

Ann spoke up. "Bailey always told Pop he was innocent."

"Well, he is!" Royce snapped. "I said that from the first. He never would have killed Jean under any circumstance."

"I'm not arguing, Pop. I'm just telling *her*."

Royce didn't bother to apologize, but his tone underwent a change. "I don't have long," he went on. "I want this squared away before I go. You find out who killed her and I'll see there's a bonus."

"That's not necessary," I said. "You'll get a written report once a week and we can talk as often as you like."

"All right, then. I own a motel up in Floral Beach. You can stay free of charge for as long as you need. Take your meals with us. Ann here cooks."

She flashed a look at him. "She might not want to take her meals with us."

"Let her say so, if that's the case. Nobody's forcing her to do anything."

She colored up at that but said nothing more.

Nice family, I thought. I couldn't wait to meet the rest. Ordinarily, I don't take on clients sight unseen, but I was intrigued by the situation and I needed the work, not for the money so much as my mental health. "What's the timetable here?"

"You can drive up tomorrow. The attorney's in San Luis. He'll tell you what he wants."

I filled out the contract and watched Royce Fowler sign. I added my signature, gave him one copy, and kept the other for my files. The check he took from his wallet was already made out to me in the amount of two grand. The man had confidence, I had to give him that. I glanced at the clock as the two of them left. The entire transaction hadn't taken more than twenty minutes.

I closed the office early and dropped my car off at the mechanic's for a tune-up. I drive a fifteen-year-old VW, one of those homely beige models with assorted dents. It rattles and it's rusty, but it's paid for, it runs fine, and it's cheap on gas. I walked home from the garage through a perfect February afternoon—sunny and clear, with the temperature hovering in the sixties. Winter storms had been blowing through at intervals since Christmas and the mountains were dark green, the fire danger laid to rest until summer rolled around again.

I live near the beach on a narrow side street that parallels Cabana Boulevard. My garage apartment, flattened by a bomb during the Christmas holidays, had now been reframed, though Henry was being coy about the plans he'd drawn up. He and the contractor had had their heads bent together for weeks, but so far he'd declined to let me see the blueprints.

I don't spend a lot of time at home, so I didn't much care what the place looked like. My real worry was that Henry would make it too large or too opulent and I'd feel obliged to pay him accordingly. My current rent is only two hundred bucks a month, unheard-of these days. With my car paid for and my office space underwritten by California Fidelity, I can live very well on a modest monthly sum. I don't want an apartment too fancy for my pocketbook. Still, the property is his and he can do with it as he pleases. Altogether, I thought it best to mind my own business and let him do what suited him.

# 2

I let myself in through the gate and circled the new construction to Henry's patio in the rear. He was standing near the back fence, chatting with our next-door neighbor while he hosed down the flagstones. He didn't miss a beat, but his gaze flicked over to the sight of me, and a slight smile crossed his face. I never think of him as elderly, though he'd celebrated his eighty-second birthday on Valentine's Day, the week before. He's tall and lean, with a narrow face, and blue eyes the color of gas jets. He's got a shock of soft white hair that he wears brushed to one side, good teeth (all his), a year-round tan. His overriding intelligence is tempered with warmth, and his curiosity hasn't diminished a whit with age. Until his retirement, he worked as a commercial baker. He still can't resist making breads and sweet rolls, cookies and cakes, which he trades to merchants in the area for goods and services. His current passion is designing crossword puzzles for those little paperback publications you can pick up in a supermarket check-out line. He also clips coupons, priding himself on all the money he saves. At Thanksgiving, for instance, he managed to buy a twenty-three-pound turkey for only seven bucks. Then, of course, he had to invite fifteen people in to help him polish it off. If I had to find fault with him, I suppose I'd have to cite his gullibility, and a tendency to be passive when he ought to take a stand and fight. In some ways, I see myself as his protector, a notion that might amuse him, as he probably sees himself as mine.

I still wasn't used to living under the same roof with him. My stay was temporary, just until my apartment was finished, perhaps another month. Peripheral damage to his place had been speedily repaired, except for the sun porch, which was demolished along with the garage. I had my own key to the house and I came and went as I pleased, but there were times when the emotional claustrophobia got to me. I like Henry. A lot. There couldn't be anyone better-natured than he, but I've been on my own for eight years plus, and I'm not used to having anyone at such close range. It was making me edgy, as if he might have some expectation of me that I could never meet. Perversely, I found myself feeling guilty for my own uneasiness.

When I let myself in the back door, I could smell something cooking: onions, garlic, tomatoes, probably a chicken dish. A dome of freshly baked bread was resting on a metal rack. The kitchen table was set for two. Henry'd had a girlfriend briefly, who'd redecorated his kitchen. At the time, she'd been hoping to rearrange his life savings— twenty thousand in cash, which she thought might look better in her own bank account. She was thwarted, thanks to me, and all that remained of her, at this point, were the kitchen curtains, green print cotton tied back with green bows. Henry was currently using the color-coordinated table napkins for handkerchiefs. We never spoke of Lila, but I sometimes wondered if he didn't secretly resent my intrusion into his romance. Sometimes being fooled by love is worth the price. At least you know you're alive and capable of feeling, even if all you end up with is chest pain.

I moved through the hallway to the small back bedroom I was currently calling home. Just walking in the door had made me feel restless and I thought ahead to the trip to Floral Beach with relief. Outside, I heard the squawk of the faucet being turned off and I could picture Henry neatly recoiling the hose. The screen door banged, and in a moment I heard the creak of his rocker, the rustle of the newspaper as he folded it over to the sports section, which he always read first.

There was a small pile of clean clothes at the foot of the bed. I crossed to the chest of drawers and stared at myself in the mirror. I looked cranky, no doubt about it. My hair is dark and I cut it myself with a pair of nail scissors every six weeks. The effect is just about what you'd expect—ragged, inexpert. Recently, someone told me it looked

like a dog's rear end. I ran my hands through my
mop, but it didn't do much good. My brow was
furrowed in a little knot of discontent, which I
smoothed with one finger. Hazel eyes, dark lashes.
My nose blows real good and it's remarkably
straight, considering it's been broken twice. Like a
chimp, I bared my teeth, satisfied to see them
(more or less) lined up right. I don't wear makeup.
I'd probably look better if I did something with
my eyes—mascara, eyebrow pencil, eye shadow in
two shades—but then I'd be forever fooling around
with the stuff, which seems like a waste of time. I
was raised, for the most part, by a maiden aunt
whose notion of beauty care was an occasional
swipe of cold cream underneath her eyes. I was
never taught to be girlish, so here I am, at thirty-
two, stuck with a face unadorned by cosmetic sub-
terfuge. As it is, we could not call mine a beautiful
puss, but it does the job well enough, distinguish-
ing the front of my head from the back. Which was
neither here nor there, as my appearance was not
the source of my disquiet. So what was my problem?

I went back to the kitchen and paused in the
doorway. Henry had poured himself a drink as he
does every night; Black Jack on the rocks. He
glanced at me idly and then did a proper double
take, fixing me with a look. "What's wrong?"

"I got a job today up in Floral Beach. I'll
probably be gone a week to ten days."

"Oh. Is that all? That's good. You need a
change." He turned back to the paper, leafing
through the section on local news.

I stood there and stared at the back of his head. A painting by Whistler came immediately to mind. In a flash, I understood what was going on. "Henry, are you mothering me?"

"What makes you say that?"

"Being here feels weird."

"In what way?"

"I don't know. Dinner on the table, stuff like that."

"I like to eat. Sometimes I eat two, three times a day," he said placidly. He found the crossword puzzle at the bottom of the funnies and reached for a ballpoint pen. He wasn't giving this nearly the attention it deserved.

"You swore you wouldn't fuss over me if I moved in."

"I don't fuss."

"You *do* fuss."

"You're the one fussing. I haven't said a word."

"What about the laundry? You've got clothes folded up at the foot of my bed."

"Throw 'em on the floor if you don't like 'em there."

"Come on, Henry. That's not the point. I said I'd do my own laundry and you agreed."

Henry shrugged. "Hey, so I'm a liar. What can I say?"

"Would you quit? I don't need a mother."

"You need a *keeper*. I've said so for months. You don't have a clue how to take care of yourself. You eat junk. Get beat up. Place gets blown to bits. I told you to get a dog, but you refuse. So now you got me, and if you ask me, it serves you right."

How irksome. I felt like one of those ducklings inexplicably bonded to a mother cat. My parents had been killed in a car wreck when I was five. In the absence of real family, I'd simply done without. Now, apparently, old dependencies had surfaced. I knew what *that* meant. This man was eighty-two. Who knew how long he'd live? Just about the time I let myself get attached to him, he'd drop dead. Ha, ha, the joke's on you, again.

"I don't want a parent. I want you as a friend."

"I am a friend."

"Well, then, cut the nonsense. It's making me nuts."

Henry's smile was benign as he checked his watch. "You've got time for a run before dinner if you quit mouthing off."

That stopped me. I'd really hoped to get a run in before dark. It was almost four-thirty, and a glance at the kitchen window showed I didn't have long. I abandoned my complaints and changed into jogging sweats.

The beach that day was odd. The passing stormclouds had stained the horizon a sepia shade. The mountains were a drab brown, the sky a poisonous-looking tincture of iodine. Maybe Los Angeles was burning to the ground, sending up this mirage of copper-colored smoke turning umber at the edge. I ran along the bike path that borders the sand.

The Santa Teresa coastline actually runs east

and west. On a map, it looks like the ragged terrain takes a sudden left turn, heading briefly out to sea before the currents force it back. The islands were visible, hovering offshore, the channel dotted with oil rigs that sparkled with light. It's worrisome, but true, that the oil rigs have taken on an eerie beauty of their own, as natural to the eye now as orbiting satellites.

By the time I made the turnaround a mile and a half down the path, twilight had descended and the streetlights were ablaze. It was getting cold and the air smelled of salt, the surf battering the beach. There were boats anchored beyond the breakers, the poor man's yacht harbor. The traffic was a comfort, illuminating the grassy strip between the sidewalk and the bike path. I try to run every day, not from passion, but because it's saved my life more than once. In addition to the jogging, I usually lift weights three times a week, but I'd had to discontinue that temporarily, due to injuries.

By the time I got home, I was in a better mood. There's no way to sustain anxiety or depression when you're out of breath. Something in the sweat seems to bring cheer in its wake. We ate supper, chatting companionably, and then I went to my room and packed a bag for the trip. I hadn't begun to think about the situation up in Floral Beach, but I took a minute to open a file folder, which I labeled with Bailey Fowler's name. I sorted through the newspapers stacked up in the utility room, clipping the section that detailed his arrest.

According to the article, he'd been out on

parole on an armed-robbery conviction at the time
his seventeen-year-old ex-sweetheart was found
strangled to death. Residents of the resort town
reported that Fowler, then twenty-three, had been
involved in drugs off and on for years, and spec-
ulated that he'd killed the girl when he learned of
her romantic entanglement with a friend of his.
With the plea bargain, he'd been sentenced to six
years in the state prison. He'd served less than a
year at the Men's Colony at San Luis Obispo when
he engineered his escape. He left California, assuming the alias of Peter Lambert. After a number
of miscellaneous sales jobs, he'd gone to work for a
clothing manufacturer with outlets in Arizona, Col-
orado, New Mexico, and California. In 1979, the
company had promoted him to western division
manager. He was transferred to Los Angeles, where
he'd been residing ever since. The newspaper indicated that his colleagues were stunned to learn
he'd ever been in trouble. They described him as
hardworking, competent, outgoing, articulate, active in church and community affairs.

The black-and-white photograph of Bailey
Fowler showed a man maybe forty years old, half-
turned toward the camera, his face blank with
disbelief. His features were strong, a refined version of his father's, with the same pugnacious jaw-
line. An inset showed the police photograph taken
of him seventeen years before, when he was booked
for the murder of Jean Timberlake. Since then, his
hairline had receded slightly and there was a suggestion that he may have darkened the color, but

then again that might have been a function of age or the quality of the photograph. He'd been a handsome kid, and he wasn't bad looking now.

Curious, I thought, that a man can reinvent himself. There was something enormously appealing in the idea of setting one persona aside and constructing a second to take its place. I wondered if serving out his sentence in prison would have had as laudatory an effect as being out in the world, getting on with his life. There was no mention of a family, so I had to guess he'd never married. Unless this new attorney of his was a legal wizard, he'd have to serve the remaining years of his original sentence, plus an additional sixteen months to two years on the felony escape charge. He could be forty-seven by the time he was released, years he probably wasn't interested in giving up without a fight.

The current paper had a follow-up article, which I also clipped. For the most part, it was a repetition of the first, except that a high school yearbook photo of the murdered girl was included along with his. She'd been a senior. Her dark hair was glossy and straight, cut to the shape of her face, parted in the middle and curving in softly at the nape of her neck. Her eyes were pale, lined with black, her mouth wide and sensual. There was the barest suggestion of a smile, and it gave her an air of knowing something the rest of us might not be aware of yet.

I slipped the clippings in the folder, which I tucked into the outside pocket of my canvas duffel.

I'd stop by the office and pick up my portable typewriter en route.

At nine the next morning, I was on the road, heading up the pass that cuts through the San Rafael Mountains. As the two-lane highway crested, I glanced to my right, struck by the sweep of undulating hills that move northward, intersected by bare bluffs. The rugged terrain is tinted to a hazy blue-gray by the nature of the underlying rock. The land here has lifted, and now the ridges of shale and sandstone project in a visible spine called the Transverse Ranges. Geological experts have concluded that California, west of the San Andreas Fault, has moved north up the Pacific coast by about three hundred miles during the last thirty million years. The Pacific Plate is still grinding away at the continent, buckling the coastal regions in earthquake after earthquake. That we continue to go about our daily business without much thought for this process is either testimony to our fortitude or evidence of lunacy. Actually, the only quakes I've experienced have been minor temblors that rattle dishes on the shelf or set the coat hangers in the closet to tinkling merrily. The sensation is no more alarming than being shaken awake gently by someone too polite to call your name. People in San Francisco, Coalinga, and Los Angeles will have a different tale to tell, but in Santa Teresa (aside from the Big One in 1925) we've had mild, friendly earthquakes that do little more than slop some of the water out of our swimming pools.

The road eased down into the valley, intersecting Highway 101 some ten miles beyond. At 10:35, I took the Floral Beach exit, heading west toward the ocean through grassy, rolling hills dotted with oaks. I could smell the Pacific long before I laid eyes on it. Screeching sea gulls heralded its appearance, but I was still surprised by the breadth of that flat line of blue. I hung a left onto the main street of Floral Beach, the ocean on my right. The motel was visible three blocks away, the only three-story structure on Ocean Street. I pulled into a fifteen-minute parking space outside the registration office, grabbed my duffel, and went in.

# 3

The office was small, the registration desk blocking off access to what I surmised were the Fowlers' personal quarters in the rear. My crossing the threshold had triggered a soft bell.

"Be right out," someone called. It sounded like Ann.

I moved to the counter and peered to my right. Through an open door, I caught a glimpse of a hospital bed. There was the murmur of voices, but I couldn't see a soul. I heard the muffled flushing of a toilet, pipes clanking noisily. The air was soon scented with the artificial bouquet of room spray, impossibly sweet. Nothing in nature has ever smelled like that.

Several minutes passed. There was no seating available, so I stood where I was, turning to survey the narrow room. The carpeting was harvest gold, the walls paneled in knotty pine. A painting of autumn birches with fiery orange and yellow leaves hung above a maple coffee table on which a rack of pamphlets promoted points of interest and local businesses. I leafed through the display, picking up a brochure for the Eucalyptus Mineral Hot Springs, which I'd passed on the road coming in. The advertisement was for mud baths, hot tubs, and rooms at "reasonable" rates, whatever that meant.

"Jean Timberlake worked there in the afternoons after school," Ann said behind me. She was standing in the doorway, wearing navy slacks and a white silk shirt. She seemed more relaxed than she had in her father's company. She'd had her hair done and it fell in loose waves to her shoulders, steering the eye away from the slightly recessed chin.

I put the pamphlet back. "Doing what?" I asked.

"Maid service, part-time. She worked for us, too, a couple of days a week."

"Did you know her well?"

"Well enough," she said. "She and Bailey started dating when he was twenty. She was a freshman in high school." Ann's eyes were mild brown, her manner detached.

"A little young for him, wasn't she?"

Her smile was brief. "Fourteen." Any other comment was curtailed by a voice from the other room.

"Ann, is someone out there? You said you'd be right back. What's happening?"

"You'll want to meet Mother," Ann murmured

in a way that generated doubts. She lifted a hinged section of the counter and I passed through.

"How's your father doing?"

"Not good. Yesterday was hard on him. He was up for a while this morning, but he's easily fatigued and I suggested he go back to bed."

"You've really got your hands full."

She flashed me a pained smile. "I've had to take a leave of absence."

"What sort of work?"

"I'm a guidance counselor at the high school. Who knows when I'll get back."

I let her lead the way into the living room, where Mrs. Fowler was now propped up in the full-sized hospital bed. She was gray-haired and heavy, her dark eyes magnified by thick glasses in heavy plastic frames. She was wearing a white cotton hospital gown that tied down the back. The neck was plain, with SAN LUIS OBISPO COUNTY HOSPITAL inked in block letters along the rim. It struck me as curious that she'd affect such garb when she could have worn a bed jacket or a gown and robe of her own. Illness as theater, perhaps. Her legs lay on top of the bedclothes like haunches of meat not yet trimmed of fat. Her pudgy feet were bare, and her toes were mottled gray.

I crossed to the bed, holding my hand toward hers. "Hi, how are you? I'm Kinsey Millhone," I said. We shook hands, if that's what you'd call it. Her fingers were as cold and rubbery as cooked rigatoni. "Your husband mentioned you weren't feeling well," I went on.

She put her handkerchief to her mouth and promptly burst into tears. "Oh, Kenny, I'm sorry. I can't help myself. I'm just all turned around with Bailey showing up. We thought he was dead and here he comes again. I've been sick for years, but this has just made it worse."

"I can understand your distress. It's Kinsey," I said.

"It's what?"

"My first name is Kinsey, my mother's maiden name. I thought you said 'Kenny' and I wasn't sure you heard it right."

"Oh Lord. I'm so sorry. My hearing's nearly gone and I can't brag about my eyes. Ann, honey, fetch a chair. I can't think where your manners went." She reached for a Kleenex and honked into it.

"This is fine," I said. "I've just driven up from Santa Teresa, so it feels good to be on my feet."

"Kinsey's the investigator Pop hired yesterday."

"I know that," Mrs. Fowler said. She began to fuss with her cotton cover, plucking it this way and that, made restless by topics that didn't pertain to her. "I hoped to get myself all cleaned up, but Ann said she had errands. I hate to interfere with her any more than I have to, but there's just things I can't do with my arthritis so bad. Now, look at me. I'm a mess. I'm Ori, short for Oribelle. You must think I'm a sight."

"Not at all. You look fine." I tell lies all the time. One more couldn't hurt.

"I'm diabetic," she said, as though I'd asked. "Have been all my life, and what a toll it's took. I got tingling and numbness in my extremities, kidney problems, bad feet, and now I've developed arthritis on top of that." She held a hand out for my inspection. I expected knuckles as swollen as a prizefighter's, but they looked fine to me.

"I'm sorry to hear that. It must be rough."

"Well, I've made up my mind I will not complain," she said. "If it's anything I despise, it's people who can't accept their lot."

Ann said, "Mother, you mentioned tea a little while ago. How about you, Kinsey? Will you have a cup?"

"I'm all right for now. Thanks."

"None for me, hon," Ori said. "My taste for it passed, but you go ahead and fix some for yourself."

"I'll put the water on."

Ann excused herself and left the room. I stood there wishing I could do the same. What I could see of the apartment looked much like the office: gold high-low carpeting, Early American furniture, probably from Montgomery Ward. A painting of Jesus hung on the wall at the foot of the bed. He had his palms open, eyes lifted toward heaven— pained, no doubt, by Ori's home decorating taste. She caught my eye.

"Bailey gave me that pitcher. It's just the kind of boy he was."

"It's very nice," I replied, then quizzed her

while I could. "How'd he get mixed up in a murder charge?"

"Well, it wasn't his fault. He fell in with bad company. He didn't do good in high school and after he got out, he couldn't find him a job. And then he ran into Tap Granger. I detested that no-account the minute I laid eyes on him, the two of 'em running around till all hours, getting into trouble. Royce was having fits."

"Bailey was dating Jean Timberlake by then?"

"I guess that's right," she said, apparently hazy on the details after so much time had passed. "She was a sweet girl, despite what everybody said about that mother of hers."

The telephone rang and she reached over to the bed table to pick it up. "Motel," she said. "Unh-hunh, that's right. This month or next? Just a minute, I'll check." She pulled the reservation book closer, removing a pencil from between the pages. I watched her flip forward into March, peering closely at the print. Her tone, as she conducted business, was completely matter-of-fact. Gone was the suggestion of infirmity that marked her ordinary speech. She licked the pencil point and made a note, discussing king-sized beds versus queen.

I took the opportunity to go in search of Ann. A doorway on the far wall led out into a hallway, with rooms opening off the central corridor in either direction. On the right, there was a staircase, leading to the floor above. I could hear water being run and then the faint tap of the teakettle on the burner in the kitchen to my left. It was hard to get a fix on the overall floor plan and I had to guess the apartment had been patched together from a number of motel rooms with the intervening walls punched out. The resulting town house was spacious, but jerry-built, with the traffic patterns of a maze. I peeked into the room across the hall. Dining room with a bath attached. There was access to the kitchen through what must have been an alcove for hanging clothes. I paused in the doorway. Ann was setting cups and saucers on an industrial-sized aluminum serving tray.

"Need any help?"

She shook her head. "Look around if you like. Daddy built the place himself when he and Mother first got married."

"Nice," I said.

"Well, it's not anymore, but it was perfect for them. Has she given you a key yet? You might want to take your bags up. I think she's putting you in room twenty-two upstairs. It's got an ocean view and a little kitchenette."

"Thanks. That's great. I'll take my bags up in a bit. I'm hoping to talk to the attorney this afternoon."

"I think Pop set up an appointment for you at one-forty-five. He'll probably want to tag along if he's feeling up to it. He tends to want to stage-manage. I hope that's all right."

"Actually, it's not. I'll want to go alone. Your

parents seem defensive about Bailey, and I don't
want to have to cope with that when I'm trying to
get a rundown on the case."

"Yes. All right. I can see your point. I'll see if
I can talk Pop out of it."

Water began to rumble in the bottom of the
kettle. She took teabags from a red-and-white tin
canister on the counter. The kitchen itself was
old-fashioned. The linoleum was a pale gridwork
of squares in beige and green, like an aerial view
of hay and alfalfa fields. The gas stove was white
with chrome trim, unused burners concealed by
jointed panels that folded back. The sink was shallow, of white porcelain, supported by two stubby
legs, the refrigerator small, round-shouldered, and
yellowing with age, probably with a freezer com-
partment the size of a bread box.

The teakettle began to whistle. Ann turned
the burner off and poured boiling water in a white
teapot. "What do you take?"

"Plain is fine."

I followed her back into the living room, where
Ori was struggling to get out of bed. She'd already
swung her feet over the side, her gown hitching
up to expose the crinkled white of her thighs.

"Mother, what are you doing?"

"I have to go sit on the pot again, and you
were taking so long I didn't think I could wait."

"Why didn't you call? You know you're not
supposed to get up without help. Honestly!" Ann
set the tray down on a wooden serving cart and

moved over to the bed to give her mother a hand. Ori descended ponderously, her wide knees trembling visibly as they took her weight. The two proceeded awkwardly into the other room.

"Why don't I go ahead and get my things out of the car?"

"Do that," she called. "We won't be long."

The breeze off the ocean was chilly, but the sun was out. I shaded my eyes for a moment, peering at the town, where pedestrian traffic was picking up as the noon hour approached. Two young mothers crossed the street at a languid pace, pushing strollers, while a dog pranced along behind them with a Frisbee in his mouth. This was not the tourist season, and the beach was sparsely populated. Empty playground equipment was rooted in the sand. The only sounds were the constant shushing of the surf and the high, thin whine of a small plane overhead.

I retrieved my duffel and the typewriter, bumping my way back into the office. By the time I reached the living room, Ann was helping Ori into bed again. I paused, waiting for them to notice me.

"I need my lunch," Ori was saying querulously to Ann.

"Fine, Mother. Let's go ahead and do a test. We should have done it hours ago, anyway."

"I don't want to fool with it! I don't feel that good."

I could see Ann curbing her temper at the

tone her mother used. She closed her eyes. "You're under a lot of stress," she said evenly. "Dr. Ortego wants you to be very careful till he sees you next."

"He didn't tell *me* that."

"That's because you didn't talk to him."

"Well, I don't like Mexicans."

"He's not Mexican. He's Spanish."

"I still can't understand a word he says. Why can't I have a real doctor who speaks English?"

"I'll be right with you, Kinsey," Ann murmured, catching sight of me. "Let me just get Mother settled first."

"I can take my bags up if you tell me where they go."

There was a brief territorial dispute as the two of them argued about which room to put me in. In the meantime, Ann was taking out cotton balls, alcohol, and some sort of testing strip sealed in a paper packet. I looked on with discomfort, an unwilling witness as she swabbed her mother's fingertip and pierced it with a lancet. I could feel myself going nearly cross-eyed with distaste. I moved over to the bookcase, feigning interest in the titles on the shelves. Lots of inspirational reading and condensed versions of Leon Uris books. I pulled out a volume at random and leafed through, blocking out the scene behind me.

I waited a decent interval, tucked the book away, and then turned back casually. Ann had apparently read the test results from the digital display on a meter by the bed and was filling a syringe from a small vial of pale, milky liquid I presumed was insulin. I busied myself with a glass paperweight—a Nativity scene in a swirling cloud of snow. Baby Jesus was no bigger than a paper clip. God, I'm a sissy when it comes to shots.

From the rustling sounds behind me, I surmised they were done. Ann broke the needle off the disposable syringe and tossed it in the trash. She tidied up the bed table and then we moved out to the desk so she could give me my room key. Ori was already calling out a request.

# 4

By one-thirty, I had driven the twelve miles to San Luis Obispo and I was circling through the downtown area, trying to orient myself and get a feel for the place. The commercial buildings are two to four stories high and immaculately maintained. This is clearly a museum town, with Spanish and Victorian structures restored and adapted to current use. The storefronts are painted in handsome dark shades, many with awnings arching over the windows. The establishments seem to be divided just about equally between trendy clothing stores and trendy restaurants. Carrotwood trees border most avenues, with strings of tiny Italian lights woven into branches bursting with green. Any businesses not catering directly to the tourists seem geared to the tastes of the Cal Poly students in evidence everywhere.

Bailey Fowler's new attorney was a man named Jack Clemson, with an address on Mill, a block from the courthouse. I pulled into a parking space

and locked my car. The office was located in a
small, brown frame cottage with a pointed gable in
the roof and a narrow wooden porch enclosed by
trellises. A white picket fence surrounded the property, with a tangle of geraniums crowding in among
the pales. Judging from the lettered sign affixed to
the gate, Jack Clemson was the sole tenant.

I climbed the wooden porch steps and moved
into the entrance hall now furnished as a reception
area. A grandfather clock on the wall to my left
gave the only sense of life, the brass pendulum
snick-snacking back and forth mechanically. The
former parlor on the right was lined with old-
fashioned, glass-fronted oak bookcases. There was
an oak desk with a typing ell, a swivel chair, a
Xerox machine, but no secretary in sight. The
screen on the computer monitor was blank, the
surface of the desk neatly stacked with legal briefs
and brown accordion files tied with string. Across
the hall, the door to the matching parlor was shut.
One of the buttons on the telephone was lighted
and I could smell fresh cigarette smoke drifting
out from somewhere in the back. Otherwise, the
office seemed deserted.

I took a seat in an old church pew with a slot
for hymnals underneath the bench. It was filled
now with alumni journals from Columbia Univer-
sity Law School, which I leafed through idly. Presently, I heard footsteps and Clemson appeared.

"Miss Millhone? Jack Clemson. Nice to meet
you. You'll have to pardon the reception. My sec-

retary's out sick and the temp's still off at lunch. Come on back."

We shook hands and I followed him. He was maybe fifty-five and heavyset, one of those men who'd probably been considered portly since birth. He was short and squat, wide-shouldered and balding. His features were babified: sparse eyebrows and a soft, undefined nose with red dents along the bridge. A pair of tortoiseshell reading glasses were shoved up on his head, and strands of hair were standing straight up on end. His shirt collar was unbuttoned and his tie was loose. Apparently he hadn't had time to shave, and he scratched at his chin experimentally as if to gauge the morning's growth. His suit was tobacco brown, impeccably tailored, but wrinkled across the seat.

His office occupied the entire rear half of the building, and had French doors that opened out onto a sunny deck. Both of the dark green leather chairs intended for clients were piled high with legal briefs. Clemson scooped up an armload of books and files and set them on the floor, motioning for me to take a seat while he went around to the far side of the desk. He caught a glimpse of himself in the mirror hanging on the wall to his left, and his hand returned involuntarily to the stubble on his chin. He sat down and pulled a portable electric razor from his desk drawer. He flicked it on and began to slide it around his face with a practiced hand, mowing a clean path across his upper lip. The shaver buzzed like a distant airplane.

"I got a court date in thirty minutes. Sorry I can't spare you any more time this afternoon."

"That's all right," I said. "When does Bailey get in?"

"He's probably here by now. Deputy drove down this morning to bring him back. I made arrangements for you to see him at three-fifteen. It's not regular visiting hours, but Quintana said it's okay. It's his case. He was rookie of the year back then."

"What about the arraignment?"

"Eight-thirty tomorrow morning. If you're interested, you can come here first and walk over with me. That'll give us a chance to compare notes."

"I'd like that."

Clemson made a note on his desk calendar. "Will you be going back over to the Ocean Street this afternoon?"

"Sure."

He tucked the electric shaver away and closed the desk drawer. He reached for some papers, which he folded and slipped into an envelope, scrawling Royce's name across the front. "Tell Royce this is ready for his signature," he said.

I tucked the envelope in my handbag.

"How much of the background on this have you been told?"

"Not much."

He lit a cigarette, coughing into his fist. He shook his head, apparently annoyed by the state of his lungs. "I had a long talk this morning with Clifford Lehto, the PD who handled Fowler's case.

He's retired now. Nice man. Bought a vineyard about sixty miles north of here. Says he's growing Chardonnay and Pinot Noir grapes. I wouldn't mind doing that myself one of these days. Anyway, he went through his old files for me and pulled the case notes."

"What's the story on that? Why'd the DA make a deal?"

Clemson gestured dismissively. "It was all circumstantial evidence. George De Witt was the district attorney. You ever run into him? Probably not. It would have been way before your time. He's a Superior Court judge now. I avoid him like the plague."

"I've heard of him. He's got political aspirations, doesn't he?"

"For all the good it's gonna do. He's into the sauce and it's the kiss of death. You never know which way he's gonna go on a case. He's not unfair, but he's inconsistent. Which is too bad. George was a hotdogger. Very flashy guy. He hated to bargain a high-publicity case, but he wasn't a fool. From what I hear, the Timberlake murder looked passable on the surface, but they were short of hard evidence. Fowler was known around town as a punk for years. His old man had thrown him out—"

"Wait a minute," I said. "Was this before he went to jail the first time or afterward? I thought he'd been convicted of armed robbery, but nobody's given me the story on that either."

"Shoot. All right, let me back up a bit. This

was two, three years before. I got the dates here somewhere, but it matters not. The deal is, Fowler and a fellow named Tap Granger hooked up right around the time Fowler got out of high school. Bailey was a good-looking kid and he was smart enough, but he never got it together. You probably know the type. He was just one of those kids who seems destined to go sour. From what Lehto says, Bailey and Tap were doing a lot of drugs. They had to pay the local dope peddler, so they started bumping off gas stations. Nickel-and-dime jobs, and they're rank amateurs. Idiots. They're wearing panty hose on their heads, trying to act like big-time hoods. Of course, they got caught. Rupert Russell was the PD on that one and he did the best he could."

"Why not a private attorney? Was Bailey indigent?"

"In essence. He didn't have the dough himself and his old man refused to pop for any legal fees." Clemson took a drag of his cigarette.

"Had Bailey been in trouble as a juvenile?"

"Nope. His record was clean. He probably figured all he'd get was a slap on the wrist. This is armed robbery, you understand, but Tap carried the gun, so I guess Bailey thought somehow that let him off the hook. Unfortunately for him, the statute doesn't read that way. Anyway, when they offered him a deal, he turned 'em down cold, pleaded not guilty, and went to trial instead. Needless to say, the jury convicted and the judge got tough. Back then, robbery was one to ten in the state prison."

"That was still indeterminate sentencing?"

"Yeah, that's right. Back then, they had a Bureau of Prison Terms that would meet and set parole and actual date of release. We had a very liberal board of prison terms at that time. Hell, we had basically a much more liberal government in California. Those people who ran the board were appointed by the governor and Pat Brown Junior . . . well, skip that tale. Point is, these guys get one to ten, but they're out in two years. Everybody starts screaming and yelling because nobody was doing nine or ten years on a one-to-ten. Bailey only served eighteen months."

"Up here?"

"Nuh-unh. Down at Chino, the country club of prisons. He got out in August. Came back to Floral Beach and started looking for work without much luck. Pretty soon he was back doing drugs again, only it was cocaine this time, along with grass. Uppers, downers, you name it."

"Where was Jean all this time?"

"Central Coast High, senior year. I don't know if anybody filled you in on this girl."

"Not at all."

"She was illegitimate. Her mom's still around in Floral Beach. You might want to talk to her. She had a reputation as the town roundheel, the mother, this is. Jean was an only child. Cute kid, but I guess she had a lot of problems. As if the rest of us don't." He took another drag from his cigarette.

"She worked for Royce Fowler, didn't she?"

"Right. Bailey got out of prison and she took up with him again. According to Lehto, Bailey claimed they were just good friends. The DA maintains they were lovers and Bailey killed her in a jealous rage when he found out she'd hooked up with Tap. Fowler says not so. It had nothing to do with Granger, even though Tap got out two months before he did."

"What about Granger? Is he still around?"

"Yeah, he operates the only gas station in Floral Beach. Owned by somebody else, but he's the manager, which is about all he can handle. He's not smart, but he seems steady enough. He was a wild one in his day, but he's mellowed out some."

I made a note about both Tap Granger and the Timberlake woman. "I didn't mean to interrupt. You were talking about Bailey's relationship with the girl after he got out of jail."

"Well, Bailey maintains the romance was over with. He and the girl hung out together and that was it. They were both outcasts anyway, Bailey because he'd been in prison, the Timberlake girl because her mother's such a slut. Besides which, the Timberlakes were poor. She was never going to amount to a hill of beans as long as she was stuck in Floral Beach. I don't know how much experience you've had with towns the size of Floral Beach. We're talking maybe eleven hundred people max, and most of 'em have been here since the year zip. Anyway, she and Bailey started running around together just like they did before. He says she was dallying with this other guy, involved in some affair that she was being real tight-lipped about. Claims she never would say who it was.

"The night she was killed, the two of 'em went out drinking. Hit about six bars in San Luis and two more in Pismo. Around midnight, they came back and parked down at the beach. He says it was closer to ten, but a witness puts 'em there at midnight. Anyway, she was upset. They had a bottle and a couple of joints with 'em. They had a tiff and he says he left her there and stomped off. Next thing he knows, it's morning and he's in his room at the Ocean Street. These kids are swarming all over the beach down below, doing clean-up detail as part of some local church do-good project. He's sick as a dog . . . so hung over he was pukin' his guts out. She's still down on the beach, passed out over by the stairs . . . only when the clean-up crew gets close, they can see she's dead, strangled with a belt that turns out to be his."

"But anybody could have done it."

"Absolutely. Of course, Bailey was favored and they might have made it stick, but De Witt had had a string of wins and he didn't want to take a chance. Lehto saw an opportunity to bargain and since Bailey'd been burned once, he went along with the deal. On the armed robbery, he was guilty, went to trial, and got himself nailed. This time he claimed he was innocent, but he didn't like the odds so when they offered him a plea of manslaughter, he took it, just like that." Clemson snapped his fingers, the sound like the clean popping of a hollow stick.

"Could he have beaten the murder rap if he'd gone to trial?"

"Hey, who knows? Going to trial is a crapshoot. You put your money on the line every time. If you roll that seven or eleven, boy, you're feeling good. But if it comes out two, three, or twelve, you're the loser. The case generated a lot of publicity. Sentiment in town was running against him. Then you had Bailey's prior, no character witnesses to speak of. He was better off with the deal. Twenty years ago, he could've been given the death penalty, too, which is something you don't want to mess with if you can help it. Talk about rolling dice."

"I thought if you were charged with murder, they wouldn't reduce that."

"True, hypothetically, but that's not the way it works. It was just discretionary with the district attorney how he filed. What Lehto did was, he goes to De Witt and says, 'Look, George, I've got evidence my guy was under the influence at the time. Evidence from your own people.' He pulls out the police report. 'If you'll note in the record, when the officers arrested him, it states he appeared to be drowsy . . .' Blah, blah, blah. Clifford does this whole number and he can see George start to sweat. He's got his ego on the line and he doesn't want to go into court with a big hole in his

case. As DA, you're expected to win ninety percent of the time, if not higher."

"So Bailey pleaded guilty to the manslaughter
and the judge maxed him out," I said.

"Exactly. You got it, but we're only talkin' six
years. Big deal. With time served and time off for
good behavior, he might have been out in half
that. The whole time, Fowler's thinking he got
screwed, but he doesn't understand how lucky he
was. Clifford Lehto did a hell of a job for him. I'd
have done the same thing myself."

"What happens next?"

Clemson shrugged again, stubbing out his cigarette. "Depends on how Bailey wants to plead on
the felony escape. What's he gonna say, 'No, I
didn't escape'? Extenuating circumstances? He can
always claim some prison goon was threatening his
life, but that hardly explains where he's been all
this time. The irony is, he should have hired some
hotshot attorney the first couple rounds. At this
point, it's not going to do him much good. I'll go
to bat for him, but no judge in his right mind is
going to set bail for some guy who's been on the
lam sixteen years."

"What do you want from me in the meantime?"

Clemson got up and started pawing through
the piles of paper on his desk. "I had my secretary
pull all the clippings from the time of the murder.
You might want to look at those. Lehto said he'd
send down everything he's got. Police reports, list
of witnesses. Talk to Bailey and see if he's got
anything to add. You know the drill. Go back

through the players and find me another suspect. Maybe we can develop evidence against somebody else and get Bailey off the hook. Otherwise, he's lookin' at a lot more years in the slammer unless I can persuade the judge no purpose would be served, which is what I'll try to do. He's been clean all this time, and personally, I can't see the point of puttin' him back in, but who knows? Here."

He unearthed an accordion file and handed it to me. I got to my feet and we shook hands again, chatting about other things as we left his office, walking toward the front. The office temp was sitting at her desk by then, trying to sustain an air of competence. She looked young and bewildered, out of her element in the world of habeas corpus, or corpuses of any kind.

"Oh yeah, one thing I almost forgot," Clemson said when we reached the porch. "What Jean was upset about that night? She was pregnant. Six weeks. Bailey swears it wasn't his."

# 5

I had about an hour to kill before I was due at the jail. I got out a city map and found the little dark square with a flag on it that marked the location of Central Coast High School. San Luis Obispo is not a large town, and the school was only six or eight blocks away. Lines painted on the main streets delineated a Path of History that I thought I might walk later in the week. I have an affection for early California history and I was curious to see the Mission and some of the old adobes as long as I was there.

When I reached the high school, I drove through the grounds, trying to imagine how it must have looked when Jean Timberlake was enrolled. Many of the buildings were clearly new: dark, smoke gray cinder block, trimmed in cream-colored concrete, with long, clean roof lines. The gymnasium and the cafeteria were of an earlier vintage, Spanish-style architecture done in darkening stucco with red tile roofs. On the upper level, where the road curved up and around to the right, there were modular units that had once served as classrooms and were now used for various businesses, Weight Watchers being one. The campus seemed more like a junior college than the high schools I'd seen. Rolling green hills formed a lush backdrop, giving the facility a feeling of serenity. The murder of a seventeen-year-old girl must have been deeply distressing to kids accustomed to pastoral surroundings such as these.

From what I remember of high school, our behavior was underscored by a hunger for sensation. Feelings were intense and events were played out in emotional extremes. While the fantasy of death satisfied a craving for self-drama, the reality was usually (fortunately) at some safe remove. We were absurdly young and healthy, and though we behaved recklessly, we never expected to suffer any consequence. The notion of a real death, whether by accident or intent, would have pushed us into a state of perplexity. Love affairs provided all the theater we could handle. Our sense of tragedy and our self-centeredness were so exaggerated that we weren't prepared to cope with any actual loss. Murder would have been beyond comprehension. Jean Timberlake's death probably still generated discussion among the people she knew, giving rise to a disquiet that marred the memories of youth. Bailey Fowler's sudden reappearance in the community was going to stir it all up again: uneasiness, rage, the nearly incomprehensible feelings of waste and dismay.

On impulse, I parked the car and searched out the library, which turned out to be much like the one at Santa Teresa High. The space was airy and open, the noise level subdued. The vinyl floor tile was a mottled beige, polished to a dull gleam. The air smelled like furniture polish, construction paper, and paste. I must have eaten six jars of LePage's during my grade-school years. I had a friend who ate pencil shavings. There's a name for that now, for kids who eat inorganic oddities like gravel and clay. In my day, it just seemed like a fun thing to do and no one ever gave it a passing thought as far as I knew.

The library tables were sparsely occupied and the reference desk was being handled by a young girl with frizzy hair and a ruby drilled into the side of her nose. She had apparently been seized by a fit of self-puncturing because both ears had been pierced repeatedly from the lobe to the helix. In lieu of earrings, she was sporting the sort of items you'd find in my junk drawer at home: paper clips, screws, safety pins, shoelaces, wing nuts. She was perched on a stool with a copy of *Rolling Stone* open on her lap. Mick Jagger was on the cover, looking sixty if a day.

"Hi."

She looked at me blankly.

"I wonder if you can give me some help. I used to be a student here and I can't find my yearbook. Do you have any copies? I'd like to take a look."

"Under the window. First and second shelves."

I pulled the annuals from three separate years and took them to a table on the far side of a row of free-standing bookcases. A bell rang and the corridor began to fill with the rustling sound of students on the move. The slamming of locker doors was punctuated by the babble of voices, laughter bouncing off the walls with the harsh echo of a racquetball court. The ghostly scent of gym socks wafted in.

I traced Jean Timberlake's picture back, volume by volume, like the aging process in reverse. During her high school years, while the rest of California's youth were protesting the war, smoking dope, and heading for the Haight, the girls at Central Coast were teasing their hair into glossy towers, putting black lines around their eyes and white gloss on their lips. The junior girls wore white blouses and bouffant hair, which curved out in a heavily sprayed flip at the sides. The guys had damp-looking crewcuts and braces on their teeth. They couldn't have guessed how soon they'd be sporting sideburns, beards, bell-bottoms, and psychedelic shirts.

Jean never looked like she had anything in common with the rest. In the few group pictures where I spotted her, she never grinned and she had none of the bouncy-looking innocence of the Debbies and the Tammies. Jean's eyes were hooded, her gaze remote, and the faint smile that played on her mouth suggested a private amuse-

ment still evident after all these years. The blurb
in the senior index listed no committees or clubs.
She hadn't been burdened with scholastic honors
or elective offices, and she hadn't bothered to
participate in any extracurricular activities. I leafed
through candid shots taken at various school func-
tions, but I never did catch sight of her. If she
went to football or basketball games, she must
have hovered somewhere beyond the range of the
school photographer. She wasn't in the senior play.
All the prom pictures focused on the queen, Barbie
Knox, and her entourage of beehived, white-lipped
princesses. Jean Timberlake was dead by then. I
jotted down the names of her more conspicuous
classmates, all guys. I figured if the girls were still
living in the area, they'd be listed in the phone
book under married names, which I'd have to get
somewhere else.

The principal at that time was a man named
Dwight Shales, whose picture appeared in an oval
on one of the early pages of the annual. The school
superintendent and his two assistant superinten-
dents were each pictured separately, seated at
their desks, holding official-looking papers. Sometimes a member of the office staff, female, peered
over some man's shoulder with interest, smiling
perkily. The teachers had been photographed
against a varied background of maps, industrial
arts equipment, textbooks, and blackboards on
which phrases had been writ large in chalk. I
noted some of their names and specialties, think-

ing I might want to return at a later date to talk to one or two. A young Ann Fowler was one of four guidance counselors photographed on a separate page with a paragraph underneath. "These counselors gave extra time, thought, and encouragement to us as they helped us plan our program for the next year wisely or advised us when we had decisions to make regarding our future plans for jobs or college." I thought Ann looked prettier then, not as tired or as soured.

I tucked my notes away and returned the books to the shelves. I headed down the hallway, passing the nurse's office and the attendance office. The administrative offices were located near the main entrance. According to the name plate on the wall beside the door, Shales was still the school principal. I asked his secretary if I could see him, and after a brief wait, I was ushered into his office. I could see my business card sitting in the center of the blotter on his desk.

He was a man in his mid-fifties, medium height, trim, with a square face. The color of his hair had changed from blond to a premature white, and he'd grown it out from its original mid-sixties crewcut. His whole manner was authoritarian, his hazel eyes as watchful as a cop's. He had that same air of assessment, as if he were checking back through his mental files to come up with my rap sheet. I felt my cheeks warm, wondering if he could tell at a glance what a troublesome student I'd been in high school.

"Yes, ma'am," he said. "What can I do for you?"

"I've been hired by Royce Fowler in Floral Beach to look into the death of a former student of yours named Jean Timberlake." I'd expected him to remember her without further prompting, but he continued to look at me with studied neutrality. Surely he couldn't know about the dope I'd smoked back then.

"You do remember her," I said.

"Of course. I was just trying to think if we'd held on to the records on her. I'm not sure where they'd be."

"I've just had a conversation with Bailey's attorney. If you need some kind of release . . ."

He gestured carelessly. "That's not necessary. I know Jack Clemson and I know the family. I'd have to clear it with the school superintendent, but I can't see that it'd be any problem . . . if we can locate 'em. It's the simple question of what we've got. You're talking more than fifteen years ago."

"Seventeen," I said. "Do you have any personal recollections of the girl?"

"Let me get clearance on the matter first and then I'll get back to you. You're local?"

"Well, I'm from Santa Teresa, but I'm staying at the Ocean Street in Floral Beach. I can give you the number . . ."

"I've got the number. I'll call you as soon as I know anything. Might be a couple of days, but we'll see what we can do. I can't make any guarantees."

"I understand that," I said.

"Good. We'll help you if we can." His hand-shake was brisk and firm.

At three-fifteen I headed north on Highway 1 to the San Luis Obispo County Sheriff's Depart-ment, part of a complex of buildings that includes the jail. The surrounding countryside is open, char-acterized by occasional towering outcroppings of rock. The hills look like soft humps of foam rub-ber, upholstered in variegated green velvet. Across the road from the Sheriff's Department is the Cal-ifornia Men's Colony, where Bailey had been in-carcerated at the time of his escape. It amused me that in the promotional literature extolling the vir-tues of life in San Luis Obispo County, there's never any mention of the six thousand prisoners also in residence.

I parked in one of the visitors' slots in front of the jail. The building looked new, similar in de-sign and construction materials to the newer por-tions of the high school where I'd just been. I went into the lobby, signs directing me to the booking and inmate information section down a short corridor to the right. I identified myself to the uniformed deputy in the glass-enclosed office, where I could see the dispatcher, the booking officer, and the computer terminals. To the left, I caught a glimpse of the covered garage where prisoners could be brought in by sheriffs' vehicles.

While arrangements were being made to bring Bailey out, I was directed to one of the small, glass-enclosed booths reserved for attorney-client conferences. A sign on the wall spelled out the rules for visitors, admonishing us that there could only be one registered visitor per inmate at any one time. We were to keep control of children, and any rude or boisterous conduct toward the staff was not going to be tolerated. The restrictions suggested past scenes of chaos and merriment I was already wishing I'd been privy to.

I could hear the muffled clanking of doors. Bailey Fowler appeared, his attention focused on the deputy who was unlocking the booth where he would sit while we spoke. We were separated by glass, and our conversation would be conducted by way of two telephone handsets, one on his side, one on mine. He glanced at me incuriously and then sat down. His demeanor was submissive and I found myself feeling embarrassed in his behalf. He wore a loosely structured orange cotton shirt over dark gray cotton pants. The newspaper photograph had shown him in a suit and tie. He seemed as bewildered by the clothing as he was by his sudden status as an inmate. He was remarkably good-looking: grave blue eyes, high cheekbones, full mouth, dark blond hair already in need of a cut. He was a tired forty, and I suspected circumstances had aged him overnight. He shifted in the straight-backed wooden chair, clasping his hands loosely between his knees, his expression empty of emotion.

I picked up the phone, waiting briefly while he picked up the receiver on his side. I said, "I'm Kinsey Millhone."

"Do I know you?"

Our voices sounded odd, both too tinny and too near.

"I'm the private investigator your father hired. I just spent some time with your attorney. Have you talked to him yet?"

"Couple of times on the phone. He's supposed to stop by this afternoon." His voice was as lifeless as his gaze.

"Is it all right if I call you Bailey?"

"Yeah, sure."

"Look, I know this whole thing's a bummer, but Clemson's good. He'll do everything possible to get you out of here."

Bailey's expression clouded over. "He better do something quick."

"You have family in L.A.? Wife and kids?"

"Why?"

"I thought there might be someone you wanted me to get in touch with."

"I don't have family. Just get me the hell out of here."

"Hey, come on. I know it's tough."

He looked up and off to one side, anger glinting in his eyes before the brief show of feeling subsided into bleakness again. "Sorry."

"Talk to me. We may not have long."

"About what?"

"Anything. When'd you get up here? How was the ride?"

"Fine."

"How's the town look? Has it changed much?"

"I can't make small talk. Don't ask me to do that."

"You can't shut down on me. We have too much work to do."

He was silent for a moment and I could see him struggle with the effort to be communicative. "For years, I wouldn't even drive through this part of the state for fear I'd get stopped." Transmission faltered and came to a halt. The look he gave me was haunted, as if he longed to speak, but had lost the capacity. It felt as if we were separated by more than a sheet of glass.

I said, "You're not dead, you know."

"Says you."

"You must have known it would happen one day."

He tilted his head, doing a neck roll to work the tension out. "They picked me up the first time, I thought it was all over. Just my luck there's a Peter Lambert out there wanted on a murder one. When they let me go, I thought maybe I had a chance."

"I'm surprised you didn't take off."

"I wish now I had, but I'd been free so long. I couldn't believe they'd get me. I couldn't believe anybody cared. Besides, I had a job and I couldn't just chuck it all and hit the road."

"You're some kind of clothing rep, aren't you? The L.A. papers mentioned that."

"I worked for Needham. One of their top salesmen last year, which is how I got promoted. Western regional manager. I guess I should have turned it down, but I worked hard and I got tired of saying no. It meant a move to Los Angeles, but I didn't see how I could get tripped up after all this time."

"How long have you been with the company?"

"Twelve years."

"What's their attitude? Can you count on them for any help?"

"They've been great. Real supportive. My boss said he'd come up here and testify . . . be a character witness and stuff like that, but what's the point? I feel like such a jerk. I've been straight all these years. Your proverbial model citizen. I never even got a parking ticket. Paid taxes, went to church."

"But that's good. That'll work in your favor. It's bound to make a difference."

"But it doesn't change the facts. You don't walk away from jail and get a slap on the wrist."

"Why don't you let Clemson worry about that?"

"I guess I'll have to," he said. "What are you supposed to do?"

"Find out who really killed her so we can get you off the hook."

"Fat chance."

"It's worth a shot. You got any ideas about who it might have been?"

"No."

"Tell me about Jean."

"She was a nice kid. Wild, but not bad. Mixed up."

"But pregnant."

"Yeah, well, the baby wasn't mine."

"You're sure of that." I framed it as a statement, but the question mark was there.

Bailey hung his head for a moment, color rising in his face. "I did a lot of booze back then. Drugs. My performance was off, especially after I got out of Chino. Not that it mattered. She was with some other guy by then."

"You were impotent?"

"Let's say, 'temporarily out of order.' "

"You do any drugs now?"

"No, and I haven't had a drink in fifteen years. Alcohol makes your tongue loose. I couldn't take the chance."

"Who was she involved with? Any indication at all?"

He shook his head again. "The guy was married."

"How do you know?"

"She told me that much."

"And you believed her?"

"I can't think why she would have lied. He was somebody respectable and she was underage."

"So this was somebody with a lot to lose if the truth came out."

"That'd be my guess. I mean, she sure didn't

want to have to tell him she was knocked up. She was scared."

"She could have had an abortion."

"I guess . . . if it came to that. She only found out about the baby that day."

"Who was her doctor?"

"She didn't have one yet for that. Dr. Dunne was the family physician, but she had the pregnancy test at some clinic down in Lompoc so nobody'd know who she was."

"Seems pretty paranoid. Was she that well known?"

"She was in Floral Beach."

"What about Tap? Could the kid have been his?"

"Nope. She thought he was a jerk and he didn't like her much either. Besides, he wasn't married and it was nothing to him even if the kid had been his."

"What else? You must have given this a lot of thought."

"I don't know. She was illegitimate and she'd been trying to find out who her old man was. Her mom refused to tell her, but money came in the mail every month, so Jean figured he had to be around someplace."

"She saw the checks?"

"I don't think he paid by check, but she was getting a line on him somehow."

"Was she born in San Luis County?"

There was a jangle of keys and we both looked

over to see the deputy at the door. "Time's up. Sorry to interrupt. You want more, Mr. Clemson has to make arrangements."

Bailey got up without argument, but I could see him zone out. Whatever energy our conversation had produced had already drained away. The numb look returned, giving him the air of someone not too bright.

"I'll see you after the arraignment," I said.

Bailey's parting look flickered with desperation.

After he left, I sat and jotted down some notes. I hoped he didn't have any suicidal tendencies.

# 6

Just to fill in another blank, I pulled into the gas station in Floral Beach and asked the attendant to top off my tank. While the kid was taking care of the windshield, I took my wallet and went into the office, where I studied the vending machine. Nothing but Cheetos for $1.25. Cheatos, I thought. There was no one at the desk, but I spotted someone working out in the service bay. I went to the door. The guy had a Ford Fiesta up on the lift, whipping lug nuts off the right rear wheel with an air-driven lug wrench.

"Can I get some change for the vending machine in here?"

"Sure thing."

The fellow set the wrench down and wiped his hands on a rag tucked into his belt. "Tap" was stitched in an embroidered script on the patch above his uniform pocket. I followed him back into the office. He moved in an aura of motor oil and tire smell, giving off that heady scent of sweat and gasoline fumes. He was wiry and small, with wide shoulders and a narrow butt, the type who might unveil a lavish tattoo when he took off his shirt. His dark hair was curly, combed into a crest on top, the sides swept into a ducktail in the back. He looked about forty, with a still-boyish face getting leathery around the eyes.

I handed him two dollars. "You know anything about VWs?"

He made eye contact for the first time. His were brown and didn't show much life. I suspected car woes were going to spark the only interest I'd be able to generate. He flicked a look out to the pumps, where the kid was just finishing up. "You got a problem?"

"Well, it may not be much. I keep hearing this high-pitched whine when I get up around sixty. Sounds kind of weird."

"You can hit sixty in a tin can like that?" he said.

A car joke. He grinned, punching open the register.

I smiled. "Well, yeah. Now and then."

"Try Gunter's in San Luis. He can fix you up." He dropped eight quarters into my palm.

"Thanks."

He moved back out to the service bay and I pocketed the change. At least I knew now who Tap Granger was. I paid for the gas and headed up two blocks to the motel.

As it turned out, I didn't talk to Royce at all that afternoon. He'd retired early, leaving word

with Ann that he'd see me in the morning. I spoke
briefly with her mother, filling her in on Bailey's
current state, and then went on upstairs. I'd picked
up a bottle of white wine on my way through San
Luis and I stashed it in the small refrigerator in
my room. I hadn't unpacked, and my duffel was
tucked in the closet where I'd left it. I tend, on
the road, to leave everything in a suitcase, digging
out my toothbrush, shampoo, and clean clothing
as the need arises. The room remains bare and
unnaturally tidy, which appeals to a streak of
monasticism in me. This room was spacious, the
designated bedroom area separated from the living/
dining/kitchenette by a partition. Factoring in the
bathroom and a closet, it was bigger than my
(former) apartment back home.

I rooted through the kitchen drawers until I
came up with a corkscrew, and then I poured
myself a glass of wine and took it out on the
balcony. The water was turning a luminous blue as
the light faded from the sky, and the dark lavender of the coastline was a vivid contrast. The sunset was a light show of deep pink and salmon
shades, gradually sinking, as if by a dimmer switch,
through magenta into indigo.

There was a tap at my door at six. I'd been
typing for twenty minutes, though the information
I'd collected, at this point, was scant. I screwed
the lid on the white-out and went to the door.

Ann was standing in the corridor. "I wondered what time you wanted supper."

"Anytime's fine with me. When do you usually eat?"

"Actually, we can suit ourselves. I fed Mother early. Her meal schedule's pretty strict, and Pop won't eat until later, if he eats at all. I'm doing pan-fried sole for us, which is a last-minute thing. I hope you don't object to fish."

"Not at all. Sounds great. You want to join me in a glass of white wine first?"

She hesitated. "I'd like that," she said. "How's Bailey doing? Is he okay?"

"Well, he's not happy, but there's not much he can do. You haven't seen him yet?"

"I'll go tomorrow, if I can get in."

"Check with Clemson. He can probably set it up. It shouldn't be hard. Arraignment's at eight-thirty."

"I think I'll have to pass on that. Mother has a doctor's appointment at nine and I couldn't get back in time anyway. Pop will want to go, if he's feeling okay. Could he go with you?"

"Sure. No problem."

I poured a glass for her and refilled my own. She settled on the couch, while I sat a few feet away at the tiny kitchen table where my typewriter was set up. She seemed ill at ease, sipping at her wine with an odd cast to her mouth, as if she'd been asked to down a glass of liniment.

"I take it you're not crazy about Chardonnay," I remarked.

She smiled apologetically. "I don't drink very

often. Bailey's the only one who ever developed a taste for it."

I thought I'd have to pump her for background information, but she surprised me by volunteering a quick family time line. The Fowlers, she said, had never been enthusiastic about alcohol. She claimed this was a function of her mother's diabetes, but to me it seemed in perfect keeping with the dour fundamentalist mentality that pervaded the place.

According to Ann, Royce had been born and raised in Tennessee and the dark strains of his Scots heritage had rendered him joyless, taciturn, and wary of excess. He'd been nineteen at the height of the Depression, migrating west on a succession of boxcars. He'd heard there was work in the oilfields in California, where the rigs were springing up like a metallic forest just south of Los Angeles. He'd met Oribelle, en route, at a dime-a-dip dinner at a Baptist church in Fayetteville, Arkansas. She was eighteen, soured by disease, resigned to a life of scriptures and insulin dependency. She was working in her father's feed store, and the most she could look forward to was the annual trip to the mule market in Fort Smith.

Royce had appeared at the church that Wednesday night, having hopped off a freight in search of a hot meal. Ann said Ori still talked of her first sight of him, standing in the door, a broad-shouldered youth with hair the color of hemp. Oribelle introduced herself as he went through the supper line, piling his plate high with macaroni and cheese, which was her specialty. By the end of the evening, she'd heard his entire life story and she invited him home with her afterward. He slept in the barn, taking all his meals with the family. He remained a guest of the Baileys for two weeks, during which she was in such a fever pitch of hormones that she'd twice gone into ketoacidosis and had had to be briefly hospitalized. Her parents took this as evidence that Royce's influence was wicked. They talked to her long and hard about her giving him up, but nothing would dissuade her from the course she had set. She was determined to marry Royce. When her father opposed the courtship, she took all the money set aside for secretarial school and ran off with him. That was in 1932.

"It's odd for me to picture either one of them caught up in high passion," I said.

She smiled. "Me too. I should show you a photo. She was actually quite beautiful. Of course, I wasn't born until six years later—1938—and Bailey came along five years after me. Whatever heat they felt was burned out by then, but the bond is still strong. The irony is, we all thought she'd die long before him, and now it looks like he'll go first."

"What's actually wrong with him?"

"Pancreatic cancer. They're saying six months."

"Which he knows?"

"Oh yes. It's one of the reasons he's so thrilled about Bailey's showing up. He talks about heartbreak but he doesn't mean a word of it."

"What about you? How do you feel?"

"Relieved, I guess. Even if he goes back to prison, I'll have someone to help me get through the next few months. The responsibility's been crushing ever since he disappeared."

"How's your mother handling this?"

"Badly. She's what they call a 'brittle' diabetic, which means she's always been in fragile health. Any kind of emotional upset is hard on her. Stress. I guess it gets to all of us one way or another, myself included. Ever since Pop was diagnosed as terminal, my life's been hell."

"You mentioned you were on a leave of absence from work."

"I had no choice. Someone has to be here twenty-four hours a day. We can't afford professional care, so I'm 'it.' "

"Rough."

"I shouldn't complain. I'm sure there are people out there who have it worse."

I shifted the subject. "You have any theories about who killed the Timberlake girl?"

Ann shook her head. "I wish I did. She was a student at the high school, as well as Bailey's girl."

"She spent a lot of time here?"

"A fair amount. Less while Bailey was off in jail."

"And you're convinced he had nothing to do with her death?"

"I don't know what to believe," she said flatly. "I don't want to think he did it. On the other hand, I've never liked the idea that the killer could still be around someplace."

"He won't like it either, now that Bailey's back in custody. Somebody must have felt pretty smug all these years. Once the investigation's opened up, who knows where it'll go?"

"You're right. I wouldn't like to be in your shoes." She rubbed her arms as if she were cold and then laughed at herself uneasily. "Well. I better get back downstairs and see how Mother's doing. She was napping when I left, but she tends to sleep in short bursts. The minute her eyes open, she wants me Johnny-on-the-spot."

"Give me time to wash my face and I'll be right down." I walked her to the door. As I passed my handbag, I caught sight of the envelope Clemson had given me. "Oh. This is for your father. Jack Clemson asked me to drop it off." I plucked it out and handed it to her.

She glanced at it idly and then smiled at me. "Thanks for the drink. I hope I haven't bored you with the family history."

"Not at all," I said. "By the way, what's the story on Jean Timberlake's mother? Will she be hard to find?"

"Who, Shana? Try the pool hall. She's there most nights. Tap Granger, too."

After supper, I snagged a jacket from my room and headed down the back stairs.

The night was cold and the breeze coming off the Pacific was briny and damp. I shrugged into

my jacket and walked the two blocks to Pearl's
Pool Hall as if through broad daylight. Floral Beach,
by night, is bathed in the flat orange glow of the
sodium vapor lights that line Ocean Street. The
moon wasn't up yet, and the ocean was as black as
pitch. The surf tumbled onto the beach in an
uneven fringe of gold, picking up illumination from
the last reaches of the street lamps. A fog was
rolling in and the air had the dense, tawny look of
smog.

Closer to the pool hall, the quiet was broken
by a raucous blast of country music. The door to
Pearl's stood open and I could smell cigarette smoke
from two doors away. I counted five Harley-
Davidsons at the curb, all chrome and black leather
seats, with convoluted tailpipes. The boys in my
junior high school went through a siege of drawing
machines like that: hot rods and racing cars, tanks,
torture devices, guns, knives, and bloodlettings of
all kinds. I should really check one day and find
out how those guys turned out.

The pool hall itself was two pool tables long,
with enough space between to allow folk to angle
for a tricky shot. Both tables were occupied by
bikers: heavyset men in their forties with Fu Man-
chu beards and long hair pulled back in ponytails.
There were five of them, a family of road pirates
on the move. The bar ran the entire length of wall
to the left, the barstools filled with the bikers'
girlfriends and assorted town folk. Walls and ceiling were covered with a collage of beer signs,
tobacco ads, bumper stickers, cartoons, snapshots,

and bar witticisms. One sign proclaimed Happy Hour from six to seven, but the hand-drawn clock under it had a 5 at every hour. A knee-slapper, that. Bowling trophies, beer mugs, and racks of potato chips lined the shelf behind the bar. There was also a display of Pearl's Pool Hall T-shirts on sale for $6.99. A leather biker's glove hung inexplicably from the ceiling, and a Miller Lite mirror on the wall was festooned with a pair of lady's underpants. The noise level was such that a hearing test might be in order later.

There was one empty stool at the bar, which I took. The bartender was a woman in her mid-sixties, perhaps the very Pearl for whom the place was named. She was short, thick through the middle, with graying, permanent-curled hair chopped straight across the nape of her neck. She was wearing plaid polyester slacks and a sleeveless top, showing arms well muscled from hefting beer cases. Maybe, at intervals, she hefted some biker out the door by the seat of his pants.

I asked for a draft beer, which she pulled and served up in a Mason jar. Since the din made conversation impossible, I had plenty of time to survey the place in peace. I turned on the stool until my back was up against the bar, watching the pool players, casting an occasional eye at the patrons on either side of me. I wasn't really sure how I wanted to present myself. I thought for the time being I'd keep hush about my occupation and the reasons for my presence in Floral Beach. The local papers had carried front-page news about Bailey's arrest, and I thought I could probably conjure up talk on the subject without appearing too inquisitive.

Down to my left, near the jukebox, two women began to dance. The bikers' girlfriends made some rude observations, but no one seemed to pay much attention aside from that. Two stools over, a woman in her fifties looked on with a sloppy smile. I pegged her as Shana Timberlake, in part because no other woman in the bar looked old enough to have had a teenage daughter seventeen years before.

At ten, the bikers cleared out, motorcycles rocketing off down the street with diminishing thunder. The jukebox was between selections, and for a moment a miraculous silence fell across the bar. Someone said, "Whew, Lord!" and everybody laughed. There were maybe ten of us left in the place, and the tension level dropped to some more familial feel. This was Tuesday night, the local hangout, the equivalent of the basement recreation room at a church, except that beer was served. There was no hard liquor in evidence and my guess was that any wine on the premises was going to come from a jug the size of an oil drum, with about that much finesse.

The man on the stool next to mine on the right appeared to be in his sixties. He was big, with a beer belly that protruded like a twenty-five-pound bag of rice. His face was broad, connected to his neck by a series of double chins. There was even a roll of fat at the back of his neck where graying hair curled over his shirt collar. I'd seen him flick a curious look in my direction. The others in the bar seemed known to one another, judging from the banter, which had largely to do with local politics, old sporting grievances, and how drunk someone named Ace had been the night before. The sheepish Ace, tall, thin, jeans, denim jacket, and baseball cap, took a lot of ribbing about some behavior of his with old Betty, whom he'd apparently taken home with him. Ace seemed to revel in the accusations of misconduct, and since Betty wasn't present to correct the impression, everyone assumed that he'd gotten laid.

"Betty's his ex-wife," the man next to me said, in one of those casual asides meant to include me in the merriment. "She kicked him out four times, but she always takes him back. Yo, Daisy. How about some peanuts down here?"

"I thought that was Pearl," I remarked, to keep the conversation alive.

"I'm Curtis Pearl," he said. "Pearl to my friends."

Daisy scooped what looked like a dog dish full of peanuts from a garbage pail under the bar. The nuts were still in the shell, and the litter on the floor suggested what we were meant to do. Pearl surprised me by chomping down a peanut, shell and all. "We're talkin' fiber here," he said. "It's good for you. I got a doctor believes in cellulose. Fills you up, he says. Gets the old system powerin' through."

I shrugged and tried it myself. No doubt about it, the shell had a lot of crunch and a sharp infusion of salt mingled nicely with the bland taste of the nut inside. Did this count as grain, or was it the same as eating the panel from a cardboard box?

The jukebox sparked to life again, this time a mellow vocalist who sounded like a cross between Frank Sinatra and Della Reese. The two women at the end of the bar began to dance again. Both were dark-haired, both slim. One taller. Pearl turned to look at them and then back at me. "That bother you?"

"Why should I care?"

"Not what it looks like anyway," he said. "Tall one likes to dance when she's feeling blue."

"What's she got to be unhappy about?"

"They just picked up the fellow killed her little girl a few years back."

# 7

I watched her for a moment. At a distance of half the bar, she looked twenty-five. She had her eyes closed, head tilted to one side. Her face was heart-shaped, her hair caught up in a clip on top, the lower portion brushing across her shoulder in a rhythm with the ballad. The light from the jukebox touched her cheek with gold. The woman she was dancing with had her back to me, so I couldn't tell anything about her at all.

Pearl was sketching in the story for me with the practiced tone of frequent telling. No details I hadn't heard before, but I was thankful he'd introduced the subject without any further prompting on my part. He was just warming up, enjoying his role as tribal narrator. "You staying at the Ocean Street? I ask because this fella's dad owns that place."

"Really," I said.

"Yep. They found her down on the beach right in front," he said. Residents of Floral Beach had been telling this tale for years. Like a stand-up comedian, he had his timing down pat, knowing just when to pause, knowing just what response he'd get.

I had to watch what I said because I didn't want to imply I knew nothing of this. While I'm not averse to lying through my teeth, I never do it when I'm apt to be caught. People get crabby about that sort of thing. "Actually, I know Royce."

"Aw, then you know all about this."

"Well, some. You really think Bailey did it? Royce says no."

"Hard to say. Naturally, he'd deny anything of the sort. None of us want to believe our kids would kill someone."

"True enough."

"You have kids?"

"Unh-unh."

"My boy was the one who spotted the two of 'em pulling into the curb that night. They got out of the truck with a bottle and a blanket and went down the steps. Said Bailey looked drunk as a skunk to him and she wasn't much better off. Probably went down there to misbehave, if you get what I mean. Maybe she sprung it on him she was in a family way."

"Hey, there. How's that little Heinie car acting?"

I glanced back to see Tap behind me, a sly grin on his face.

Pearl didn't seem thrilled to see him, but he made polite noises with his mouth. "Say, Tap.

What're you up to? I thought that old lady of yours didn't like you comin' in here."

"Aw, she don't care. Who's this we're talking to?"

"I'm Kinsey. How're you?"

Pearl raised an eyebrow. "You two know each other?"

"She had her bug in this afternoon and wanted me to take a look. Said it was kind of whiny up around sixty. Whiny Heinie," he said, and got real tickled with himself. At close range, I could smell the pomade on his hair.

Pearl turned and stared at him. "You got something against the Germans?"

"Who, me?"

"My folks is German, so you better make it good."

"Naw, hell. I don't care. That Nazi business wasn't such a bad idea. Hey, Daisy. Gimme a beer. And hand me a bag of them barbecued potato chips. Big one. This gal looks like she could use a bite to eat. I'm Tap." He hiked himself up on the barstool to my left. He was the sort of man who saved his handshakes for meetings with other men. A woman, if known to him, might warrant a pat on the butt. As a stranger, I lucked out.

"What kind of name is Tap?" I asked.

Pearl cut in. "Short for tapioca. He's a real puddin' head."

Tap cut loose with a laugh again, but he didn't seem that amused. Daisy showed up with the beer and chips so I never did find out what Tap was short for.

"We're just talking about your old friend Bailey," Pearl said. "She's stayin' down at the Ocean Street and Royce is fillin' her head full of all kind of thing."

"Aw, that Bailey's something else," Tap said. "He's quick. He had a million schemes. Talk you into anything. We had us a good time, I can tell you that."

"I just bet you did," Pearl said. He was seated on my right, Tap on my left, the two of them conversing back and forth across me like a tennis match.

"Made more money than you ever seen," Tap said.

"Tap and him did a little business together in the old days," Pearl said to me, his tone confidential.

"Really. What kind of business?"

"Now come on, Pearl. She doesn't want to hear about that stuff."

"Eat a man's chips, you might want to know what kind of company you're in."

Tap was starting to squirm. "I straightened myself up now and that's a fact. I got me a good wife and kids and I keep my nose clean."

I leaned toward Pearl with mock concern. "What'd he do, Pearl? Am I safe with this man?"

Pearl loved it. He was looking for ways to prolong the aggravation. "I'd keep a hand on my wallet if I was you. Him and Bailey took to putting ladies' panties on their heads . . . stickin' up gas stations with their little toy guns."

"Pearl! Now, goddamn. You know that ain't true."

Tap apparently wasn't good at being teased about these things. His choice was to let the story stand, or make corrections that would perhaps have him looking even worse.

Pearl retracted his statement with all the contrition of a prosecuting attorney who knows the jury's already got the point. "Oh hell, I'm sorry. You're right, Tap. There was only the one gun," Pearl said. "Tap, here, carried it."

"Well, it wasn't my idea in the first place and the damn thing wasn't loaded."

"Bailey thought up the gun. It was Tap's idea about the ladies' underpants."

Tap made a stab at recovering. "This guy don't know ladies' pants from panty hose. That's his problem. We had stockings pulled over our faces."

"Kept gettin' runs in the hose," Pearl said, ad-libbing. "Spent all their profits at the five-and-dime buyin' more."

"Don't mind him. He's jealous is all. We got them panty hose off that wife of his. She put her legs up and they come right off." Tap snickered at himself. Pearl didn't seem to take offense.

I allowed myself to laugh, more from discomfort than amusement. It was odd being caught between these two male energies. It felt like the equivalent of two dogs barking at each other across the safety of a fence.

There was a commotion at the far end of the bar, and Pearl's attention strayed. Daisy, standing close to us, seemed to understand what it was about. "Jukebox is broke again. It's been eating quarters all day. Darryl claims he's down a dollar twenty-five."

"Give him back his money from the register and I'll take a look." Pearl eased off the stool and moved down to the jukebox. Shana Timberlake was still dancing, by herself this time, to music no one else could hear. There was a touch of exhibitionism in her grief, and a couple of guys playing pool were eyeing her with undisguised interest, calculating the odds of cashing in on her mood. I've known women like that, who use their troubles as a reason to get laid, as if sex were a balm with healing properties.

Once Pearl absented himself, the tension level in the air dropped by half and I could feel Tap relax. "Hey, Daze. Gimme another beer, here, babe. This is Crazy Daisy. She's worked for Pearl since before the rocks cooled."

Daisy glanced at me. "How about it? You ready for another one?"

Tap caught her eye. "Go ahead and make it two. On me."

I smiled briefly. "Thanks. That's nice."

"I didn't want you to think you were settin' here with a crook."

"He sure likes to hassle you, doesn't he?"

"Now that's the truth," Tap said. He reared back and looked at me, surprised that anyone but he had picked up on it. "He don't mean any harm by it, but it gets on my nerves, I can tell you that. If this wasn't the only bar in town, I'd tell him to get . . . well, I'd tell him what he could do with it."

"Really. Anyone can make mistakes," I said. "I pulled all kinds of pranks when I was a kid. I'm just lucky I didn't get caught. Not that sticking up gas stations is a prank, of course."

"That ain't even the half of it. That's just what they nailed us for," he said. A slight note of bragging had crept into his tone. I'd heard it before, usually from men who longed for the remembered hype of past sports triumphs. I seldom thought of crime as a peak experience, but Tap might.

I said, "Listen, if we got nailed for everything we did, we'd all be in jail."

He laughed. "Hey, I like you. I like your attitude."

Daisy brought our beers and I watched while Tap pulled out a ten. "Run us a tab," he said to her.

She picked up the bill and moved back toward the register where I saw her make a note. Meanwhile, Tap studied me, trying to figure out where I was coming from. "I bet you never robbed nobody at gunpoint."

"No, but my old man did," I said easily. "Did time for it, too." Oh, I liked that. The lie rolled right off my tongue without a moment's thought.

"You're b.s.-in' me. Your old man did time? Don't give me that. Where?" The "where" came out sounding like "were."

"Lompoc," I said.

"That's federal," he said. "What'd he do, rob a bank?"

I pointed at him, aiming my finger like a gun.

"Goddamn," he said. "God*damn*." He was

excited now, as if he'd just found out my father was a former president. "How'd he get caught?"

I shrugged. "He'd been picked up before for passing bad checks, so they just matched the prints on the note he handed the teller. He never even had a chance to spend the money."

"And you never done any time yourself?"

"Not me. I'm a real law-and-order type."

"That's good. You keep that up. You're too nice to get mixed up with prison types. Women are the worst. Do all kind of things. I've heard tales that'd make your hair stand right up on end. And not the hair on your head neither."

"I'll bet," I said. I changed the subject, not wanting to lie any more than I had to. "How many kids you got?"

"Here, lemme show you," he said, reaching in his back pocket. He took out his wallet and flipped it open to a photo tucked in the window where his driver's license should have been. "That's Joleen."

The woman staring out of the picture looked young and somewhat amazed. Four little children surrounded her, scrubbed, grinning, and shiny-faced. The oldest was a boy, probably nine, snaggle-toothed, his hair still visibly damp where she'd combed it into a pompadour just like his dad's. Two girls came next, probably six and eight. A plump-armed baby boy was perched on his mother's lap. The picture had been shot in a studio, the five of them posed in the midst of a faux picnic scene complete with a red-and-white checked cloth and artificial tree branches overhead. The baby held a fake apple in one chubby fist like a ball.

"Well, they're cute," I said, hoping he didn't pick up on the note of astonishment.

"They're rascals," he said fondly. "This was last year. She's pregnant again. She's wishin' she didn't have to work, but we do pretty good."

"What's she do?"

"She's a nurse's aide up at Community Hospital on the orthopedic ward, night shift. She'll work eleven to seven. Then she gets home and I take off, drop the kids at school, and swing back around to the station. We got a babysitter for the little guy. I don't know quite what we'll do when the new one comes along."

"You'll figure something out," I said.

"I guess," he said. He flopped the wallet shut and tucked it back in his pocket.

I bought a round of beers and then he bought one. I felt guilty about getting the poor man sloshed, but I had another question or two for him and I wanted his inhibitions out of the way. Meanwhile, the population in the bar was thinning down from ten to maybe six. I noticed, with regret, that Shana Timberlake had left. The jukebox had been fixed and the volume of the music was just loud enough to guarantee privacy without being so obtrusive we'd be forced to shout. I was relaxed, but not as loose as I allowed Tap to think. I gave his arm a bump.

"Tell me something," I said soddenly. "I'm just curious."

"What's that?"

"How much money did you and this Bailey fellow net?"

"Net?"

"In round numbers. About how much you make? I'm just asking. You don't have to say."

"We paid restitution on two thousand some-odd dollar."

"Two thousand? Bulll. You made more than that," I said.

Tap flushed with pleasure. "You think so?"

"Even bumpin' off gas stations, you made more, I bet."

"That's all I ever saw," he said.

"That's all they caught you for," I said, correcting him.

"That's all I put in my pocket. And that's the honest truth."

"But how much else? How much altogether?"

Tap studied up on that one, extending his chin, pulling at his lip in a parody of deep thought. "In the neighborhood, I would say, of . . . would you believe, forty-two thousand six hunderd and six."

"Who got that? Bailey got that?"

"Oh, it's gone now. He never did see a dime of it neither, as far as I know."

"Where'd it come from?"

"Couple little jobs we pulled they never found out about."

I laughed with delight. "Well, you old devil, you," I said, and gave his arm another push. "Where'd it go?"

"Beats me."

I laughed again and he got tickled, too. Somehow, it seemed like the funniest thing either of us
ever heard. After half a minute, the laughter trick-
led out and Tap shook his head.

"Whoo, that's good," he said. "I haven't
laughed like that since I don't know when."

"You think Bailey killed that little girl?"

"Don't know," he said, "but I will tell you
this. When we went off to jail? We give the money
to Jean Timberlake to hold. He got out and next
thing I know, she's dead and he says he don't
know where the money's at. It was long gone."

"Why didn't you get it when the two of you
got out?"

"Ah, no. Huh-unh. The cops prob'ly had their
eye on us, waitin' to see if we'd make a move.
Goddamn. Everybody figured he killed her for
sure. Me, I don't know. Doesn't seem like him.
Then again, she might of spent all the money and
he choked her in a fit."

"Naw. I don't believe that. I thought Pearl
said she was knocked up."

"Well, she was, but Bailey wouldn't kill her
for that. What's the point? The money's all we
cared about, and why in hell not? We done jail
time. We paid. We get out and we're too smart to
start throwin' cash around. We laid low. After she
died, Bailey told me she was the only one knew
for sure where it was and she never told. He
didn't want to know in case he ever had to take a
lie detector test. Gone for good by now. Or maybe
it's still hid, only nobody knows where."

"Maybe he has it after all. Maybe that's what he's lived on the whole time he's been gone."

"I don't know. I doubt it, but I'd sure like to have me a little talk with him."

"What do you think, though? Honestly."

"The honest truth?" he said, fixing me with a look. He leaned closer, winking. "I think I gotta go see a man about a dog. Don't go 'way now." He eased off the stool. He turned and pointed a finger at me solemnly like a gun. I fired a digit right back at him. He proceeded to the john, walking with the exaggerated nonchalance of a man who's drunk.

I waited fifteen minutes, nursing my beer, with an occasional glance at the door to the unisex facility. The woman who'd been dancing with Shana Timberlake was now playing pool with a kid who looked eighteen. It was nearly midnight by then, and Daisy started cleaning off the bar with a rag.

"Where'd Tap go?" I said when she had worked her way down within range of me.

"He got a phone call and took off."

"Just now?"

"Few minutes ago. He still owes a couple bucks on that tab."

"I'll take care of it," I said. I laid a five on the bar and waved away any change.

She was looking at me. "You know Tap's the biggest bullshitter ever lived."

"I gathered as much."

Her gaze was dark. "He might have been in trouble some years ago, but these days he's a decent family man. Nice wife and kids."

"Why tell me? I'm not hustling his buns."

"Why all the questions about the Fowler boy? You been pumping him all night."

"I talked to Royce. I'm curious about this business with his son, that's all."

"What's it to you?"

"It's just something to jaw about. There's nothing else going on."

She seemed to soften, apparently satisfied at the benevolence of my intent. "You here on vacation?"

"Business," I replied. I thought she'd pursue it, but she let the subject drop.

"We close about this time weeknights," she said. "You're welcome to stay while I lock up in back, but Pearl doesn't like anyone around when I close out the register."

I realized then that I was the last person in the place. "I guess I better let you get on with it, then. I've had enough anyway."

The fog had curled right up to the road, obscuring the beach in a bunting of yellow mist. In the distance, a foghorn repeated its warning note. There were no cars passing and no sign of anyone on foot. Behind me, Daisy flipped the dead bolt and turned off the exterior lights, leaving me on my own. I walked briskly back to my motel room, wondering why Tap hadn't said good-bye.

# 8

Bailey's arraignment was scheduled for room
B of the Municipal Court, on the lower level of
the San Luis Obispo County Courthouse on Monterey Street. Royce rode with me. He didn't really
seem well enough for the trip into town, but he
was determined to have his way. Since Ann was
taking her mother to the doctor that morning and
couldn't accompany us, we tried to minimize the
exertions he'd be subjected to. I dropped him out
in front, watching as he made his way painfully up
the wide concrete steps. We had arranged for him
to wait for me in the airy lobby coffee shop with its
skylights and potted ficus plants. I had already
briefed him in the car coming over and he'd seemed
satisfied with the state of my inquiries to that
point. Now I wanted the opportunity to bring Jack
Clemson up to speed.

I left my car parked in a small private lot
behind the attorney's office, a block away. Clemson
and I walked over to the courthouse together,
using the time to talk about Bailey's frame of mind,
which he found worrisome. With me, Bailey had

seemed to alternate betwen numbness and despair. By the time he and Clemson chatted later in the day, his mood had darkened considerably. He was convinced he was never going to beat the escape charge. He was certain he'd end up at the Men's Colony again and equally certain he'd never survive incarceration.

"The guy's a basket case," Jack said. "I can't seem to talk any sense into him."

"But what are his chances, realistically?"

"Hey, I'm doing what I can. Bail's been set at half a million bucks, which is ridiculous. We're not talkin' Jack the Ripper here. I'll enter a motion to reduce. And maybe I can talk the prosecuting attorney into letting him plead to escape for the minimum. The time'll be added on, of course, but there's no way around that."

"And if I come up with some convincing evidence that someone else killed Jean Timberlake?"

"Then I'd move to set aside the original plea, or maybe file a coram nobis. Either way, we'd be set."

"Don't count on it, but I'll do what I can."

He flashed a smile at me, holding up crossed fingers.

When we got to the courthouse, he left me in the lobby while he went down to meet with the prosecuting attorney and the judge in chambers. The coffee shop was really no more than a wide expanse of central lobby, jammed with people now, the press in evidence. Royce was seated at a small table near the stairs, his hands folded across the top of his cane. He seemed tired. His hair had that matted, slightly sweaty cast of someone in ill health. He had ordered coffee, but it sat in the cup looking cold and untouched. I took a seat. The waitress swung by with a fresh pot of coffee, but I shook my head. Royce's anxiety enveloped the table like a sour, hopeless scent. He was clearly a proud man, accustomed to bending the world to his will. Bailey's arraignment already bore all the trappings of a public spectacle. The local paper had been running the story of his capture on the front page for days, and the local radio stations made mention of it at the top of each hour and again in the quick news summaries on the half hour.

A crew with a minicam passed just to the right of us, heading down the stairs without realizing Bailey Fowler's father was sitting within camera range. He turned a baleful eye on them and the ensuing smile was bitter and brief.

"Maybe we better go on down," I said.

We descended the stairs, walking slowly. I controlled an urge to give him physical support, sensing that he might take offense. His stoicism had a hint of self-mockery to it. He was grimly amused to have prevailed thus far, forcing his body to do his bidding regardless of the cost.

The corridor below was lined on one side with big plate-glass windows, with two exits into a sunken courtyard. Both the interior passageway and the exterior stairways were filling with spectators, some of whom seemed to recognize Royce as we passed. There was a silent parting in the crowd; gazes averted as we made our way into the courtroom. In the third row, people squeezed together to make room for us. There was the same hushed murmuring as in a church before services start. Most had dressed in their Sunday best, and the air seemed to stir with conflicting perfumes. No one spoke to Royce, but I could sense the rustling and nudging going on all around us. If he was humbled by the reaction, he gave no sign. He had been a respected member of the community, but Bailey's notoriety had tainted him. To have a son accused of murder is the same as being accused of a crime oneself—parental failure of the direst sort. Unfair though it may be, there is always that unspoken question: What did these people do to turn this once-innocent child into a cold-blooded killer of another human being?

I had checked the docket posted in the upstairs corridor. There were ten other arraignments scheduled that morning in addition to Bailey's. The door to the judge's chambers was closed. The court clerk, a slim, handsome woman in a navy blue suit, was seated at a table below and to the right of the judge's bench. The court reporter, also female, sat at a matching table to the left. There were a dozen attorneys present, most in dark, conservatively cut suits, all with white shirts, muted ties, black shoes. Only one was female.

While we waited for the proceedings to begin, I scanned the crowd. Shana Timberlake was seated across the aisle from us, one row back.

Under the flat fluorescent lights, the illusion of
youth vanished and I could see the dark streaks at
the corners of her eyes, suggesting age, weariness,
too many nights in bad company. She was wide-
shouldered, heavy-breasted, slender through the
waist and hips, wearing jeans and a flannel shirt.
As mother of the victim, she was free to dress any
way she liked. Her hair was nearly black, with a
few strands of silver here and there, combed straight
back from her face and held with a clip on top.
She turned her hot, dark eyes on me and I looked
away. She knew I was with Royce. When I glanced
back, I could see her gaze lingering on him with a
blunt appraisal of his physical condition.

One other woman caught my attention as she
came down the aisle. She was in her early thirties,
sallow, thin, wearing an apricot knit dress with a
big stain across the hem. She had on a white
sweater and white heels with short white cotton
socks. Her hair was a dishwater blond, held back
with a wide, tatty-looking headband. She was ac-
companied by a man I assumed was her husband.
He appeared to be in his mid-thirties, with curly
blond hair and the sort of pouty good looks I've
never liked. Pearl was with them, and I wondered
if this was the son he'd referred to who had seen
Bailey with Jean Timberlake the night she was
killed.

There was a faint escalation of murmurs at the
rear of the courtroom and I turned my head. The
crowd's attention focused in the way it does at a
wedding when the bride appears, ready to begin

her walk down the aisle. The prisoners were being brought in and the sight was oddly disturbing: nine men, handcuffed, shackled together, shuffling forward with their leg chains. They wore jail garb: unconstructed cotton shirts in orange, light gray, or charcoal, and gray or pale blue cotton pants with JAIL stenciled across the butt, white cotton socks, the type of plastic sandals known as "jellies." Most of them were young: five Latinos and three black guys. Bailey was the only white. He seemed acutely self-conscious, high color in his cheeks, his eyes downcast, the modest star of this chorus line of thugs. His fellow prisoners seemed to take the proceedings for granted, nodding to the scattering of friends and relatives. Most of the spectators had come to see Bailey Fowler, but nobody seemed to begrudge him his status. A uniformed deputy escorted the men into the jury box up front, where their leg chains were removed in case one of them had to approach the bench. The prisoners settled in, like the rest of us, to enjoy the show.

The bailiff went through his "all rise" recital, and we dutifully rose as the judge appeared and took his seat. Judge McMahon was in his forties and bristled with efficiency. Trim and fair-haired, he looked like the kind of man who played handball and squash, and risked dropping dead of a heart attack despite his prior history of perfect health. Bailey's case was being called next to last, so we were treated to a number of minor procedural dramas. A translator had to be summoned from somewhere in the building to aid in the arraignments of two of the accused who spoke no English. Papers had been misfiled. Two cases were kicked over to another date. Another set of papers had been sent but never received, and the judge was irked about that because the attorney had no proof of service and the other side wasn't ready. Two additional defendants, out on OR, were seated in the audience and each stepped forward in turn as his case was called.

At one point, one of the deputies pulled out a set of keys and unlocked an accused's handcuffs so that he could talk to his attorney at the back of the room. While that conference was going on, another prisoner engaged the judge in a lengthy discussion, insistent on representing himself. Judge McMahon was very opposed to the idea and spent ten minutes warning and admonishing, advising and scolding. The defendant refused to budge. The judge was finally forced to concede to the fellow's wishes since it was his right, but he was clearly cross about the matter. Through all of this, an undercurrent of restlessness was agitating the spectators into side-conversations and titters of laughter. They were primed for the lead act, and here they were, having to suffer through this second-rate series of burglaries and sexual assault cases. I half expected them to start clapping in unison, like a movie audience when the film is delayed.

Jack Clemson had been leaning against the wall in murmured conversation with the attorney next to him. As the time approached for Bailey's case to be called, he broke away and crossed the room. He spoke to the deputy and she unlocked Bailey's handcuffs. The two of them had just stepped to one side when there was a shout from the back. The judge's head snapped up and everybody turned simultaneously. A man in a red ski mask stood in the doorway, brandishing a sawed-off shotgun. The effect was electric, a ripple running through the room.

"FREEZE!" he yelled. "Everybody just hold it right there."

He fired once, apparently to make his point. The boom from the gun was deafening and the blast took one of the overhead lights right off its chain and sent it crashing to the floor. Shattered glass rained down like a cloudburst, and people screamed and scrambled for cover. A baby started shrieking. Everybody hit the floor, including me. Bailey's father was still sitting upright, immobilized by surprise. I reached up and grabbed him by the shirt front. I pulled him down to the floor with me, sheltering him with my body weight. He struggled, trying to get up, but in his condition it didn't take much to subdue him. I glanced over in time to see one of the deputies belly-crawl up the aisle to my right, shielded from the gunman's view by the wooden benches.

I'd caught a glimpse of the gunman and I could have sworn it was Tap, his hands shaking badly. He seemed too small to be a threat, his entire body tensed by fear. The true menace was the shotgun, with its broad, lethal spray, the indiscriminate destruction if his finger slipped. Any

unexpected movement might startle him into firing. Two women on the other side of Royce were
burbling hysterically, clinging to one another like
lovers.

"BAILEY, COME ON! GET THE FUCK
OUTTA HERE!!" the gunman screamed. His voice
broke from fright and I felt a chill as I peered over
the seat. It had to be Tap.

Bailey was transfixed. He stared in disbelief
and then he was in motion. He leaped the wooden
railing and ran, pounding down the aisle toward
the rear door while Tap blasted again. A large
framed photograph of the governor jumped off the
wall, disintegrating as the pellets ripped through
glass, wood frame, and matting in a spray of white.
A second round of wails and screams erupted from
the crowd. Bailey had disappeared by then. Tap
cracked the shotgun and jammed in two more
shells as he backed out of the courtroom. I heard
running. An outside door slammed and then there
were shouts and the sound of shots.

In the courtroom, there was chaos. The clerk
and the court reporter were nowhere to be seen
and I could only guess that the judge had made his
way out of the room at floor level, crawling on his
hands and knees. Once the immediate threat was
gone, people surged forward in a panic, shoving
toward the bench, pushing through to the safety of
the judge's chambers beyond. Pearl was hustling
his son and daughter-in-law out the fire exit, setting off an alarm bell that clanged at a piercing
pitch.

More screams sounded from the corridor, where someone was shouting incomprehensibly. I headed in that direction, bent double until I could get a sense of what was happening. If more gunfire broke out, I didn't want to get caught by flying bullets. I passed a woman bleeding badly from the glass shards that had cut into her face. Someone was already applying pressure to the worst of her wounds, while beside her, two little children huddled together and wept. I reached the rear door and pushed out. Shana Timberlake was leaning against the wall to my left, her face blanched, the shadows under her eyes as emphatic as stage makeup.

Outside, police sirens were already spiraling against the morning air.

Through the big plate-glass walls that formed one side of the corridor, I could see uniformed police officers spilling down the steps into the courtyard outside. Several women screamed in continuous shrill tones, as if the shooting had unleashed years of suppressed anguish. The jam of hysterical people in the hallway surged forward and then parted abruptly.

Tap Granger lay on his back, his arms flung out like he was taking a sunbath. The red ski mask had been pulled back off his face and it rested on the back of his head, as flabby as a rooster's crest. He wore a short-sleeved shirt and I could see where his wife had ironed the creases in. His arms looked skinny. His whole body looked dead. Bailey was nowhere in sight.

I went back into the courtroom, aware for the first time that I was crunching my way through broken glass and grit. Royce Fowler was on his feet, swaying uncertainly among the rows of empty benches. His mouth trembled.

"Tell me you had nothing to do with this," I said to him.

"Where's Bailey? Where's my boy? They'll shoot him down like a dog."

"No, they won't. He's unarmed. They'll find him. I take it you didn't know this was going to happen."

"Who was that in the mask?"

"Tap Granger. He's dead."

Royce sank onto the bench and lowered his head into his hands. The debris underfoot made a crackling sound. Looking down, I realized the floor was littered with white specks.

I stared in confusion, then bent down and picked up a handful. "What is this?" I said. Comprehension came in the same moment, but it still made no sense. Tap's shotgun shells had been loaded with rock salt.

# 9

By the time we got back to the motel, Royce was close to collapse and I had to help him into bed. Ann and Ori had heard the news in the doctor's office and they came straight home, pulling in soon after I did. Bailey Fowler was being billed as "a killer on the loose, believed armed and dangerous." The streets of Floral Beach already looked deserted, as if in the wake of some natural disaster. I could practically hear the doors slamming all up and down the block, little children jerked to safety, old ladies peering out from behind their curtains. Why anyone thought Bailey would be foolish enough to come back to his parents' house, I don't know. The sheriff's department must have considered it a good possibility because a deputy, in a tan uniform, stopped by the motel and had a long, officious chat with Ann, one hand on his gun butt, his gaze shifting from point to point, searching (I assumed) for some indication that the escapee was being harbored on the premises.

As soon as the patrol car pulled away, friends began to arrive with solemn expressions, dropping off casseroles. Some of these people I'd seen at the courthouse and I couldn't tell if their appearance was motivated by sympathy or a craven desire to be part of the continuing drama. Two neighbor ladies came, introduced to me as Mrs. Emma and Mrs. Maude, aging sisters who'd known Bailey since he was a boy. Robert Haws, the minister from the Baptist church, appeared along with his wife, June, and yet another woman who introduced herself as Mrs. Burke, the owner of the Laundromat two blocks away. She just popped over for a minute, she said, to see if there was anything she could do. I was hoping she'd offer cut rates on the Fluff 'n' Fold, but apparently this didn't occur to her. Judging from Mrs. Maude's expression, she disapproved of the store-bought frozen cheesecake the Laundromat lady handed over so blithely. Mrs. Maude and Mrs. Emma exchanged a look that suggested this was not the first time Mrs. Burke had flaunted her lack of culinary zealousness. The phone rang incessantly. Mrs. Emma appointed herself the telephone receptionist, fielding calls, keeping a log of names and return numbers in case Ori felt up to it later.

Royce refused to see anyone, but Ori entertained from her bed, repeating endlessly the circumstances under which she'd heard the news, what she'd first thought, when the facts had finally penetrated, and how she'd commenced to howl with misery until the doctor sedated her. Whatever Tap Granger's fate or her son's fugitive status, she experienced events as peripheral to "The Ori Fowler Show," in which she starred. Before I had a chance to slip out of the room, the minister asked us to join him in a word of prayer. I have to confess, I've never been taught proper prayer etiquette. As far as I can tell, it consists of folded hands, solemnly bowed heads, and no peeking at the other supplicants. I don't object to religious practices, per se. I'm just not crazy about having someone else inflict their beliefs on me. Whenever Jehovah's Witnesses appear at my door, I always ask for their addresses first thing, assuring them that I'll be around later in the week to plague them with my views.

While the minister interceded with the Lord in Bailey Fowler's behalf, I absented myself mentally, using the time to study his wife. June Haws was in her fifties, no more than five feet tall and, like many women in her weight class, destined for a sedentary life. Naked, she was probably dead white and dimpled with fat. She wore white cotton gloves with some sort of amber-staining ointment visible at the wrist. With her face blocked out, hers were the kind of limbs one might see in a medical journal, illustrative of particularly scabrous outbreaks of impetigo and eczema.

When Reverend Haws's interminable prayer had come to a close, Ann excused herself and went into the kitchen. It was clear that the appearance of servitude on her part was actually a means of escaping whenever she could. I followed her and, in the guise of being helpful, began to set out cups and saucers, arranging Pepperidge Farm cookies on plates lined with paper doilies while she hauled out the big stainless-steel coffee urn that usually sat in the office. On the kitchen counter, I could see a tuna casserole with crushed potato chips on top, a ground beef and noodle bake, and two Jell-O molds (one cherry with fruit cocktail, one lime with grated carrots), which Ann asked me to refrigerate. It had only been an hour and a half since Bailey fled the courthouse in a blaze of gunfire. I didn't think gelatin set up that fast, but these Christian ladies probably knew tricks with ice cubes that would render salads and desserts in record time for just such occasions. I pictured a section in the ladies' auxiliary church cookbook for Sudden Death Quick Snacks . . . using ingredients one could keep on the pantry shelf in the event of tragedy.

"What can I do to help?" June Haws asked from the kitchen door. With her cotton gloves, she looked like a pallbearer, possibly for someone who had died recently from the same skin disease. I moved a plate of cookies just out of range and pulled a chair out so she could have a seat.

"Oh, not for me, hon," she said. "I never sit. Why don't you let me take over, Ann, and you can get off your feet."

"We're doing fine," Ann said. "If you can

keep Mother's mind off Bailey, that's all the help we need."

"Haws is reading Scriptures with her even as we speak. I can't believe what that woman's been through. It's enough to break your heart. How's your daddy doing? Is he all right?"

"Well, it's been a shock, of course."

"Of course it has. That poor man." She looked over at me. "I'm June Haws. I don't believe we've been introduced."

Ann broke in. "I'm sorry, June. This is Kinsey Millhone. She's a private detective Pop hired to help us out."

"Private *detective*?" she said, with disbelief. "I didn't think there was such a thing, except on television shows."

"Nice to meet you," I said. "I'm afraid the work we do isn't quite that thrilling."

"Well, I hope not. All those gun battles and car chases? It's enough to make my blood run cold! It doesn't seem like a fit occupation for a nice girl like you."

"I'm not that nice," I said modestly.

She laughed, mistaking this for a joke. I avoided any further interaction by picking up a cookie plate. "Let me just take these on in," I murmured, moving toward the other room.

Once in the hallway, I slowed my pace, caught between Bible readings in the one room and relentless platitudes in the other. I hesitated in the doorway. The high school principal, Dwight Shales, had appeared while I was gone, but he was deep in conversation with Mrs. Emma and didn't seem to notice me. I eased into the living room where I handed the cookie plate to Mrs. Maude, then excused myself again and headed toward the office. Reverend Haws was intoning an alarming passage from the Old Testament full of besiegedness, pestilence, consuming locusts, and distress. Ori's lot must have seemed pretty tame by comparison, which was probably the point.

I went up to my room. It was almost noon and my guess was the assembled would hang around for a hot lunch. With luck, I could slip down the outside stairs and reach my car before anybody realized I was gone. I washed my face and ran a comb through my hair. I had my jacket over my arms and a hand on the doorknob when somebody knocked. For a moment I flashed on the image of Dwight Shales. Maybe he'd gotten the okay to talk to me. I opened the door.

Reverend Haws was standing in the corridor. "I hope you don't mind," he said. "Ann thought you'd probably come up here to your room. I didn't have an opportunity to introduce myself. I'm Robert Haws of the Floral Beach Baptist Church."

"Hi, how are you?"

"I'm just fine. My wife, June, was telling me what a nice chat she had with you a short while ago. She suggested you might like to join us for Bible study over at the church tonight."

"How nice," I said. "Actually, I'm not sure where I'll be tonight, but I appreciate the invitation." I'm embarrassed to admit it, but I was mimicking the warm, folksy tone they all used with one another.

Like his wife, Reverend Haws appeared to be in his fifties, but aging better than she was, I thought. He was round-faced, handsome in a Goody-Two-Shoes sort of way: bifocals with wire frames, sandy hair streaked with gray, cut full (with just the faintest suggestion of styling mousse). He was wearing a business suit in a muted glen plaid and a black shirt with a clerical collar that seemed an affectation for a Protestant. I didn't think Baptists wore things like that. He had all the easy charm of someone who spent his entire adult life on the receiving end of pious compliments.

We shook hands. He held on to mine and gave it a pat, making lots of Christian eye contact. "I understand you're from Santa Teresa. I wonder if you know Millard Alston from the Baptist church there in Colgate. He and I were seminarians together. I hate to tell you how long ago that's been."

I extracted my hand from his moist grip, smiling pleasantly. "The name doesn't sound familiar. Of course, I don't have much occasion to be out in that direction."

"What's your congregation? I hope you're not going to tell me you're an ornery Methodist." He said this with a laugh, just to show what a wacky sense of humor he had.

"Not at all," I said.

He peered toward the room behind me. "Your husband traveling with you?"

"Uh, no. Actually he's not." I glanced at my watch. "Oh golly. I'm late." The "golly" rather stuck in my throat, but it didn't seem to bother him.

He put his hands in his pants pockets, subtly adjusting himself. "I hate to see you run off so soon. If you're in Floral Beach come Sunday, maybe you can make it to the eleven-o'clock service and then join us for lunch. June doesn't cook anymore because of her condition, but we'd enjoy having you as our guest at the Apple Farm Restaurant."

"Oh gee. I wish I could, but I'm not sure I'll be here for the weekend. Maybe another time."

"Well, you're a tough little gal to pin down," he said. His manner was a trifle irritated and I had to guess he was unaccustomed to having his unctuous overtures rebuffed.

"I sure am," I said. I put on my jacket as I moved out into the corridor. Reverend Haws stepped aside, but he was still standing closer to me than I would have liked. I pulled the door shut behind me, making sure it was locked. I walked toward the stairs and he followed me.

"Sorry to be in such a rush, but I have an appointment." I'd cut the warm, folksy tone to a minimum.

"I'll let you get on your way, then."

The last I saw of him, he was standing at the head of the exterior stairs, looking down at me with a chilly gaze that contradicted his surface benevolence. I started my car and then waited in the parking slot until I'd seen him walk by, returning to the Fowlers. I didn't like the idea of his being anywhere near my room if I was off the premises.

I drove half a mile along the two-lane access road that connected Floral Beach to the highway, another mile due north. I reached the entrance to the Eucalyptus Mineral Hot Springs and turned into the parking lot. The brochure in the motel office indicated that the sulfur-based springs had been discovered in the late 1800s by two men drilling for oil. Instead of the intended rigs, a spa was built, serving as a therapeutic center for ailing Californians who arrived by train, alighting at the tiny station just across the road. A staff of doctors and nurses attended the afflicted, offering cures that included mud baths, nostrums, herbal treatments, and hydroelectric therapy. The facility flourished briefly and then fell into disuse until the 1930s, when the present hotel was constructed on the site. A second incarnation occurred in the early seventies when spas became fashionable again. Now, in addition to the fifty or so hot tubs that dotted the hillside under the oak and eucalyptus trees, there were tennis courts, a heated pool, and aerobics classes available, along with a full program of facials, massage, yoga instruction, and nutritional counseling.

The hotel itself was a two-story affair, a curious testament to thirties architecture, art deco Spanish, complete with turrets, sensuously rounded corners, and walls of block glass. I approached the office by way of a covered walk, the air chilled by deep shade unrelieved by sunlight. At close range, the building's stucco exterior showed bulging cracks that snaked up from the foundations to the terra-cotta roof tiles that had aged to the color of cinnamon. The sulfurous aroma of the mineral springs blended dankly with the smell of wet leaves. There was the suggestion of subtle leakages, something permeating the soil, and I wondered if, later, drums of poisonous wastes would be excavated from the spot.

I took a quick detour, climbing a set of steep wooden stairs that cut up along the hill behind the hotel. There were gazebos at intervals, each sheltering a hot tub sunk into a wooden platform. Weathered wooden fences were strategically placed to shield the bathers from public view. Each alcove had a name, perhaps to facilitate some scheduling procedure in the office down below. I passed "Serenity," "Meditation," "Sunset," and "Peace," uncomfortably aware of how similar the names were to the "sleep rooms" in certain funeral homes of my acquaintance. Two of the tubs were empty, littered with fallen leaves. One had an opaque plastic cover lying on the surface of the water like a skin. I picked my way down the steps again, thankful that I wasn't in the market for a hot soak.

At the main building, I pushed through glass doors into the reception area. The lobby seemed more inviting, but it still had the feel of a YWCA in need of funds. The floors were a mosaic of black and white tiles, the smell of PineSol suggesting a recent swabbing with a wet mop. From the far reaches of the interior, I could hear the hollow echoes of an indoor pool where a woman with a German accent called out authoritatively, "Kick! Resist! Kick! Resist!" Her commands were punctuated by a torpid splashing that called to mind the clumsy mating of water buffalo.

"May I help you?"

The receptionist had emerged from a small office behind me. She was tall, big-boned, one of those women who probably shopped in the "full figured" department of women's clothing stores. She must have been in her late forties, with white-blond hair, white lashes, and pale, unblemished skin. Her hands and feet were large, and the shoes she wore were the prison-matron-lace-up sort.

I handed her my business card, introducing myself. "I'm looking for someone who might remember Jean Timberlake."

She kept her eyes pinned on my face, her expression blank. "You'll want to talk to my husband, Dr. Dunne. Unfortunately, he's away."

"Can you tell me when he's expected back?"

"I'm not certain. If you leave a number, I can have him call when he returns."

We locked eyes. Hers were the stony gray of winter skies before snow. "What about you?" I said. "Did you know the girl yourself?"

There was a pause. Then, carefully, "I knew who she was."

"I understand she was working here at the time of her death."

"I don't think this is something we should discuss" —she glanced down at the card—"Miss Millhone."

"Is there some problem?"

"If you'll tell me how to reach you, I'll have my husband get in touch."

"Room twenty-two at the Ocean Street Motel in—"

"I know where it is. I'm sure he'll call if he has time."

"Wonderful. That way we won't have to bother about subpoenas." I was bluffing, of course, and she might have guessed as much, but I did enjoy the pale wash of color that suffused her cheeks. "I'll check back if I don't hear from him," I said.

It wasn't until I reached the car again that I remembered the owners mentioned in the brochure I'd seen. Dr. and Mrs. Joseph Dunne had bought the hotel the same year Jean Timberlake died.

# 10

It was 12:35 when I swung back around to the main street of Floral Beach and parked my car out in front of Pearl's Pool Hall. Weekday business hours were listed as 11:00 A.M. to 2:00 A.M. The door stood open. Last night's air tumbled out in a sluggish breeze that smelled of beer spills and cigarettes. The interior was stuffy, slightly warmer than the ocean-chilled temperature outside. I caught sight of Daisy at the back door, hauling out a massive plastic sack of trash. She gave me a non-committal look, but I sensed that her mood was dark. I took a seat at the bar. I was the only customer at that hour. Empty, the place seemed even more drab than it had the night before. The floors had been swept and I could see peanut shells and cigarette butts in a heap near the broom, waiting to be nudged into the dustpan propped nearby. The back door banged shut and Daisy reappeared, wiping her hands on the toweling she'd tucked in her belt. She approached warily, her gaze not quite meeting mine. "How's the detective work?"

"I'm sorry I didn't identify myself last night."

"What's it to me? I don't give a damn who you are."

"Maybe not, but I wasn't quite straight with Tap and I feel bad about that."

"You look real tore up."

I shrugged. "I know it sounds lame, but it's the truth. You thought I was hustling him, and in a way, I was."

She said nothing. She stood and stared at me. After a while she said, "You want a Co'-Cola? I'm having one."

I nodded, watching as she picked up a couple of Mason jars and filled them from the hose dispenser under the bar. She set mine in front of me.

"Thanks."

"I hear by the grapevine Royce hired you," she said. "What'd he do that for?"

"He's hoping to have Bailey cleared of the murder charge."

"He'll have a hell of a time after what happened this morning. If Bailey's innocent like he claims, why take off?"

"People get impulsive under pressure. When I talked to him at the jail, he seemed pretty desperate. Maybe when Tap showed up, he saw a way out."

Daisy's tone was contemptuous. "Kid never did have a lick of sense."

"So it would seem."

"What about Royce? How's he doing?"

"Not that well. He went right to bed. A lot of people are over there with Ori."

"I don't have much use for her," Daisy said. "Anybody heard from Bailey?"

"Not as far as I know."

She busied herself behind the bar, running a sinkful of hot soapy water and a second sinkful of rinse water. She began to wash Mason jars left over from the night before, her motions automatic as she ran through the sequence, setting clean jars to drain on a towel to the right. "What'd you want with Tap?"

"I was curious what he had to say about Jean Timberlake."

"I heard you askin' him about the stickups them two pulled."

"I was interested in whether his version would match Bailey's."

"Did it?"

"More or less," I said. I studied her as she worked, wondering why she was suddenly so interested. I wasn't about to mention the $42,000 Tap claimed had disappeared. "Who called him here last night? Did you recognize the voice?"

"Some man. Not anyone I knew right off. Might have been someone I'd talked to before, but I couldn't say for sure. There was something queer about the whole conversation," she remarked. "You think it was related to the shooting?"

"It almost had to be."

"That's what I think, too, the way he tore out

of here. I'd be willing to swear it wasn't Bailey, though."

"Probably not," I said. "He wouldn't have been permitted to use the jail phone at that hour and he couldn't have met with Tap in any event. What made the call seem so queer?"

"Odd voice. Deep. And the speech was kind of drug out, like someone who'd had a stroke."

"Like a speech impediment?"

"Maybe. I'd have to think about that some. I can't quite put my finger on it." She was silent for a moment and then shook her head, shifting the subject. "Tap's wife, Joleen, is who I feel sorry for. Have you talked to her?"

"Not yet. I guess I will at some point."

"Four little kids. Another due any day."

"Nasty business. I wish he'd used his head. There's no way he could have pulled it off. The deputies are always armed. He never had a chance," I said.

"Maybe that's the way they wanted it."

"Who?"

"Whoever put him up to it. I knew Tap since he was ten years old. Believe me, he wasn't smart enough to come up with a scheme like that on his own."

I looked at her with interest. "Good point," I said. Maybe Bailey was meant to get whacked at the same time, thus eliminating both of them. I reached into my jeans pocket and pulled out the list of Jean Timberlake's classmates. "Any of these guys still around?"

She took the list, pausing while she removed a pair of bifocals from her shirt pocket. She hooked the stems across her ears. She held the paper at arm's length and peered at the names, tilting her head back. "This one's dead. Ran his car off the road about ten years back. This fella moved up to Santa Cruz, last I heard. The rest are either here in Floral Beach or San Luis. You going to talk to every one of 'em?"

"If I have to."

"David Poletti's a dentist with an office on Marsh. You might want to start with him. Nice man. I've known his mother for years."

"Was he a friend of Jean's?"

"I doubt it, but he'd probably know who was."

As it turned out, David Poletti was a children's dentist who spent Wednesday afternoons in the office, catching up on his paperwork. I waited briefly in a pastel-painted reception suite with scaled-down furniture and tattered issues of *Highlights for Children* stacked on low tables, along with *Jack and Jill* and *Young Miss*. Of special interest to me in the last was a column called "Was My Face Red!" in which young girls gushingly related embarrassing moments—most of which were things I'd done not that long ago. Knocking a full cup of Coke off a balcony railing was one. The people down below really yell, don't they?

Dr. Poletti's office staff was composed of three women in their twenties, Alice-in-Wonderland types with big eyes, sweet smiles, long straight hair, and nothing threatening about them. Soothing music oozed out of the walls like whiffs of nitrous oxide. By the time I was ushered into his inner office, I would almost have been willing to sit in a tot-sized dental chaise and have my gums probed with one of those tiny stainless-steel pruning hooks.

When I shook hands with Dr. Poletti, he was still wearing a white jacket with an alarming blood-stain on the front. He caught sight of it about the same time I did, and peeled his jacket off, tossing it across a chair with a soft, apologetic smile. Under the jacket he was wearing a dress shirt and a sweater vest. He indicated that I should take a seat while he shrugged into a brown tweed sport coat and adjusted his cuffs. He was maybe thirty-five, tall, with a narrow face. His hair frizzed in tight curls already turning gray along the sides. I knew, from his yearbook pictures, that he'd played high school basketball and I imagined sophomore girls gushing over him in the cafeteria. He wasn't technically handsome, but he had a certain appeal, a gentleness in his demeanor that must have been reassuring to women and little kids. His eyes were small and drooped slightly at the corners, the color a mild brown behind lightweight metallic frames.

He sat down at his desk. A color studio por-trait of his wife and two young boys was promi-nently displayed, probably to dispel any fantasies his staff might entertain about his availability. "Tawna says you have some questions about an old high school classmate. Given recent events, I'm assuming it's Jean Timberlake."

"How well did you know her?"

"Not very well. I knew who she was, but I don't think I ever had a class with her." He reached for a set of plaster-of-Paris impressions that sat on his desk, upper plate positioned above the lower in a jutting overbite. He cleared his throat. "What sort of information are you looking for?"

"Whatever you can tell me. Bailey Fowler's father hired me to see if I could come up with some new evidence. I thought I'd start with Jean and work forward from there."

"Why come to me?"

I told him about my conversation with Daisy and her suggestion that he might be of help. His manner seemed to shift, becoming less suspicious, though a certain wariness remained. Idly he lifted the mold's upper plate and stuck his finger in, feeling the crowded lower incisors. If I had banged a fist down on the mold, I could have bitten his finger off. The thought made it hard to concentrate on what he was saying. "I've been thinking a lot about the murder since Bailey Fowler's arrest. Terrible thing. Just terrible."

"Were you in that group of kids who found her, by any chance?"

"No, no. I'm a Catholic. That was the youth group from the Baptist church."

"The one in Floral Beach?"

He nodded and I made a mental note, thinking of Reverend Haws. "I've heard she was a bit free with her favors," I said.

"That's the reputation she had. Some of my patients are young girls her age. Fourteen, fifteen.

They just seem so immature. I can't imagine them sexually active and yet I'm sure some of them are."

"I've seen pictures of Jean. She was a beautiful girl."

"Not in any way that served her. She wasn't like the rest of us. Too old in some ways, innocent in others. I guess she thought she'd be popular if she put out, so that's what she did. A lot of guys took advantage." He paused to clear his throat. "Excuse me," he said. He poured himself half a tumbler of water from the thermos sitting on his desk. "You want some water?"

I shook my head. "Anybody in particular?"

"What?"

"I'm wondering if she was involved with anyone you knew."

He gave me a bland look. "Not that I recall."

I could feel the arrow on my bullshit meter swing up into the red. "What about you?"

A baffled laugh. "Me?"

"Yeah, I was wondering if you got involved with her." I could see the color come and go in his face, so I ad-libbed a line. "Actually, someone told me you dated her. I can't remember now who mentioned it, but someone who knew you both."

He shrugged. "I might have. Just briefly. I never dated her steadily or anything like that."

"But you were intimate."

"With Jean?"

"Dr. Poletti, spare me the wordplay and tell

me about your relationship. We're talking about things that happened seventeen years ago."

He was silent for a moment, toying with the plaster jaw, which seemed to have something on it he had to pick off. "I wouldn't want this to go any further, whatever we discuss."

"Strictly confidential."

He shifted in his chair. "I guess I've always regretted my association with her. Such as it was. I'm ashamed of it now because I knew better. I'm not sure she did."

"We all do things we regret," I said. "It's part of growing up. What difference does it make after all this time?"

"I know. You're right. I don't know why it's so hard to talk about."

"Take your time."

"I did date her. For a month. Less than that. I can't say my intentions were honorable. I was seventeen. You know how guys are at that age. Once word got out that Jeannie was an easy lay, we became obsessed. She did things we'd never even heard about. We were lined up like a pack of dogs, trying to get at her. It was all anybody ever talked about, how to get in her pants, how to get her in ours. I guess I was no better than the other guys." He shot me an embarrassed smile.

"Go on."

"Some of 'em didn't even bother going through the motions. Just picked her up and took her out to the beach. They didn't even take her out on a date."

"But you did."

He lowered his gaze. "I took her out a few times. I felt guilty even doing that. She was kind of pathetic . . . and scary at the same time. She was bright enough, but she wanted desperately to believe someone cared. It made you feel sheepish, so you'd get together with the guys afterward and bad-mouth her."

"For what you'd done," I supplied.

"Right. I still can't think about her without feeling kind of sick. What's strange is I can still remember things she did." He paused for a moment, eyebrows going up. He shook his head once, blowing out a puff of air. "She was really outrageous . . . insatiable's the word . . . but what drove her wasn't sex. It was . . . I don't know, self-loathing or a need to dominate. We were at her mercy because we wanted her so much. I guess our revenge was never really giving her what she wanted, which was old-fashioned respect."

"And what was hers?"

"Revenge? I don't know. Creating that heat. Reminding us that she was the only source, that we could never have enough of her or anything even halfway like her for life. She needed approval, some guy to be nice. All we ever did was snicker about her behind her back, which she must have known."

"Did she get hung up on you?"

"I suppose. Not for long, I don't think."

"It would help if you could tell me who else might have been involved with her."

He shook his head. "I can't. You're not going to get me to blow the whistle on anybody else. I still hang out with some of those guys."

"How about if I read you some names off a list?"

"I can't do that. Honestly. I don't mind owning up to my own part in it, but I can't implicate anybody else. It's an odd bond and something we don't talk about, but I'll tell you this—her name gets mentioned, we don't say a word, but we're all thinking the same damn thing."

"What about guys who weren't friends of yours?"

"Meaning what?"

"At the time of the murder, she was apparently having an affair and got herself knocked up."

"Don't know."

"Make a guess. There must have been rumors."

"Not that I heard."

"Can you ask around? Somebody must know."

"Hey, I'd like to help, but I've probably already said more than I should."

"What about some of the girls in your class? Someone must have been clued in back then."

He cleared his throat again. "Well. Barb might know. I could ask her, I guess."

"Barbara who?"

"My wife. We were in the same class."

I glanced at the photograph on his desk, recognizing her belatedly. "The prom queen?"

"How'd you know about that?"

"I saw some pictures of her in the yearbook. Would you ask her if she could help?"

"I doubt if she knows anything, but I could mention it."

"That'd be great. Have her give me a call. If she doesn't know anything about it, she might suggest someone who would."

"I wouldn't want anything said about . . ."

"I understand," I said.

I gave him my card with a little note on the back, with my telephone number at the Ocean Street. I left his office feeling faintly optimistic and more than a little disturbed. There was something about the idea of grown men haunted by the sexuality of a seventeen-year-old girl that seemed riveting—both pitiable and perverse. Somehow the glimpse he'd given me of the past made me feel like a voyeur.

# 11

At two o'clock I slipped up the outside stairs at the motel and changed into my running clothes. I hadn't had lunch, but I was feeling supercharged, too wired to eat. After the hysteria at the courthouse, I'd spent hours in close contact with other human beings and my energy level had risen to an agitated state. I pulled on my sweats and my running shoes and headed out again, room key tied to my laces. The afternoon was slightly chilly, with a haze in the air. The sea blended into the sky at the horizon with no line of demarcation visible between. Southern California seasons are sometimes too subtle to discern, which I'm told is disconcerting to people who've grown up in the Midwest and the East. What's true, though, is that every day is a season in itself. The sea is changeable. The air is transformed. The landscape registers delicate alterations in color so that gradually the saturated green of winter bleaches out to the straw shades of summer grass, so quick to burn. Trees

explode with color, fiery reds and flaming golds
that could rival autumn anywhere, and the charred
branches that remain afterward are as bare and
black as winter trees in the East, slow to recover,
slow to bud again.

I jogged along the walkway that bordered the
beach. There was a sprinkling of tourists. Two kids
about eight were dodging the waves, their shrieks
as raucous as the birds that wheeled overhead.
The tide was almost out and a wide, glistening
band divided the bubbling surf from the dry sand.
A twelve-year-old boy with a boogie board slid
expertly along the water's edge. Ahead, I could
see the zigzagging coastline, banded with asphalt
where the road followed the contours of the shore.
At the road's end was the Port San Luis Harbor
District, a fuel facility and launching area that
serviced the local boats.

I reached the frontage road and angled left,
jogging along the causeway that spanned the slough.
Up on the hill to my right was the big hotel with
its neatly trimmed shrubs and manicured lawns. A
wide channel of seawater angled back along the
fairways of the hotel's golf course. The distance
was deceptive and it took me thirty minutes to
reach the cul-de-sac at the end of the road where
the boats were launched. I slowed to a walk, catching my breath. My shirt was damp and I could feel
sweat trickling down the sides of my face. I've
been in better shape in my life and I didn't relish
the misery of regaining the ground I'd lost. I did
the turnaround, watching with interest as three

men lowered a pleasure craft into the water from a crane. There was a fishing trawler in drydock, its exposed hull tapering to a rudder as narrow as the blade of an ice skate. I found a spigot near a corrugated metal shed and doused my head, drinking deeply before I headed back, my leg muscles protesting as I increased my pace. By the time I reached the main street of Floral Beach again, it was nearly four and the February sun was casting deep shadows along the side of the hill.

I showered and dressed, pulling on jeans, tennis shoes, and a clean turtleneck, ready to face the world.

The Floral Beach telephone directory was about the size of a comic book, big print, skimpy on the Yellow Pages, light on advertising space. There was nothing to do in Floral Beach and what there was, everybody knew about. I looked up Shana Timberlake and made a note of her address on Kelley, which, by my calculation, was right around the corner. On my way out, I peered into the motel office, but everything was still.

I left my car in the slot and walked the two blocks. Jean's mother lived in what looked like a converted 1950s motor court, an inverted U of narrow frame cottages with a parking space in front of each. Next door, the Floral Beach Fire Department was housed in a four-car garage painted pale blue with dark blue trim. By the time I got back to Santa Teresa, it would seem like New York City compared with this.

There was a battered green Plymouth parked

beside unit number one. I peered in the window on the driver's side. The keys had been left in the ignition, a big metal initial T dangling from the key ring—for Timberlake, I assumed. Trusting, these folk. Auto theft must not be the crime of choice in Floral Beach. Shana Timberlake's tiny front porch was crowded with coffee cans planted with herbs, each neatly marked with a Popsicle stick labeled with black ink: thyme, marjoram, oregano, dill, and a two-gallon tomato sauce can filled with parsley. The windows flanking the front door were opened a crack, but the curtains were drawn. I knocked.

Presently, I heard her on the other side. "Yes?"

I talked through the door to her, addressing my remarks to one of the hinges. "Mrs. Timberlake? My name is Kinsey Millhone. I'm a private detective from Santa Teresa. I wonder if I might talk to you."

Silence. Then, "You the one Royce hired to get Bailey off?" She didn't sound happy about the idea.

"I guess that's one interpretation," I said. "Actually, I'm in town to look into the murder. Bailey says now he's innocent."

Silence.

I tried again. "You know, there never was much of an investigation once he pled guilty."

"So what?"

"Suppose he's telling the truth? Suppose whoever killed her is still running around town, thumbing his nose at the rest of us?"

There was a long pause and then she opened the door.

Her hair was disheveled, eyes puffy, mascara smeared, nose running. She smelled like bourbon. She tightened the sash on her flowered cotton kimono and stared at me blearily. "You were in court."

"Yes."

She swayed slightly, working to focus. "You believe in justice? You b'lieve justice is done?"

"On occasion."

"Yeah, well, I don't. So what's there to talk about? Tap's been shot down. Jean's choked to death. You think any of this is going to bring my daughter back?"

I said nothing, but I kept my gaze on her, waiting for her to wind down.

Her expression darkened with contempt. "You prob'ly don't even have kids. I bet you never even had a dog. You look like somebody breezing through life without a care in this world. Stand there talking about 'innocence.' What do you know about innocence?"

I kept my temper intact, but my tone was mild. "Let's put it this way, Mrs. Timberlake. If I had a kid and somebody'd killed her, I wouldn't be drunk in the middle of the day. I'd be out pulling this town apart until I found out who did it. And then I'd manufacture some justice of my own if that's what it took."

"Well, I can't help you."

"You don't know that. You don't even know what I want."

"Why don't you tell me?"

"Why don't you invite me in and we'll talk."

She glanced back over her shoulder. "Place looks like shit."

"Who cares?"

She focused on me again. She could barely stand up. "How many kids you got?"

"None."

"That's how many I got," she said. She pushed the screen door open and I stepped in.

The place was essentially one long room with a stove, sink, and refrigerator lined up at the far end. Every available surface was stacked with dirty dishes. A small wooden table with two chairs divided the kitchen from the living room, one corner of which was taken up by a brass bed with the sheets half pulled off. The mattress sagged in the middle and it looked as if it would erupt in a symphony of springs if you sat on it. I caught a glimpse of bathroom through a curtained doorway to the right. On the other side of the bathroom, there was a closet, and beyond that was the back door.

I followed her to the kitchen table. She sank into one of the chairs and then got up again, frowning, and moved with great care to the bathroom where she threw up at length. I hate listening to people throw up. (This is big news, I'll bet.) I moved over to the sink and cleared the dirty dishes out, running hot water to mask the sounds coming from the bathroom. I squirted dish-washing liquid into the tumbling water and watched with satisfaction as a cloud of bubbles began to form. I slid plates into the depths, tucking silverware around the edges.

While the dishes soaked, I emptied the garbage, which consisted almost exclusively of empty whiskey bottles and beer cans. I peered into the refrigerator. The light was out and the interior smelled like mold, the metal racks crusted with what looked like dog doo. I closed the door again, worried I was going to have to take a turn in the bathroom with her.

I tuned an ear to Shana again. I heard the toilet galumphing and, after that, the reassuring white noise of a shower being run. Being an incurable snoop at heart, I turned my attention idly to the mail stacked up on the kitchen table. Since I was being mother's little helper, I felt almost entitled to nose around in her business. I walked my fingers through some unopened bills and junk mail. Nothing of interest on the face of it. There was only one piece of personal mail, a big square envelope postmarked Los Angeles. A greeting card? Curses. The envelope was sealed so tight I couldn't even pick the flap loose. Nothing visible when I held it to the light. No scent. Shana's name and address were handwritten in ink, a genderless script that told me nothing about the person who'd penned it. Reluctantly I tucked it back and returned to the sink.

By the time I had the dishes clean and piled in a perilous mound in the rack, Shana was emerging from the bathroom, her head wrapped in one towel and her body in another. Without any modesty at all, she dried herself off and got dressed. Her body was much older than her face. She sat down at the kitchen table in jeans and a T-shirt, barefoot. She looked exhausted, but her skin was scrubbed and her eyes had cleared to some extent. She lit an unfiltered Camel. This lady took smoking seriously. I didn't think unfiltered cigarettes were available these days.

I sat down across from her. "When did you last eat?"

"I forget. I started drinking this morning when I got back. Poor Tap. I was standing right there." She paused and her eyes filled with tears again, her nose turning pink with emotion. "I couldn't believe what was happening. I just lost it. Couldn't cope. I wasn't crazy about him, but he was an okay guy. Kind of dumb. A goofball who made awful jokes. I can't believe this is starting all over. What was he thinking about? He must have been nuts. Bailey comes back to town and look what happens. Somebody else dead. This time it's his best friend."

"Daisy figures somebody put Tap up to it."

"Bailey did," she snapped.

"Just wait," I said. "He got a telephone call last night at Pearl's. He talked briefly and then took off."

She blew her nose. "Must have been after I left," she said, unconvinced. "You want some coffee? It's instant."

"Sure, I'll have some."

She left her cigarette on the lip of the ashtray

and got up. She filled a saucepan with water and stuck it on the back burner, turning on the gas. She extracted two coffee mugs from the dish rack. "Thanks for cleaning up. You didn't have to do that."

"Idle hands . . ." I said, not mentioning that I'd also managed a little of the devil's work.

She unearthed a jar of instant coffee and a couple of spoons, which she set on the table while we waited for the water to boil. She took another drag from her cigarette and blew the smoke toward the ceiling. I could feel it settle around me like a fine veil. I was going to have to shampoo my hair again and change my clothes.

She said, "I still say Bailey killed her."

"Why would he do that?"

"Why would anybody else?"

"Well, I don't know, but from what I've heard, he was the only real friend she had."

She shook her head. Her hair was still wet, separated into long strands that dampened the shoulders of her T-shirt. "God, I hate this. Sometimes I wonder how she would have ended up. I've thought about that a lot. I never was much of a mom in terms of the ordinary stuff, but that kid and I were close. More like sisters."

"I saw some pictures of her in the yearbook. She was beautiful."

"For all the good it did. Sometimes I think her looks were what caused all her problems."

"Do you know who she was involved with?"

She shook her head. "I didn't know she was

pregnant until I heard about the coroner's report. I knew she was sneakin' out at night, but I have no idea where she went. And what was I supposed to do, nail the door shut? You can't control a kid that age. I guess maybe I should correct myself. We'd always *been* close. I thought we still were. If she was in trouble, she could have come to me. I'd have done anything for her."

"I heard she'd been trying to find out about her father."

Shana shot me a startled look, then covered her surprise with busyness. She stubbed out her cigarette and moved over to the stove, where she picked up a pot holder and shifted the saucepan unnecessarily. "Where'd you hear that?"

"Bailey. I talked to him at the jail yesterday. You never told her who her father was?"

"No."

"Why not?"

"I made a deal with him years ago and I kept my part. I might have broken down and told her, but I couldn't see what purpose it'd serve."

"Did she ask?"

"She might have mentioned it, but she didn't seem all that intent on the answer and I didn't think much of it."

"Bailey thought she was getting a line on the guy. Was there a way she could have tracked him down?"

"Why would she do that when she had me?"

"Maybe she wanted acknowledgment, or maybe she needed help."

"Because she was pregnant?"

"It's possible," I said. "As I understand it, she'd just had it confirmed, but she must have suspected if her period was late. Why else go all the way to Lompoc for a test?"

"I have no idea."

"What if she'd found him? What would his reaction have been?"

"She didn't find him," she said flatly. "He'd have told me."

"Unless he didn't want you to know."

"What are you getting at?"

"*Somebody* killed her."

"Well, it wasn't him." Her voice had risen and I could see the heat in her face.

"It could have been an accident. He might have been upset or incensed."

"She's his daughter, for God's sake! A seventeen-year-old girl? He'd never do such a thing. He's a nice man. A prince."

"Why not take responsibility if he was so nice?"

"Because he couldn't. It wasn't possible. Anyway, he did. He sent money. Still does. That's all I ever asked."

"Shana, I need to know who he is."

"It's none of your business. It's nobody's business except his and mine."

"Why all the secrecy? What's the big deal? So he's married. So what?"

"I didn't say he was married. You said that. I don't want to discuss it. He's got nothing to do with this, so just drop it. Ask me any more about him and I'll throw your ass out the door."

"What about Bailey's money? Did she ever mention that?"

"What money?"

I watched her carefully. "Tap told me the two of them had a stash nobody knew about. They asked her to hold it till they got out of jail. That's the last anybody heard of it."

"I don't know about any money."

"What about Jean? Did she seem to spend more than she might have made at work?"

"Not that I ever saw. If she'd had some, you wouldn't have caught her livin' like this."

"You were living here at the time of her death?"

"We had an apartment a couple blocks over, but it wasn't much better."

We talked on for a bit, but I couldn't elicit any more information. I got back to my room at six o'clock, not much smarter than I was when I'd started out. I typed up a report, fudging the language to disguise the fact that I hadn't gotten much.

# 12

I ate an early dinner with the Fowlers that night. Ori's meals had to come at fixed intervals to keep her blood sugar on track. Ann had made a beef stew, with salad and French bread, all of it yummy, I thought. Royce had problems with the meal. His illness had sapped his appetite along with his strength, and some deep-seated impatience made it hard for him to tolerate social occasions in any event. I couldn't imagine how it must have been to grow up with a man like him. He was gruff to the point of churlishness except when Bailey's name was mentioned, and then he shifted into a sentimentality he made no attempt to disguise. Ann didn't show much reaction to the fact that Bailey was the preferred child, but then she'd had a lifetime to get used to it. Ori, wanting to be certain Royce's illness didn't outshine her own, picked at her food, not complaining about it, but sighing audibly. It was obvious she was feeling "poorly," and Royce's refusal to inquire about her health only caused her to double her efforts. I made myself inconspicuous, tuning out the content of their conversation so I could concentrate on the interplay between them. As a child, I didn't experience much in the way of family and I usually find myself somewhat taken aback to see one at close range. "The Donna Reed Show" this was not. People talk about "dysfunctional" families; I've never seen any other kind. I turned up my interior volume control.

Ori put her fork down and pushed her plate back. "I best get things picked up. Maxine's coming by in the morning."

Ann took note of how much Ori'd eaten, and I could see her debating whether to speak up or not. "Did she switch days again? I thought she came on Mondays."

"I asked her to come special. Time to spring-clean."

"You don't have to do that, Mother. Nobody does any spring cleaning out here."

"Well, I know I don't *have* to. What's that got to do with it? Place is a mess. Dirt everywhere. It gets on my nerves. I may be an invalid, but I'm not infirm."

"Nobody said you were."

Ori plowed right on. "I still have some use, even if it's not appreciated."

"Of course you're appreciated," Ann murmured dutifully. "What time's she coming?"

"About nine, she said. We'll have to tear this whole place apart."

"I'll take care of my room," Ann said. "Last time she was in there, I swear she went through everything I owned."

"Well, I'm sure Maxine wouldn't do that. Besides, I already told her to do the floors in there and take down the drapes. I can't turn around and tell her the opposite."

"Don't worry about it. I'll tell her myself."

"Don't you hurt her feelings," Ori warned.

"All I'm going to do is tell her I'll clean my own room."

"What do you have against the woman? She's always liked you."

Royce stirred irritably. "Goddamn it, Ori. There's such a thing as privacy. If she doesn't want Maxine in her room, then so be it. Keep her out of my room, too, while you're at it. I feel the same way Ann does."

"Well, pardon me, I'm sure!" Ori snorted.

Ann seemed surprised by Royce's support, but she didn't dare comment. I'd seen his loyalties alter inexplicably, but there didn't seem to be any pattern to the shift. As a result, she was often caught up short or in some way made to look foolish.

Ori was now annoyed and her face was set with stubbornness. She lapsed into silence. Ann studied her dinner plate. I was casting about desperately for a reason to excuse myself.

Royce focused on me. "Who'd you talk to today?"

I hate being quizzed at the table. It's one of

the reasons I choose to eat alone. I mentioned my conversation with Daisy and the brief interview with the dentist. I was detailing some of the background information I'd picked up on Jean when he cut me off.

"Waste of time," he said.

I paused, losing my train of thought. "That isn't clear."

"I'm not paying you to talk to that pansy of a dentist."

"Then I'll do it on my own time," I said.

"Man's an idiot. Never had a thing to do with Jean. Wouldn't give her the time of day. Thought he was too good. She told me that herself." Royce coughed into his fist.

"He did date her briefly."

Ann's face lifted. "David Poletti did?"

"Do what I say and leave him out of this."

"Pop, if Kinsey thinks he might provide useful information, why not let her pursue it?"

"Who's paying the woman, you or me?"

Ann retreated into silence. Ori gestured with impatience and struggled to her feet. "You have ruint this meal," she snapped at him. "Just go on to bed if you can't be civil to our company. Lord a day, Royce, I can't stand no more of your crankiness."

Now the pouting crossed the table from Ori to Royce. Ann got up and moved to the kitchen counter, probably driven by the same tension that was making my stomach hurt. My orphanhood was becoming more appealing by the minute.

Ori snatched her cane and began to hobble toward the living room.

"Sorry for the interruption. Her temper's kind of short," he said to me.

"Is not," she fired back over her shoulder.

Royce ignored her so he could concentrate on me. "That's all you talked to? Daisy and that . . . tooth fairy?"

"I spoke to Shana Timberlake."

"What for?"

Ori paused at the door, not wanting to miss a trick. "Maxine says she's took up with Dwight Shales. Can you believe that?"

"Oh, Mother. Don't be ridiculous. Dwight wouldn't have anything to do with her."

"It's the truth. Maxine saw her getting out of his car over by the Shop 'n' Go last Saturday."

"So what?"

"At six A.M.?" Ori said.

"Maxine doesn't know what she's talking about."

"She most certainly does. She was right about Sarah Brunswick and her yardman, wasn't she?"

Royce turned around and stared at her pointedly. "Do you *mind*?" Ann's face was beginning to flush darkly as the conflict between the two sparked to life again. He turned back to me. "What's Shana Timberlake got to do with my son?"

"I'm trying to find out who fathered Jean's baby. I gather he was married."

"She mention any names?" Royce asked. Ann had returned with a fresh basket of bread, which she passed to him. He took a piece and passed the basket on to me. I placed it on the table, unwilling to be distracted by ritual gestures.

"She says Jean didn't tell her, but she must suspect someone. I'll let a little time pass and try her again. Bailey indicated Jean was trying to find out who her own father was, and that might open up some possibilities."

Royce pinched his nose, sniffing, and then he waved the idea away. "Probably some trucker she took up with. Woman never was particular. Long as a fella had money in his pocket, she'd do anything he asked." A second mild bout of coughing shook him and I had to wait till it had passed before I responded.

"If it was a trucker, why conceal his identity? It almost has to be somebody in the community, and probably somebody respectable."

"Hogwash. Nobody respectable would be caught dead with that whore. . . ."

"Somebody who didn't want it known, then," I said.

"Bullshit! I don't believe a word of it—"

I cut him off in a flash. "Royce, I know what I'm doing. Would you just back off and let me get on with it?"

He stared at me dangerously, his face growing dark. "What?"

"You hired me to do a job and I'm doing it. I don't want to have to justify and defend every move."

Royce's temper flared like lighter fluid squirted

on a fire. His hand shot out and he pointed a shaking finger in my face. "I'm not taking any sass from you, sis!"

"Great. And I won't take any sass from you. Either I do this my way or you can find somebody else."

Royce came halfway out of his chair, leaning on the table. "How dare you talk to me that way!" His face was flaming and his arms trembled where they bore his weight.

I sat where I was, watching him remotely through a haze of anger. I was on the verge of a comment so rude that I hesitated to voice it, when Royce started to cough. There was a pause while he tried to suppress it. He sucked in a breath. The coughing doubled. He pulled out a handkerchief and clamped it across his mouth. Ann and I both gave him our undivided attention, alerted by the fact that he couldn't seem to get his breath. His chest heaved in a wrenching spasm that gathered momentum, flinging him about.

"Pop, are you all right?"

He shook his head, unable to speak, his tongue protruding as the coughing shook him from head to toe. He wheezed, clutching at his shirt front as if for support. Instinctively, I reached for him as he staggered backward into his chair, struggling for air. It was suffocating to watch. The coughing tore at him, bringing up blood and phlegm. Sweat broke out on his face.

Ann said, "My God." She rose to her feet, hands cupped across her mouth. Ori was transfixed in the doorway, horrified by what was happening. Royce's whole body was wracked. I banged on his back, grabbing one arm, which I held aloft to give his lungs room to inflate.

"Get an ambulance!" I yelled.

Ann turned a blank look on me and then mobilized herself sufficiently to reach for the phone, punching 911. She kept her eyes pinned on her father's face while I loosened his collar and fumbled with his belt. Through a rush of adrenaline, I heard her describe the situation to the dispatcher on the other end, reciting the address and directions.

By the time she put the phone down, Royce was gaining control, but he was soaked in perspiration, his breathing labored. Finally the coughing subsided altogether, leaving him pale and clammy-looking, his eyes sunken with exhaustion, hair plastered to his scalp. I wrung a towel out in cold water and wiped his face. He started to tremble. I murmured nonsense syllables, patting at his hands. There was no way Ann and I could lift him, but we managed to lower him to the floor, thinking somehow to make him more comfortable. Ann covered him with a blanket and tucked a pillow under his head. Ori stood there in tears, mewing helplessly. She seemed to grasp the severity of his illness for the first time and she cried like a three-year-old, giving herself up to grief. He would go first. She seemed to understand that now.

In the distance we heard the sirens from the emergency vehicle. The paramedics arrived, taking in the situation with a practiced eye, their demeanor so studiously neutral that the crisis was reduced to a series of minor problems to be solved. Vital signs. Oxygen administered and an IV started. Royce was hefted with effort onto a portable gurney, which was angled out of the room to the vehicle at the curb. Ann went with him in the ambulance. The next thing I knew, I was alone with Ori. I sat down abruptly. The room looked as if it had been ransacked.

I heard a tentative voice from the office. "Hello? Ori?"

"That's Bert," Ori murmured. "He's the night manager."

Bert peered into the living room. He was maybe sixty-five, slight, no more than five feet tall, dressed in a suit he must have bought in the boys' wear department. "I saw the ambulance pull away. Is everything all right?"

Ori told him what had happened, the narrative apparently restoring some of the balance in her universe. Bert was properly sympathetic, and the two swapped a few long-winded tales about similar emergencies. The phone started to ring and he was forced to return to the front desk.

I got Ori into bed. I was worried about her insulin, but she wouldn't discuss it so I had to drop the subject. The episode with Royce had thrown her into a state of clinging dependency. She wanted physical contact, incessant reassurances. I made her some herb tea. I dimmed the lights. I stood by the bed while she clutched my hand. She talked on about Royce and the children at length while I supplied questions to keep the conversation afloat. Anything to get her mind off Royce's collapse.

She finally drifted off to sleep, but it was midnight before Ann got back. Royce had been admitted and she'd stayed until he was settled. A number of tests had been scheduled for first thing in the morning. The doctor was guessing that the cancer had invaded his lungs. Until the chest X rays came back, he couldn't be sure, but things weren't looking good.

Ori stirred. We'd been speaking in whispers, but it was clear we were disturbing her. We moved out through the kitchen and sat together on the back steps. It was dark out there, the building shielding us from the smudged yellow of the streetlights. Ann pulled her knees up and rested her head wearily on her arms. "God. How am I going to get through the next few months?"

"It'll help if we can get Bailey cleared."

"Bailey," she said. "That's all I hear about." She smiled bitterly. "So what else is new?"

"You were what, five when he was born?"

She nodded. "Mom and Pop were so thrilled. I'd been sickly as an infant. Apparently, I didn't sleep more than thirty minutes at a stretch."

"Colic?"

"That's what they thought. Later, it turned out to be some kind of allergy to wheat. I was sick as a dog . . . diarrhea, ferocious stomachaches. I was thin as a stick. It seemed to straighten out for a while. Then Bailey came along and it started all over again. I was in kindergarten by then and the teacher decided I was just acting up because of him."

"Were you jealous?" I asked.

"Absolutely. I was horribly jealous. I couldn't help myself. They doted on him. He was everything. And of course he was good . . . slept like an angel, blah, blah, blah. Meanwhile, I was half-dead. Some doctor caught on. I don't even know now who it was, but he insisted on a bowel biopsy and that's when they diagnosed the celiac disease. Once they took me off wheat, I was fine, though I think Pop was always half-convinced I'd done it out of spite. Ha. The story of my life." She glanced at her watch. "Oh hell, it's almost one. I better let you go."

We said our good-nights and then I went upstairs. It wasn't until I was ready for bed that I realized someone had been in my room.

# 13

What I spotted was the partial crescent of a heel print on the carpet just inside the sliding door. I don't even know now what made me glance down. I had gone into the kitchen to pour myself a glass of wine. I popped the cork back in the bottle and tucked it in the refrigerator door. I crossed to the sliding glass door and opened the drapes, then flipped the lock and slid the door open about a foot, letting in a dense shaft of ocean breeze. I stood for a moment, just breathing it all in. I loved the smell. I loved the sound the ocean made and the line of frothy silver curling up onto the sand whenever a wave broke. The fog was in and I could hear the plaintive moo of the foghorn against the chill night air.

My attention strayed to a small kink in the hem of the drape. There was a trace of wet sand adjacent to the metal track in which the door rode. I peered at it, uncomprehending. I set my wineglass aside and went down on my hands and knees to inspect the spot. The minute I saw what it was, I got up and backed away from the door, whipping my head around so I could scan the room. There was no place anyone could hide. The closet consisted of an alcove without a door. The bed was bolted to the wall and quite low, framed in at the bottom with wood strips mounted flush with the carpeting. I'd just come out of the bathroom, but I checked it again, moving automatically. The frosted-glass shower door was open, the stall empty. I knew I was alone, but the sense of that other presence was so vivid that it made my hair stand on my arms. I was seized by an involuntary tremor of fear so acute that it generated a low sound in my throat, like a growl reflex.

I surveyed my personal belongings. My duffel seemed untouched, though it was perfectly possible that someone had eased a sly hand among the contents. I went back to the kitchen table and checked my papers. My portable Smith-Corona was sitting open as it had been, my notes in a folder to the left. Nothing was missing as far as I could tell. I couldn't tell if the papers had been disturbed because I hadn't paid any particular attention to them when I tucked them away. That had been before supper, six hours ago.

I checked the lock on the sliding glass door. Now that I knew what I was looking for, the tool marks were unmistakable and I could see where the aluminum frame had been forced out around the bolt. The lock was a simple device in any event, and hardly designed to withstand brute force. The thumb bolt still turned, but the mechanism had been damaged. Now the latch lever didn't fully meet the strike plate, so that any locking capacity was strictly illusory. The intruder must have left the bolt in its locked position and used the corridor door for egress. I got the penlight out of my handbag and checked the balcony with care. There were additional traces of sand near the railing. I peered the one floor down, trying to figure out how someone could have gotten up here— possibly through one of the rooms on the same floor, climbing from balcony to balcony. The motel driveway ran right under my room and led to covered parking along the perimeter of the courtyard formed by the four sides of the building. Someone could have parked in the driveway, then climbed up on the car roof, and from there swung up onto the balcony. It wouldn't have taken long. The driveway might have been blocked temporarily, but at this hour there was little or no traffic. The town was shut down and the tenants of the motel were probably in for the night.

I called down to the desk, told Bert what had happened, and asked him to move me to another room. I could hear him scratch his chin. His voice, when it came, was papery and frail.

"Gee, Miss Millhone. I don't know what to tell you this time of night. I could move you first thing tomorrow morning."

"Bert," I said, "someone broke into my room! There's no way I'm going to stay here."

"Well. Even so. I'm not sure what we can do at this hour."

"Don't tell me you don't have another room somewhere. I can see the 'vacancy' sign from here."

There was a pause. "I suppose we *could* move you," he said skeptically. "It's awful late, but I'm not saying we can't. When do you think it might have happened, this break-in you're referring to?"

"What difference does it make? The lock on the sliding glass door's been jimmied. I can't even get it to shut properly, let alone lock."

"Oh. Well, even so. Things can fool you sometimes. You know some of those fittings have warped over the years. Doors down here, some of them at any rate, you have to—"

"Could you connect me with Ann Fowler, please?"

"I believe she's asleep. I'd be happy to come up myself and take a look. I don't believe you're in danger. I can understand your concern, but you're up on the second floor there and I don't see how anyone could get up on that balcony."

"Probably the same way they got up here in the first place," I said snappishly.

"Unh-hunh. Well, why don't I come up there and take a look? I guess I can leave the desk for a minute. Maybe we can figure something out."

"Bert. Goddamn it, I want another room!"

"Well, I can see your point. But now there's the question of liability, too, you know. I don't know if you've considered it in that light. Truth is, we've never had any kind of break-in all the years I've been here, which is, oh . . . nearly eighteen years now. Over at the Tides, it's different of course . . ."

"I . . . want . . . another . . . room," I said, giving full measure to each syllable.

"Oh. Well." A pause here. "Let me check and see what I can do. Hang on and I'll pull the registration."

He put me on hold, giving me a restful few minutes in which to get my temper under control. In some ways it felt better to be irritated than unnerved.

He cut back into the line. I could hear him flipping through registration cards in the background, probably licking his thumb for traction. He cleared his throat. "You can try the room next door," he said. "That's number twenty-four. I can bring you up a key. Connecting door might be open if you want to give it a try. Unless, of course, you got some notion that's been tampered with, too. . . ."

I hung up on him, which seemed preferable to going mad.

I hadn't paid much attention to the fact that my room connected to the one next door to it. Access to room 24 was actually effected through two doors with a kind of air space between. I unlocked the door on my side. The second door was ajar, the room in shadow. I flashed my penlight around. The room was empty, orderly, with the slightly musty smell of carpeting that's been dampened too often by the trampling of summer feet. I found the switch and turned the light on, then checked the sliding door that opened out onto the balcony adjacent to mine.

Once I determined the room could be secured, I tossed my few loose personal items into my duffel and moved it next door. I gathered up my typewriter, papers, wine bottle. Within minutes, I was settled. I pulled some clothes on, took my keys and went down to the car. My gun was still locked in my briefcase in the backseat. I stopped in at the office and picked up the new room key, curtly refusing to engage with Bert in any more of his rambling dialogues. He didn't seem to mind. His manner was tolerant. Some women just seem to worry more than others, he remarked.

I took the briefcase up to my room, where I locked the door and chained it. Then I sat at the kitchen table, loaded seven cartridges in the clip, and smacked it home. This was my new handgun. A Davis .32, chrome and walnut, with a five-and-a-quarter-inch barrel. My old gun had gotten blown to kingdom come when the bomb went off in my apartment. This one weighed a tidy twenty-two ounces and already felt like an old friend, with the added virtue that the sights were accurate. It was 1:00 A.M. I was feeling a deadly rage by then and I didn't really expect to sleep. I turned the light out and pulled the fishnet drapes across the glass doors, which I felt compelled to keep locked. I peered out at the empty street. The surf was pounding monotonously, the sound reduced to a mild rumble through the glass. The muffled foghorn intoned its hollow warning to any boats at sea. The sky was dense with clouds, moon and stars blanked out. Without fresh air coming in, the room felt like a prison cell, stuffy and dank. I left my clothes on and got in bed, sitting bolt upright, my gaze pinned on the sliding glass doors, half expecting to see a shadowy figure slip over the railing from below. The sodium-vapor streetlights washed the balcony with a tawny glow. The incoming light was filtered by the curtains. The neon "vacancy" sign had begun to sputter off and on, causing the room to pulsate with red. Someone knew where I was. I'd told a lot of people I was staying at the Ocean Street, but not which room. I got up again and padded over to the table, where I picked up my file notes and tucked them in my briefcase. From now on, I'd take them with me. From now on, I'd tote the gun with me, too. I got back in bed.

At 2:47 A.M. the phone rang and I jumped a foot, unaware that I'd been asleep. The jolt of adrenaline made my heart clatter in my chest like a slug of white-hot metal on a stone floor. Fear and the shrilling of the phone became one sensation. I snatched up the receiver. "Yes?"

His tone was low. "It's me."

Even in the dark, I squinted. "Bailey?"

"You alone?"

"Of course. Where *are* you?"

"Don't worry about that. I don't have much time. Bert knows it's me, and I don't want to take a chance on his calling the cops."

"Forget it. They can't get a trace on a call that fast," I said. "Are you all right?"

"I'm fine. How are things there, pretty bad?"

I gave him a brief rundown on what was happening. I didn't dwell on Royce's collapse because I didn't want to worry him, but I did mention that someone had broken in. "Was it you, by any chance?"

"Me? No way. This is the first time I've been out," he said. "I heard about Tap. God, poor bastard."

"I know," I said. "What a chump he was. It looks like he didn't even have a real load in the gun. He was firing rock salt."

"Salt?"

"You got it. I checked the residue at the scene. I don't know if he realized what it was or not."

"Jesus," Bailey breathed. "He never had a chance."

"Why did you take off? That was the worst move you could possibly have made. They probably have every cop in the state out. Were you the one who set it up?"

"Of course not! I didn't even know who it was at first, and then all I could think to do was get the hell out of there."

"Who could have put him up to it?"

"I have no idea, but somebody did."

"Joleen might know. I'll try to see her tomorrow. In the meantime, you can't stay on the loose. They've got you listed as armed and dangerous."

"I figured as much, but what am I supposed to do? The minute I show up, they're going to blow me off the face of the earth, same as Tap."

"Call Jack Clemson. Turn yourself in to him."

"How do we know it wasn't him set me up?"

"Your own attorney?"

"Hey, if I die, it's over. Everybody's off the hook. Anyway, I gotta get myself out of here before—" I heard an intake of breath. "Hang on." There was a silence. His end of the conversation had reverberated with the hollow echo of a phone booth. Now I heard the metal bi-fold door squeak. "All right, I'm back. I thought there was somebody out there, but it doesn't look like it."

"Listen, Bailey. I'm doing what I can, but I could use some help."

"Like what?"

"Like what happened to the money from the bank job you did?"

A pause. "Who told you about that?"

"Tap, last night at the pool hall. He says you left it with Jean, but then the last he heard, the whole forty-two thousand had disappeared. Could she have taken it herself?"

"Not Jean. She wouldn't have done that to us."

"What was the story she told you? She must have said something."

"All I know is she went to lay hands on it and the whole stash was gone."

"Or so she said," I put in.

I could hear him shrug. "Even if she did take it, what was I going to do, turn her in to the cops?"

"Did she tell you where she'd hidden it?"

"No, but I got the impression it was somewhere up there at the hot springs where she
worked."

"Oh, great. Place is huge. Who else knew
about the money?"

"That's all as far as I know." He hissed into
the phone.

I could feel my heart do a flip-flop. "What's
wrong?"

Silence.

"Bailey?"

He severed the connection.

Almost immediately, the phone rang again. A
sheriff's deputy advised me to remain where I was
until a car could pick me up. Good old Bert. I
spent the rest of the night at the county sheriff's
department, being variously questioned, accused,
abused, and threatened—quite politely, of course
—by a homicide detective named Sal Quintana,
who wasn't in a much better mood than I was at
that point. A second detective stood against the
wall, using a broken wooden match to clean the
plaque off his teeth. I was certain his dental hygien-
ist would applaud his efforts when he saw her
next.

Quintana was in his mid-forties, with closely
cropped black hair, big, dark eyes, and a face
remarkable for its impassivity. Dwight Shales's face
had the same deadpan look: obdurate, unresponsive, aggressively blank. This man was probably
twenty pounds overweight, with a shirt size that
hadn't quite conceded the point. The extra weight

across his back had pulled his sleeves up an inch, and where his wrist extended, there were already a few gray hairs mingled with the black. He had good teeth, and my assessment of his looks might have been upgraded if he'd smiled. No such luck. He seemed to be operating on the theory that Bailey Fowler and I were in cahoots.

"You're crazy," I said. "I only saw the man once."

"When was that?"

"You know when. Yesterday. I signed in at the desk. You've got it right there in front of you."

His gaze flicked down to the papers on the table. "You want to tell us what you talked about?"

"He was depressed. I tried to cheer him up."

"You fond of Mr. Fowler?"

"That's none of your business. I'm not under arrest and I'm not charged with anything, right?"

"That's right," he said patiently. "We're just trying to understand the situation here. I'm sure you can appreciate that, given the circumstances." He paused while the second detective leaned down and murmured something indistinct. Quintana looked back at me. "I believe you were present in the courtroom when Mr. Fowler escaped. You have any contact with him at the time?"

"None. Zippity-doo-dah."

He didn't react at all to my flippancy. "When you spoke with Mr. Fowler on the telephone, did he give you any indication where he was calling from?"

"No."

"Was it your impression he was still in the area?"

"I don't know. I guess so. He could have called from anyplace."

"What'd he tell you about the escape?"

"Nothing. We didn't talk about that."

"You have any idea who picked him up?"

"I don't even know which direction he went. I was still in the courtroom when the shots were fired."

"What about Tap Granger?"

"I don't know anything about Tap."

"You spent enough time with him the night before," he remarked.

"Yeah, well, he wasn't that informative."

"You know who might have paid him off?"

"Somebody paid Tap off?" I said.

Quintana was unresponsive, simply waiting me out.

"He didn't even mention the arraignment. I was astonished when I turned around and realized it was him."

"Let's get back to Bailey's phone call," Quintana said.

"I've covered most of it."

"What else was said?"

"I told him to get in touch with Jack Clemson and turn himself in."

"He say he'd do that?"

"Uh, no. He didn't seem real thrilled at that, but maybe he'll have a change of heart."

"We're having a hard time believing he could

disappear without a trace. He almost had to have assistance."

"Well, he didn't get it from me."

"You think somebody's hiding him?"

"How do I know?"

"Why'd he get in touch?"

"I have no idea. The call was interrupted before he got to that."

We continued in this monotonous, circular fashion till I thought I'd drop. Quintana was unfailingly civil, unsmiling, persistent—nay, relentless —and finally agreed to let me go back to the motel only after he'd milked me of all conceivable information. "Miss Millhone, let me make one thing crystal clear," he said, shifting in his seat. "This is a police matter. We want Bailey Fowler back in custody. I better not find out you're helping him in any way. Do you understand that?"

"Absolutely," I said.

He gave me a look that said he doubted my sincerity.

I staggered back to bed at 6:22 A.M. and slept until nine, which was when Ann tapped on my door and got me up.

# 14

Ann was on her way to the hospital to see her father. The house cleaner, Maxine, had been delayed, but swore she'd be there by ten. In the meantime, Ann felt Ori was too anxious to be left alone. "I've called Mrs. Maude. She and Mrs. Emma agreed to sit with Mother, but neither one can make it till this afternoon. I feel like a dog asking you to fill in . . ."

"Don't worry about it. I'll be right down."

"Thanks."

I still had my clothes on, so I didn't have to waste any time getting dressed. I brushed my teeth and threw some water on my face, ignoring the dark smudges around my eyes. There was a time in my youth when staying up all night had felt adventuresome. Dawn then was exhilarating and there didn't seem to be any end to the physical resources at my command. Now the lack of sleep was creating an odd high that foreshadowed a stomach-churning descent. I was still on the upswing, gathering momentum as I dragged my body out. Coffee might help, but it would only postpone the inevitable crash. I was going to pay for this.

Ori was sitting up in bed, fussing with the ties on her gown. Paraphernalia on the night table and the faint scent of alcohol indicated that Ann had done Ori's glucose test and had already administered her morning dose of insulin. The trace of blood streaked on the reagent strip had dried to a rusty brown. Old adhesive tape was knotted up on the bed tray like a wad of chewing gum. Stuck to it was a cotton ball with a linty-looking dot of red. This before breakfast. Mentally, I could feel my eyes cross, but I bustled about in my best imitation of a visiting nurse. I was accustomed, from long experience, to steeling myself to the sight of violent death, but this residue of diabetic odds and ends nearly made my stomach heave. Resolutely, I swept it all into a plastic wastebasket and tucked it out of sight, tidying pill bottles, water glass, carafe, and Ace bandages. Usually, Ori had her legs bound in heavy pink stretch wraps, but she was apparently airing them today. I avoided the sight of her mottled calves, the ice-cold feet in which so little circulation pumped, the blue-gray toes, dry and cracked. She had an ulcerated area about the size of a nickel on the inside aspect of her right ankle.

"I think I'll sit down a minute," I murmured.

"Well, honey. You're pale as a ghost. Go out to the kitchen and get a glass of juice."

The orange juice helped and I ate a piece of toast, cleaning up the kitchen afterward as a way of avoiding the woman in the other room. Three thousand hours of investigative training hadn't quite prepared me for a sideline as a drudge. I felt like I'd spent half my time on this case washing dirty dishes. How come Magnum, P.I., never had to do stuff like this?

At twenty minutes after ten, Maxine appeared, cleaning supplies in a plastic bucket on her arm. She was one of those women with an extra hundred pounds wobbling around her body like a barrel made of flesh. She had one eyetooth the size and color of a rusty nail. Without any pause, she took out a dustrag and began to work her way around the room. "Sorry I'm late, but I couldn't get that old car to start to save my neck. I finally called and asked John Robert to come over with a set of jumper cables, but it took him a good half hour just to get there. I heard about Royce. God love his heart."

"I'm going to have Ann take me over there this evening," Ori said. "Provided I feel well enough."

Maxine just clucked and shook her head. "I tell you," she said. "And I bet you haven't heard a word from Bailey. No telling where he's at."

"Aw, and I'm worried sick. I never even laid eyes on him after all this time. And here he's took off again."

Maxine made a face that conveyed sympathy and regret, then flapped her dustrag to indicate a shift in tone. "Mary Burney's making a perfect fool of herself. Windows boarded up, big lock on the gate, convinced he'll go over there and carry her off."

"Well, whatever for?" Ori asked, completely mystified.

"I never said she had brains, but then half the people I talked to are loading their guns. Radio says he 'may be seeking refuge among former acquaintances.' Just like that. 'May be seeking refuge.' Now, if that's not the silliest thing I ever heard. I told John Robert, 'Bailey's got more sense than that,' I said. 'For one thing, he doesn't know Mary Burney from a hole in the ground and besides which, he wouldn't go anywhere near that place of hers because it backs right up to the National Guard Armory. Chain-link fence and all what kind of thing. Floodlights? Lord God,' I said. 'Bailey may be a criminal, but he's not a *re*tard.' "

As soon as I could decently insert myself into the conversation, I told Ori I'd be taking off. Maxine got conspicuously quiet, hoping no doubt to pick up some information she could pass along to John Robert and Mary Burney next chance she had. I avoided giving any indication where I meant to go. The last glimpse I had of them, Maxine was handing Ori a fistful of junk mail to sort through while she applied Lemon Pledge to the top of the bookshelf where the mail had been stacked.

Tap Granger's widow lived on Kaye Street in a one-story frame house with a screened-in porch. The exterior was painted an ancient turquoise

trimmed in buttercup, the porch steps eaten
through by something that left ominous holes in
the wood. She came to the door looking pale and
thin, except for the belly that jutted out in front of
her like a globe. Her nose was a dull pink from
tears, her eyes swollen, with all the makeup cried
off. Her hair had the tortured appearance of a
recent home permanent. She wore faded jeans
that hung on her narrow behind, a sleeveless T-shirt
that left her bare arms bony-looking and puckered
from the chilly morning air. She had a plump baby
affixed to one hip, his massive thighs gripping her
bulk like a horseman preparing to post. The pacifier in his mouth looked like some kind of plug you
might pull if you wanted to let all the air out.
Solemn eyes, runny nose.

"I'm sorry to bother you, Mrs. Granger. My
name's Kinsey Millhone. I'm a private investigator. Could I talk to you?"

"I guess," she said. She couldn't have been
much more than twenty-six, with the lackluster air
of a woman drained of youth. Where was she
going to find someone who'd take on another man's
five kids?

The house was small and rustic, the construction crude, but the furnishings looked new. All
Sears Revolving Charge Account items, still under
warranty. The couch and two matching Barcaloungers
were green Naugahyde, the coffee table and the
two end tables flanking the couch were blond wood
laminate, still unscarred by little children's shoes.
The squat table lamps had pleated shades still

wrapped in clear cellophane. She'd be paying it all off till the kids were in high school. She sat down on one couch cushion, which buckled up slightly and let out a sigh as the air was forced out. I perched on the edge of one lounge chair, uneasy about the half-eaten Fluffer-nutter sandwich that kept me company on the seat.

"Linnetta, quit doin' that!" she sang out suddenly, though there didn't seem to be anyone else in the room. I realized belatedly that the twanging sound of a kid jumping up and down on a bed had just ceased. She shifted the baby, setting him on his feet. He swayed, clutching at her jeans, the pacifier wriggling around in his mouth as he started working it with a little humming sound.

"What'd you want?" she said. "The police have been here twice and I already told 'em everything I know."

"I'll try to be brief. It must be hard on you."

"Doesn't matter," she shrugged. The stress of Tap's death had made her face break out, her chin splotched and fiery pink.

"Did you know what Tap was getting involved in yesterday?"

"I knew he had some money, but he said he won a bet with this guy who finally paid up."

"A bet?"

"Might not have been true," she said, somewhat defensively, "but God knows we needed it and I wasn't about to ask after it too close."

"Did you see him leave the house?"

"Not really. I'd come in from work and I went

straight to bed as soon as him and the kids left. I guess he dropped Ronnie and the girls off and then took Mac to the sitters. He must have drove into San Luis Obispo after that. I mean, he had to, since that's where he ended up."

"But he never said anything about the break-out or who put him up to it?"

"I wouldn't have stood for it if I'd known."

"Do you know how much he was paid?"

Her eyes became wary in the blank of her face. She began to pick idly at her chin. "Nuh-unh."

"No one's going to take it back. I just wondered how much it was."

"Two thousand," she murmured. God, a woman with no guile, married to a man with no sense. Two thousand dollars to risk his life?

"Are you aware that the shotgun shells were loaded with rock salt?"

Again, she gave me that cagy look. "Tap said that way nobody'd get hurt."

"Except him."

Light dawned in that faraway world of the 98 IQ. "Oh."

"Was the shotgun his?"

"Nuh-unh. Tap never had a gun. I wouldn't have one in the house with these kids," she said.

"Do you have any idea at all who he was dealing with?"

"Some woman, I heard."

That got my attention. "Really."

Back went the hand to her chin. Pick, pick. "Somebody saw 'em together at the pool hall night before he died."

It took a split second. "Shit, that was *me*. I was trying to get a lead on this Bailey Fowler business and I knew they'd been friends."

"Oh. I thought maybe him and some woman . . ."

"Absolutely not," I said. "In fact, he spent half the time showing me pictures of you and the kids."

She colored faintly, tears welling. "That's sweet. I wish I could help. You seem awful nice."

I took out my card and jotted down the number of the motel on the back. "Here's where I'll be for the next couple of days. If you think of anything, get in touch."

"Are you coming to the funeral? It's tomorrow afternoon at the Baptist church. It should be a good turnout because everybody liked Tap."

I had my doubts about that, but it was clearly something she needed to believe. "We'll see. I may be tied up, but I'll be there if I can." My recollection of Reverend Haws made attendance unlikely, but I couldn't rule it out. I'd been present at a number of funerals over the last several months, and I didn't think I could endure another. Organized religion was ruined for me when I was five years old, subjected to a Sunday-school teacher with hairs sticking out of her nose and bad breath. Trust me to point that out. The Presbyterians had suggested the Vacation Bible School at the Congregational Church down the road. Since I'd already been expelled by the Methodists, my aunt was losing heart. Personally, I was looking forward to another flannel board. You could make Baby Jesus with some fuzzies on his back and stick him right up in the sky like a bird, then make him dive-bomb the manger.

Joleen left the baby sidestepping his way down the length of the couch while she walked me to the door. The bell rang almost simultaneously with her opening it. Dwight Shales stood on the doorstep, looking as surprised as we were. His glance shifted from her face to mine and then back again. He nodded at Joleen. "Thought I'd stop by and see how you were."

"Thanks, Mr. Shales. That's real nice of you. This is, unh . . ."

I held my hand out. "Kinsey Millhone. We've met." We shook hands.

"I remember," he said. "I just stopped by the motel, as a matter of fact. If you can hold on a minute, we can have a chat."

"Sure," I said. I stood there while he and Joleen talked briefly. From their conversation, I gathered that she'd been at the high school not that many years before.

"I just lost my wife, and I know how it feels," he was saying. The authoritarian air I remembered was gone. His pain seemed so close to the surface, it made tears well up in Joleen's eyes again.

"I appreciate that, Mr. Shales. I do. Mrs. Shales was a nice woman and I know she suffered something fierce. You want to come in? I can fix you some tea."

He glanced at his watch. "I can't right this

minute. I'm late as it is, but I'll stop by again. I wanted you to know we're all thinking of you over at the high school. Can I help you with anything? You have enough money?"

Joleen seemed completely overwhelmed, nose turning rosy, her voice cracking when she spoke. "I'm all right. Mom and Daddy are coming up from Los Angeles tonight. I'll be fine as soon as they get here."

"Well, you let us know if there's anything we can do. I can have one of the senior girls look after the kids tomorrow afternoon. Bob Haws said the services are scheduled for two."

"I'd appreciate the help. I hadn't even thought about who'd be keeping the kids. Will you be at the funeral? Tap'd be awful glad."

"Of course, I'll be there. He was a fine man and we were all proud of him."

I followed him out to the street, where his car was parked. "I pulled school records on Jean Timberlake," he said. "If you want to stop by the office, you can see what we've got. You have a car? I can give you a lift."

"I better take mine. It's back at the motel."

"Hop in. I'll drop you off."

"Are you sure? I don't want to hold you up."

"Won't take a minute. I'm headed back in that direction anyway."

He held the door for me and I got in, the two of us chatting inconsequentially during the brief ride back to the Ocean Street. I could have walked, but I was trying to ingratiate myself with the man in the hope that he might have personal recollections of his own to add to whatever data I found in Jean's file.

Ann had returned from the hospital and I saw her peer out of the office window as we pulled up. She and Shales exchanged a smile and a wave and she disappeared.

I stepped out of the car, leaning back toward the open window. "I have another errand to run and then I'll pop by."

"Good. Meanwhile, I'll check and see if any of the staff have information to contribute."

"Thanks," I said.

As he took off, I turned to find Ann right behind me. She seemed surprised to see him pull away. "He's not coming in?"

"I think he had to get back to the school. I just ran into him over at Joleen Granger's. How's your father?"

Reluctantly, Ann's gaze flicked back to my face. "About what you'd expect. Cancer's spread to his lungs, liver, and spleen. They're saying now he probably has less than a month."

"How's he taking it?"

"Poorly. I thought he'd made his peace, but he seemed real upset. He wants to talk to you."

My heart sank. It was the last thing I needed, a conversation with the doomed. "I'll try to get up there sometime this afternoon."

# 15

I sat in the vestibule outside Dwight Shales's office, variously picking my way through the papers in Jean Timberlake's school file and eavesdropping on an outraged senior girl who'd been caught in the restroom shampooing her hair. Apparently the drill in disciplinary matters was for the culprit to use the pay phone in the school office to notify the appropriate parent about the nature of the offense.

" . . . Well, guy, Mom. How was I to know? I mean, big fuckin' deal," she said. " . . . Because I didn't have time! Guuuyyy . . . Well, nobody ever told me . . . It's a fuckin' free country. All I did was wash my hair! . . . I did noooot . . . I'm not smarting off! Yeah, well, you have a big mouth, too." Her tone shifted here from exasperation to extreme martyrdom, voice sliding up and down the scale. "Okaaay! I said, okay. Oh, right, Mom. God . . . Why'n't you ground me for life. Right. Oh, rilly, I'm sure. Fuck you, okay? You are such an asshole! I just hate you!!" She slammed the phone down resoundingly and burst noisily into tears.

I suppressed a temptation to peer around the corner at her. I could hear the low murmur of a fellow conspirator.

"God, Jennifer, that is just *so* unfair," the second girl said.

Jennifer was sobbing inconsolably. "She is such a bitch. I hate her fuckin' guts. . . ."

I tried to picture myself at her age, talking to my aunt like that. I'd have had to take out a loan for the ensuing dental work.

I leafed through Jean's Scholastic Aptitude Test scores, attendance records, the written comments her teachers had added from time to time. With the weeping in the background, it was almost like having Jean Timberlake's ghost looking on. She certainly seemed to have had her share of grief in high school. Tardiness, demerits, detention, parent-teacher conferences scheduled and then canceled when Mrs. Timberlake failed to show. There were repeated notes from sessions with first one and then another of the four school counselors, Ann Fowler being one. Jean had spent a large part of her junior year consigned to Mr. Shales's office, sitting on the bench, perhaps sullenly, perhaps with the total self-possession she seemed to display in the few yearbook photographs I'd seen. Maybe she'd sat there and recollected, in tranquillity, the lewd sexual experiments she'd conducted with the boys in the privacy of parked cars. Or maybe she'd flirted with one of the senior honors students manning the main desk. From the moment she reached puberty, her grade point average had slid steadily downward despite the contradictory evidence of her IQ and past grades. I could practically feel the heat of noxious hormones seeping through the pages, the drama, confusion, finally the secrecy. Her confidences in the school nurse ceased abruptly. Where Mrs. Berringer had jotted down folksy notes about cramps and heavy periods, advising a consultation with the family physician, there was suddenly concern about the girl's mounting absenteeism. Jean's problems didn't go unnoticed or unremarked. To the credit of the faculty, a general alarm seemed to sound. From the paper trail left behind, it looked as if every effort had been made to bring her back from the brink. Then, on November 5, someone had noted in dark blue angular ink that the girl was deceased. The word was underlined once, and after that, the page was blank.

"Is that going to help?"

I jumped. Dwight Shales had emerged from his inner office and he stood now in the door. The weeping girl was gone, and I could hear the tramp of footsteps as the students passed between classes. "You scared me," I said, patting myself on the chest.

"Sorry. Come into the office. I've got a conference scheduled at two, but we can talk till then. Bring the file."

I gathered up Jean's records and followed him in.

"Have a seat," he said.

His manner had changed. The easygoing man I'd seen earlier had disappeared. Now he seemed guarded, careful of his words, all business—slightly curt, as if twenty years of dealing with unruly teenagers had soured him on everyone. I suspected his manner tended toward the autocratic anyway, his tone edged with combativeness. He was used to being in charge. On the surface, he was attractive, but his good looks were posted with warning signs. His body was trim. He had the build and carriage of a former military type, accustomed to operating under fire. If he was a sportsman, I'd peg him as an expert in trap and skeet shooting. His games would be handball, poker, and chess. If he ran, he'd feel compelled to lower his finish by a few seconds each time out. Maybe once he'd been open, vulnerable or soft, but he was shut down now, and the only evidence I'd seen of any warmth at all was in his dealings with Joleen. Apparently his wife's death had ruptured the bounds of his self-control. In matters of mourning, he could still reach out.

I took a seat, placing the fat, dog-eared manila folder on the desk in front of me. I hadn't found anything startling, but I'd made a few notes. Her former address. Birth date, social security number, the bare bones of data made meaningless by her death. "What did you think of her?" I asked him.

"She was a tough little nut. I'll tell you that."

"So I gathered. It looks like she spent half her time in detention."

"At least that. What made it frustrating—for me, at any rate, and you're welcome to talk to some of the other teachers about this—is that she was a very appealing kid. Smart, soft-spoken, friendly—with adults, at any rate. I can't say she was well liked among her classmates, but she was pleasant to the staff. You'd sit her down to have a chat and you'd think you were getting through. She'd nod and agree with you, make all the proper noises, and then she'd turn around and do exactly what she'd been reprimanded for in the first place."

"Can you give me an example?"

"Anything you name. She'd ditch school, show up late, fail to turn in assignments, refuse to take tests. She smoked on campus, which was strictly against the rules back then, kept booze in her locker. Drove everybody up the wall. It's not like what she did was worse than anybody else. She simply had no conscience about it and no intention whatever of cleaning up her act. How do you deal with someone like that? She'd say anything that got her off the hook. This girl was convincing. She could make you believe anything she said, but then it would evaporate the minute she left the room."

"Did she have any girlfriends?"

"Not that I ever saw."

"Did she have a rapport with any teacher in particular?"

"I doubt it. You can ask some of the faculty if you like."

"What about the promiscuity?"

He shifted uncomfortably. "I heard rumors about that, but I never had any concrete information. Wouldn't surprise me. She had some problems with self-esteem."

"I talked with a classmate who implied that it was pretty steamy stuff."

Shales wagged his head reluctantly. "There wasn't much we could do. We referred her two or three times for professional counseling, but of course she never went."

"I take it the school counselors didn't make much progress."

"I'm afraid not. I don't think you could fault us for the sincerity of our concern, but we couldn't force her to do anything. And her mother didn't help. I wish I had a nickel for every note we sent home. The truth is, we liked Jean and thought she had a chance. At a certain point, Mrs. Timberlake seemed to throw up her hands. Maybe we did, too. I don't know. Looking back on the situation, I don't feel good, but I don't know how we could have done it any differently. She's just one of those kids who fell between the cracks. It's a pity, but there it is."

"How well do you know Mrs. Timberlake at this point?"

"What makes you ask?"

"I'm being paid to ask."

"She's a friend," he said, after the barest hesitancy.

I waited, but he didn't amplify. "What about the guy Jean was allegedly involved with?"

"You've got me on that. A lot of stories started circulating right after she died, but I never heard a name attached."

"Can you think of anything else that might help? Someone she might have taken into her confidence?"

"Not that I recall." A look crossed his face. "Well, actually, there was one thing that always struck me as odd. A couple times that fall, I saw her at church, which seemed out of character."

"Church?"

"Bob Haws's congregation. I forget who told me, but the word was she had the hots for the kid who headed up the youth group over there. Now what the hell was his name? Hang on." He got up and went to the door to the main office. "Kathy, what was the name of the boy who was treasurer of the senior class the year Jean Timberlake was killed? You remember him?"

There was a pause and a murmured response that I couldn't quite hear.

"Yeah, he's the one. Thanks." Dwight Shales turned back to me. "John Clemson. His dad's the attorney representing Fowler, isn't he?"

I parked in the little lot behind Jack Clemson's office, taking the flagstone path around the cottage to the front. The sun was out, but the breeze was cool and the pittosporum shading the side yard were being hedged up by a man in a landscape company uniform. The Little Wonder electric trimmer in his hands made a chirping sound as he passed it across the face of the shrub, which was raining down leaves.

I went up on the porch, pausing for a moment before I let myself in. All the way over, I'd been rehearsing what I'd say, feeling not a little annoyed that he'd withheld information. Maybe it would turn out to be insignificant, but that was mine to decide. The door was ajar and I stepped into the foyer. The woman who glanced up must have been his regular secretary. She was in her forties, petite—nay, toy-sized—hair hennaed to an auburn shade, with piercing gray eyes and a silver bracelet, in a snake shape, coiled around her wrist.

"Is Mr. Clemson in?"

"Is he expecting you?"

"I stopped by to bring him up to date on a case," I said. "The name is Kinsey Millhone."

She took in my outfit, gaze traveling from turtleneck to jeans to boots with an almost imperceptible flicker of distaste. I probably looked like someone he might represent on a charge of welfare fraud. "Just a moment, I'll check." Her look said, *Not bloody likely.*

Instead of buzzing through, she got up from her desk and tippy-tapped her way down the hall to his office, flared skirt twitching on her little hips as she walked. She had the body of a ten-year-old. Idly, I surveyed her desk while she was gone, scanning the document that she was working from. Reading upside down is only one of several obscure talents I've developed working as a private eye. ". . . And he is enjoined and restrained from annoying, molesting, threatening, or harming petitioner . . ." Given the average marriage these days, this sounded like pre-nups.

"Kinsey? Hey, nice to see you! Come on back."

Clemson was standing in the door to his office. He had his suit jacket off, shirt collar unbuttoned, sleeves rolled up, and tie askew. The gabardine pants looked like the same ones he'd had on two days ago, bunched up in the seat, pleated with wrinkles across the lap. I followed him into his office in the wake of cigarette smoke. His secretary tippy-tapped back to her desk out front, radiating disapproval.

Both chairs were crowded with law books, tongues of scrap paper hanging out where he'd marked passages. I stood while he cleared a space for me to sit down. He moved around to his side of the desk, breathing audibly. He stubbed out his cigarette with a shake of his head.

"Out of shape," he remarked. He sat down, tipping back in his swivel chair. "What are we going to do with that Bailey, huh? Guy's a fuckin' lunatic, taking off like that."

I filled him in on Bailey's late-night call, repeating his version of the escape while Jack Clemson pinched the bridge of his nose and shook his head in despair. "What a jerk. No accounting for the way these guys see things."

He reached for a letter and gave it a contemptuous toss. "Look at this. Know what that is? Hate mail. Some guy got put away twenty-two years ago when I was a PD. He writes me every year from jail like it's something I did to him. Jesus. When I was in the AG's office, the AG did a survey of prisoners as to who they blamed for their conviction—you know, 'why are you in prison and whose fault is it?' Nobody ever says, 'It's my fault . . . for being a jerk.' The number-one guy who gets blamed is their own lawyer. 'If I'da had a real lawyer instead of a PD, I'da got off.' That's the number-one guy, okay? His own lawyer. The number-two guy that was blamed was the witness who testified against him. Number three—are you ready?—is the judge who sentenced him. 'If I'da had a fair judge, this woulda never happened.' Number four was the police who investigated the case, the investigating officer, whoever caught 'im. And way down there at the bottom was the prosecuting attorney. Less than ten percent of the people they surveyed could even remember the prosecutor's name. I'm in the wrong end of the business." He snorted and leaned forward on his elbows, shoving files around on his desk. "Anyway, skip that. How's it going from your end? You comin' up with anything?"

"I don't know yet," I said carefully. "I just talked to the principal at Central Coast High. He tells me he saw Jean at the Baptist church a couple of times in the months before she was killed. Word was she was infatuated with your son."

Dead silence. "Mine?" he said.

I shrugged noncommittally. "Kid named John

Clemson. I assume he's your son. Was he the student leader of the church youth group?"

"Well, yeah, John did that, but it's news to me about her."

"He never said anything to you?"

"No, but I'll ask."

"Why don't I?"

A pause. Jack Clemson was too much the professional to object. "Sure, why not?" He jotted an address and a telephone number on a scratch pad. "This is his business."

He tore the leaf off and passed it across the desk to me, locking eyes with me. "He's not involved in her death."

I stood up. "Let's hope not."

# 16

The business address I'd been given turned out to be a seven-hundred-square-foot pharmacy at one end of a medical facility half a block off Higuera. The complex itself bore an eerie resemblance to the padres' quarters of half the California missions I'd seen: thick adobe walls, complete with decorator cracks, a long colonnade of twenty-one arches, with a red tile roof, and what looked like an aqueduct tucked into the landscaping. Pigeons were misbehaving up among the eaves, managing to copulate on a perilously tiny ledge.

The pharmacy, amazingly, did not sell beach balls, lawn furniture, children's clothing, or motor oil. To the left of the entrance were tidy displays of dental wares, feminine hygiene products, hot water bottles and heating pads, corn remedies, body braces of divers kinds, and colostomy supplies. I browsed among the over-the-counter medications while the pharmacist's assistant chatted with a customer about the efficacy of vitamin E for hot flashes. The place had a faintly chemical scent, reminiscent of the sticky coating on fresh Polaroid prints. The man I took to be John Clemson was standing behind a shoulder-high partition in a white coat, his head bent to his work. He didn't look at me, but once the customer left, he murmured something to his assistant, who leaned forward.

"Miss Millhone?" she said. She wore pants and a yellow polyester smock with patch pockets, one of those uniforms that would serve equally for a waitress, an au pair, or an LVN.

"Yes."

"You want to step back here, please? We're swamped this morning, but John says he'll talk to you while he works, if that's all right."

"That's fine. Thanks."

She lifted a hinged portion of the counter, holding it for me while I ducked underneath and came up in a narrow alleyway. The counter on this side was lined with machinery: two computer monitors, a typewriter, a label maker, a printer, and a microfiche reader. Storage bins below the counter were filled with empty translucent plastic pill vials. Ancillary labels on paper rolls were hung in a row, stickers cautioning the recipient: SHAKE WELL; THIS RX CANNOT BE REFILLED; WILL CAUSE DISCOLORATION OF URINE OR FECES; EXTERNAL USE ONLY; and DO NOT FREEZE. On the right were the drug bays, floor-to-ceiling shelves stocked with antibiotics, liquids, topical ointments and oral medications, arranged alphabetically. I had, within easy reach, the cure for most of life's ills: depression, pain, tenderness, apathy, insomnia, heartburn, fever, infection, obsession, and dizziness, excitability, seizures, histrionics, remorse. Given my poor night's sleep, what I needed were uppers, but it seemed unprofessional to whine and beg.

I'd expected John Clemson to look like his father, but he couldn't have been more different. He was tall and lean, with a thatch of dark hair. His face, in profile, was thin and lined, his cheeks sunken, cheekbones prominent. He had to be my age, but he had a worn air about him, an aura of weariness, ill health, or despair. He made no eye contact, his attention fixed on the task in front of him. Using a spatula, he was sliding pills, by fives, across the surface of a counting tray. With a rattle, he tumbled pills into a groove on the side, funneling them into an empty plastic vial, which he sealed with a child-proof cap. He affixed a label, set the vial aside, and started again, working with the same automatic grace as a dealer in Vegas. Thin wrists, long, slender fingers. I wondered if his hands would smell of PhisoDerm.

"Sorry I can't interrupt what I'm doing," he said mildly. "What can I help you with?" His tone had a light mocking quality, as if something amused him that he might or might not reveal.

"I take it your father called. How much did he tell you?"

"That you're investigating the murder of Jean Timberlake at his request. I know, of course, that he was hired to represent Bailey Fowler. I don't know what you want with me."

"You remember Jean?"

"Yes."

I had hoped for something a little more informative, but I was willing to press. "Can you tell me about your relationship with her?"

His mouth curved up slightly. "My relationship?"

"Somebody told me she used to hang out at the Baptist church. As I understand it, you were a classmate of hers and headed up the youth group back then. I thought maybe the two of you developed a friendship."

"Jean didn't have friends. She had conquests."

"Were you one?"

A bemused smile. "No."

What was the damn joke here? "Do you remember her coming to church?"

"Oh yes, but it wasn't me she was interested in. I wish I could say it was. She was very particular, our Miss Timberlake."

"Meaning what?"

"Meaning she'd never have tumbled for the likes of me."

"Oh, really? Why is that?"

He turned his face. The whole right side was disfigured, right eye missing, the lid welded shut by shiny pink and silver scar tissue that extended from his scalp to his jaw. His good eye was large and dark, filled with self-awareness. The missing eye created the illusion of a constant wink. I could see now that his right arm was also badly scarred.

"What was it?"

"Automobile accident when I was ten. The gas tank blew up. My mother died and I was left looking like this. It's better now. I've had surgery twice. Back then, the church was my salvation, literally. I was baptized when I was twelve, dedicating my life to Jesus. Who else would have me? Certainly not Jean Timberlake."

"Were you interested in her?"

"Sure, I was. I was seventeen years old and doomed to be a virgin for life. My bad luck. Good looks ranked high with her because she was so beautiful herself. After that came money, power . . . sex, of course. I thought about her incessantly. She was so completely venal."

"But not with you?"

He went back to his work, sliding pills into the trough. "Unfortunately not."

"Who, then?"

The lips curved up again in that nearly beatific smile. "Well, let's see now. How much trouble should I make?"

I shrugged, watching him carefully. "Just tell me the truth. What else can you do?"

"I could keep my mouth shut, which is what I've done to date."

"Maybe it's time to speak up," I said.

He was quiet for a moment.

"Who was she involved with?"

His smile finally disappeared. "The Right Reverend Haws. What a pal he turned out to be. He knew I lusted after her, so he counseled me in matters of purity and self-control. He never mentioned what he did with her himself."

I stared at him. "Are you sure of that?"

"She worked at the church, cleaning Sunday-school rooms. Wednesdays at four o'clock before choir practice started, he would pull his pants down around his knees and lie back across his desk while she worked on him. I used to watch from the vestry . . . Mrs. Haws, our dear June, suffers from a peculiar stigmata that originated just about that time. Resistant to treatment. I know because I fill the prescriptions, one right after the other. Amusing, don't you think?"

A chill rippled down my back. The image was vivid, his tone matter-of-fact. "Who else is aware of this?"

"No one, as far as I know."

"You never mentioned it to anybody at the time?"

"Nobody asked, and I've since left the church. It turned out not to be the kind of comfort I was hoping for."

The San Luis county clerk's office is located in the annex, right next door to the County Courthouse on Monterey. It was hard to believe that only yesterday we were all convening for Bailey's arraignment. I found a parking place across the street, inserted coins in the meter, then headed past the big redwood and into the annex entrance. The corridor was lined with marble, a cold gray with darker streaks. The county clerk's office was on the first floor, through double doors. I set to work. Using Jean Timberlake's full name and the date of birth I'd pulled from her school records, I found the volume and page number listing her birth certificate. The records clerk looked up the original certificate and, for eleven dollars, made me a certified copy. I didn't much care if it was certified or not. What interested me was the information it contained. Etta Jean Timberlake was born at 2:26 A.M. on June 3, 1949, 6 lbs., 8 oz., 19 inches long. Her mother was listed as gravida 1, para 1, fifteen years old and unemployed. Her father was "unknown." The attending physician was Joseph Dunne.

I found a public phone and looked up his office. The number rang four times and then his answering service picked up. He was out on Thursdays, not due in again till Monday morning at ten. "Do you know how I can reach him?"

"Dr. Corsell's on call. If you'll leave your name and number, we can have him get in touch."

"What about the Hot Springs? Could Dr. Dunne be up there?"

"Are you a patient of his?"

I set the receiver back in the cradle and let myself out of the booth. Since I was already downtown, I debated briefly about stopping by the hospital to see Royce. Ann had said he was asking for me, but I didn't want to talk to him just yet. I drove back toward Floral Beach, taking one of the back roads, an undulating band of asphalt that

wound past ranches, walled tract "estates," and
new housing developments.

There were very few cars in the spa's parking
lot. The hotel couldn't be doing enough business
to sustain the good doctor and his wife. I angled
my VW in close to the main building, noting as I
had before the dense chill in the air. The sulfur
smell of spoiled eggs conjured up images of some
befouled nest.

This time I bypassed the spa entrance and
went around to the front, up wide concrete stairs
to the wraparound porch. A row of chaise longues
lent the veranda the look of a ship's deck. Under a
canopy of oaks, the ground sloped down gradually,
leveling out then for a hundred yards until it met
the road. On my left, in an area cleared of trees, I
caught a glimpse of the deserted swimming pool in
a flat oblong of sunlight. Two tennis courts occupied the only other portion of the property graced
with sun. The surrounding fence was screened by
shrubs, but the hollow *pok . . . pok* suggested that
at least one court was in use.

I pushed through a double-wide door of carved
mahogany, the upper half inset with glass. The
lobby was built on a grand scale, rimmed with
wooden balustrades, flooded with light from two
translucent glass skylights. The main salon was
currently undergoing renovation. The carpeting
was obscured by yards of gray canvas dropcloth,
speckled with old paint. Scaffolding erected along
two walls suggested that the wood paneling was in
the process of being sanded and refinished. Here,

at least, the harsh smell of varnish overrode the pungent aroma of the mineral springs that burbled under the property like a cauldron.

The registration desk ran the width of the lobby, but there was no one in evidence. No reception clerk, no bellman, no painters at work. The silence had a quality about it that caused me to glance back over my shoulder, scanning the second-floor gallery. There was no one visible. Shadows hung among the eaves like spiderwebs. Wide, carpeted hallways extended on either side of the desk back into the gloomy depths of the hotel. I waited a decent interval in the silence. No one appeared. I pivoted, doing a one-eighty turn while I surveyed the place. Time to nose around, I thought.

Casually, I ambled down the corridor on the right, my passage making no sound on the densely carpeted floors. Halfway down the hall, glass-paned doors opened into a vast semicircular dining room with a wooden floor, furnished with countless round oak dining tables and matching ladder-backed chairs. I crossed to the bay windows on the far side of the room. Through the watery ripples of old glass, I saw the tennis players leave the courts, heading my way.

There were two sets of wooden swinging doors down to my left. I tiptoed the length of the room and peered into the hotel kitchen. A dull illumination from the kitchen windows cast a gray light against the expanses of stainless-steel counter. Stainless-steel fixtures, chrome, old linoleum. Heavy white crockery was stacked on open shelves. The room might have been a museum exhibit—the "moderne" style revisited, the kitchen of the future, circa 1966. I moved back toward the corridor. The murmur of voices.

I slipped into the triangle formed by the dining room door and the wall, pressing myself flat. Through the hinged crack, I saw Mrs. Dunne pass in a tennis outfit, racket under one arm. She had legs about as shapely as a pair of Doric columns, capped by the rims of her underpants, which extended unbecomingly from the flounce of short skirt. A varicose vein wound along one calf like a vine. Not one strand of her white-blond hair was out of place. I assumed her companion was her husband, Dr. Dunne. They were gone in a flash, voices receding. The only impression I had of him was of curly white hair, pink skin, and portliness.

As soon as they'd disappeared from sight, I slipped out of my hiding place and returned to the lobby. A woman in a burnt orange hotel blazer was now standing at the registration desk. Her gaze flicked toward the corridor when she saw me emerge, but she was apparently too schooled in proper desk-clerk behavior to quiz me about where I'd been.

"I was just having a look around," I said. "I may want to book a room."

"The hotel's closed for three months for renovation. We'll be open again April first."

"Do you have a brochure?"

"Certainly." She reached under the counter,

automatically producing one. She was in her thirties, probably with a degree in hotel management, no doubt wondering if she was wasting her professional training in a place that smelled like a faulty garbage disposal. I glanced at the pamphlet she'd handed me, a match for the one I'd seen at the motel.

"Is this Dr. Dunne around? I'd like to talk to him."

"He just came in from the tennis courts. You must have passed him in the hall."

I shook my head, baffled. "I didn't see anyone."

"Just a moment. I'll ring."

She picked up an in-house telephone, turning away from me so I couldn't read her lips while she murmured to someone on the other end. She replaced the receiver. "Mrs. Dunne will be right out."

"Great. Uh, do you have a rest room close by?"

She pointed toward the corridor to the left of the desk. "Second door down."

"I'll be right back."

I was telling a little fib. The minute I was out of sight I race-walked down the corridor to the far end where it met a transverse corridor with administrative offices on either side. All of them were empty except for one. A nice brass plaque identified it as Dr. Dunne's. I went in. He didn't seem to be there, but the chair was piled with sweaty tennis togs, and I could hear the patter of a shower being run behind a door marked Private. I took the liberty of a stroll around his desk while I waited for him. I let my fingers tippy-toe among his papers, but there was nothing of interest. A detail man had been there and had left some samples of a new anticholinergic, with accompanying literature. The glossy color enlargement showed a duodenal ulcer as large as the planet Jupiter. Oh, barf. Picture that sucker sitting in your gut.

The file cabinets were locked. I had hoped to explore his desk drawers, but I didn't want to push my luck. Some people get cranky when you snoop around like that. I cupped one hand to my ear. Shower off. Ah, that was good. The doctor and I were going to have a little chat.

# 17

Dr. Dunne emerged from the bathroom fully dressed, wearing kelly green slacks with a white belt, a pink and green plaid sports shirt, white loafers, pink socks. All he needed was a white sportcoat to constitute what's known as a "full Cleveland," very popular among middle-aged bon vivants in the Midwest. He had a full head of white hair, still damp, combed straight back. Tendrils were already curling up around his ears. His face was full, his complexion hot pink, eyes very blue under unruly white brows. He was probably six foot two, toting an extra fifty pounds' worth of rich food and drink, which he carried in the front like six months' worth of pregnancy. How come all the men in this town were out of shape?

He stopped in his tracks when he caught sight of me. "Yes, ma'am," he said, in response to some question I hadn't asked him yet.

I infused my tone with warmth, feigning graciousness. "Hi, Dr. Dunne. I'm Kinsey Millhone,"

I said, extending my hand. He responded with a minimal squeeze, three fingers pressing mine.

"Personnel's down the hall, but we're not hiring presently. The hotel won't open for business until April first."

"I'm not looking for work. I need some information about a former patient of yours."

His eyes took on that doctor-privilege look. "And who would that be?"

"Jean Timberlake."

His body language switched over to a code I couldn't read. "Are you with the police?"

I shook my head. "I'm a private detective, hired by—"

"I can't help you, then."

"Mind if I sit?"

He stared at me blankly, accustomed to his pronouncements being taken as law. He probably never had to deal with pushy people like me. He was protected from the public by his receptionist, his lab tech, his nurse, his billing clerk, his answering service, his office manager, his wife—an army of women keeping Doctor safe and untouched. "I must not have made myself clear, Miss Millhone. We have nothing to discuss."

"Sorry to hear that," I said equably. "I'm trying to find out who her father was."

"Who let you in here?"

"The desk clerk just talked to your wife," I said, which was true but not relevant.

"Young lady, I'm going to have to ask you to leave. There's no way in the world I'd give you information about the Timberlakes. I've been the personal physician to that family for years."

"I understand that," I said. "I'm not asking you to breach confidentiality—"

"You most certainly are!"

"Dr. Dunne, I'm trying to get a line on a murder suspect. I know Jean was illegitimate. I've got a copy of the birth certificate, listing her father as unknown. I don't see any reason to protect the man if you know who he was. If you don't, just say so and save us both some time."

"This is a damn outrage, barging in on me like this! You have no right to pry into that poor girl's past. Excuse me," he said darkly, crossing to the door. "Elva!" he yelled. "El!!"

I could hear someone thumping purposefully down the corridor. I put a business card on the edge of his desk. "I'm at the Ocean Street Motel if you decide to help."

I was halfway out the door when Mrs. Dunne appeared. She was still in tennis clothes, her pale cheeks flushed. I could see that she recognized me from my first visit to the place. My return wasn't greeted with the delight I had hoped for. She was holding her racket like a hatchet, the wooden rim edgewise. I eased away, keeping an eye on her. I don't usually feel that threatened by horsey women with big legs, but she had already stepped across the line into my psychological space. She moved forward a step, standing so close now I could smell her breath, no big treat.

"I was hoping to get some help on a case, but I guess I was wrong."

"Call the police," she said flatly to him.

Without any warning, she lifted the racket like a samurai sword.

I skipped back as the racket swopped down at me. "Whoa, lady! You better watch that," I said.

She struck out at me again, missing.

I had dodged in reflex. "Hey! Knock it off!"

She whacked at me again, fanning the air within an inch of my face. I jerked back. This was ludicrous. I wanted to laugh, but the racket had hissed with a savagery that made my stomach lurch. I danced backward as she advanced. She swatted again with the Wilson and missed. Her face had taken on an expression of avid concentration, eyes glittering, lips parted slightly. Behind her, I was dimly aware that Dr. Dunne's attitude had shifted from wariness to concern.

"Elva, that's enough," he said.

I didn't think she'd heard him, or if she had, she didn't care. The racket whacked at me sideways, wielded this time like a broadax. She shifted her weight, her grip two-handed as she sliced diagonally, and sliced again.

Whack, whack!

Missing me by a hair's breadth and only because I was quick. She was totally focused and I was afraid if I turned to run, she'd catch me in the back of the head. Take a crack like that and you're talkin' blood, folks. Not a fatal impact, but one you'd prefer to skip.

Up came the racket again. The wood rim descended like a blade, too swift this time to evade.

I took the brunt of it on my left forearm, raised instinctively to shield my face. The racket connected with a cracking sound. The blow was like a white flash of heat up my arm. I can't say I felt pain. It was more like a jolt to my psyche, unleashing aggression.

I caught her in the mouth with the heel of my hand, knocking her back into him. The two of them went down with a mingled yelp of surprise. The air around me felt white and empty and clean. I grabbed her shirt with an unholy strength, hauling her to her feet. Without any thought at all, I punched her once, registering an instant later the smacking sound as my fist connected with her face.

Somebody snagged my arm from behind. The desk clerk was hanging on to me, screaming incoherently. My left hand was still knotted in Elva's shirt. She tried to backstroke out of range, arms flailing as she yodeled with fear, eyes wide.

My self-control reasserted itself and I lowered my fist. She fairly crowed with relief, staring at me with astonishment. I don't know what she'd seen in my face, but I knew what I'd seen in hers. I felt giddy with power, happiness surging through me like pure oxygen. There's something about physical battle that energizes and liberates, infusing the body with an ancient chemistry—a cheap high with a sometimes deadly effect. A blow to the face is as insulting as you can get, and there's no predicting what you'll garner in return. I've seen petty barroom disputes end in death over a slap on the cheek.

Her mouth was already puffy, her teeth washed with blood. Exhilaration peaked and drained at the sight. Now I could feel pain throb in my arm and I bent with the pulse of it, panting hard. The bruise was a sharp blue vertical line, red welt spreading its blood cloud under the skin. I would swear I could see a raised line where the gut had been strung along the edge of the racket. Set upon by an evil-tempered tennis buff. It was all so damn dumb. Lucky I hadn't interrupted her at a round of golf. She'd have pounded me to a pulp with her pitching wedge. My knuckles were stinging where the skin had ripped. I hoped her rabies vaccinations were up to date.

Elva began to cry piteously, adopting the victim stance when it was she who had tried to savage me! I felt something stir and I yearned to go after her again, but the truth was I hurt, and the need to tend to myself took precedence. Dr. Dunne shepherded his wife into his office. The desk clerk in the orange blazer scurried after them while I leaned against the wall, trying to catch my breath. He might have been calling the sheriff's department, but I didn't much care.

In a moment the doctor returned, full of soothing apologies and solicitous advice. All I wanted was to get the hell out of there, but he insisted on examining my arm, assuring me it wasn't broken. God, did the man think I was an idiot? Of course it wasn't broken. He steered me into the hotel infirmary where he cleaned my battered hand. He was clearly worried, and that interested me more than anything that had transpired so far.

"I'm sorry you and Elva had a falling-out." He dabbed a stinging disinfectant on my hand, his gaze flicking quickly to my face to see if I'd react.

I said, "You know women. We get into these little tiffs." The irony was apparently lost on him.

"She's protective. I'm sure she didn't mean to offend. She was so upset, I had to give her a sedative."

"I hope you've got all your hand tools locked up. I'd hate to see the lady with a crescent wrench."

He began to put his first-aid supplies away. "I think we should try to forget the incident."

"Easy for you to say," I said. I was flexing my right hand, admiring the way the butterfly Band-Aid closed the cleft in my knuckle formed by Elva's front teeth. "I take it you still won't give me information on Jean Timberlake."

He had crossed the room to the sink, where he was washing his hands, his back turned. "I saw her that day," he said tonelessly. "I explained as much to the police at the time."

"The day she was killed?"

"That's right. She came to my office when she got the results of her pregnancy test."

"Why not have you run the test to begin with?"

"I couldn't tell you that. Perhaps she was embarrassed about the predicament she was in. She said she'd pleaded with the Lompoc doctor to abort her. He'd turned her down and I was next on her list."

He dried his hands thoroughly and hung the towel on the rack.

"And you refused?"

"Of course."

"Why 'of course'?"

"Aside from the fact that back then abortion was illegal, it's something I would never do. Her mother survived an illegitimate pregnancy. No reason this girl couldn't have done the same. The world doesn't end, though she didn't seem to see it that way. She said it would ruin her life, but that simply wasn't true."

While he talked, he unlocked a cabinet and took out a big jar of pills. He shook five into a small white envelope, which he handed to me.

"What are these?"

"Tylenol with codeine."

I couldn't believe I'd need painkillers, but I tucked the envelope in my handbag. In my line of work, I get bashed around a lot. "Did you tell Jean's mother what was going on?"

"Unfortunately, no. Jean was a minor and I should have informed her mother, but I agreed to keep the matter confidential. I wish now I'd spoken up. Maybe things would have turned out differently."

"And you have no idea who Jean's father was?"

"I'd try ice on that arm," he said. "If the swelling persists, come back and see me. At the office, if you don't mind. There'll be no charge."

"Did she give you *any* indication who she was involved with?"

Dr. Dunne left the room without another word.

\*     \*     \*

I scrounged a long-sleeved shirt out of the backseat of my car and pulled it on over my T-shirt so the rainbow of bruises on my arm wouldn't show. I sat there for a moment, leaning my head back against the seat, trying to marshal my forces for whatever was coming next. I was done in. It was only four o'clock and I felt as if the day had gone on forever. So many things bothered me. Tap with his shotgun shells loaded with rock salt. The $42,000 unaccounted for. Someone was maneuvering, slipping in and out like a dim figure in the fog. I had caught glimpses, but there was no way to identify the face. I pulled myself upright and started the car, heading into town again so I could talk to Royce.

I found the hospital on Johnson, just a few blocks from the high school, the architecture chunky and nondescript. No design awards for this one.

Royce was on the medical-surgical floor. The soles of my boots squeaked faintly against the highly polished vinyl tiles. I passed the nurses' station, following the room numbers. Nobody paid any attention to me as I made my way down the hall, averting my eyes when I passed an open door. The sick, the injured, and the dying have very little privacy as it is. Out of the corner of my eye, I could see that most of them lay abed in a cluster of flower arrangements, get-well cards propped open, their television sets on. I could smell green beans. Hospitals always smell like canned vegetables to me.

I came to Royce's room. I paused just outside

the door and disconnected my feelings. I went in. Royce was asleep. He looked like a captive, sides pulled up around his bed, an IV like a tether connecting him to a pole. A clear blue plastic oxygen cone covered his nose. The only sound was the breath whiffling through his lips in an intermittent snore. His teeth had been taken away from him, lest he bite himself to death. I stood by the bed and watched him.

He'd been sweating and his white hair was lank, plastered in long strands across his forehead. His hands lay palms-up on the covers, large and raw, fingers twitching now and then. Was he dreaming, like a dog, of his hunting days? In a month he'd be gone, this ornery mass of protoplasm driven by countless irritations, by dreams, by desires unfulfilled. I wondered if he'd live long enough to have what he wanted most—his son, Bailey, whose fate he'd entrusted to my care.

# 18

At five-thirty I was knocking on Shana Timber-lake's door, already convinced there was no one home. Her battered green Plymouth was no longer in the drive. The cottage windows were dark and the drawn front curtains had that blank look of no occupancy. I tried the knob without luck, always interested in the notion of an unsupervised inspection of the premises, a specialty of mine. I did a quick detour around to the back, checking the rear door. She'd put a second bag of trash out, but I could see through the kitchen window that the dirty dishes were piling up again and the bed was unmade. The place looked like a flophouse.

I went back to the motel. What I wanted most in the world was to lay my little head down and go to sleep, but I couldn't see a way to pull that off. I had too much work to do, too many troubling questions yet to ask. I stepped into the office. As usual, the desk was unmanned, but I could hear Ori on the telephone in the family living room. I slipped under the counter and knocked politely on the door frame. She glanced up, catching sight of me, and motioned me in.

She was taking reservations for a family of five, negotiating a sofa bed, a crib, and a cot with variations in the room rate. Maxine, the cleaning lady, had come and gone with very little evidence of her effectiveness. All she'd done, as far as I could see, was to clear off a few surfaces, leaving a residue of furniture oil in which dust was settling. The counterpane on Ori's hospital bed was now littered with junk mail, news clippings, and old magazines, along with that mysterious collection of coupons and fliers that seems to accumulate on end tables everywhere. The wastebasket beside the bed was already spilling over. Ori was idly sorting and discarding as she talked. She concluded her business and set the telephone aside, fanning herself with a windowed envelope.

"Aw, Kinsey. What a day it's been. I think I'm comin' down with something. Lord only knows what. Everybody I talk to has the twenty-four-hour flu. I feel so achy all over and my head's about to bust."

"I'm sorry to hear that," I said. "Is Ann around?"

"She's inspecting some rooms. Every time we get a new maid we have to check and double-check, makin' sure the job's done right. Of course, the minute one's trained, off she goes again and you have to start from scratch. Well, look at you. What'd you do to your hand there, poke it through a winda screen?"

I glanced at my knuckles, trying to think of a convincing fib. I didn't think I'd been hired to punch out the local doctor's wife. Bad form, and I was embarrassed now that I'd lost control of myself. Fortunately, my ills were of only passing interest, and before I could answer, she was back to her own.

She scratched at her arm. "I got this rash," she said, mystified. "Can you see them little bumps? Itch? It's like to drove me insane. I never heard of any kind of flu like that, but I don't know what else it could be, do you?"

She held her arm up. I peered dutifully, but all I could see were the marks she'd made while clawing at herself. She was the kind of woman who would launch, any minute, into a long monologue about her bowels, thinking perhaps that her flatulence had some power to fascinate. How Ann Fowler survived in this atmosphere of medical narcissism was beyond me.

I glanced at my watch. "Oh gee, I better get upstairs."

"Well, I'm not gonna let you do that. You sit right down here and visit," Ori said. "With Royce gone, and my arthritis acting up, I don't know where my manners have went. We never had a chance to get to know one another." She patted the side of the bed as if I might be a lucky pup, allowed at last on the furniture.

"I wish I could, Ori, but you know I have to—"

"Oh no, you don't. It's after five o'clock and

not even suppertime yet. Why would you have to run off at this hour?"

My mind went blank. I stared at her mutely, unable to think of any plausible excuse. I have a friend named Leo who became phobic about old ladies after one wrapped a turd in waxed paper and put it in his trick-or-treat bag. He was twelve at the time and said that aside from spoiling Halloween for him, it ruined all his candy corn. He never could trust old folks after that. I'd always been fond of the elderly, but now I was developing much the same distaste.

Ann appeared in the doorway, a clipboard in hand. She shot me a distracted look. "Oh, hello, Kinsey. How are you?"

Ori launched right in, not wanting to let anybody else establish a conversational beachhead. She held her arm out again. "Ann, honey, look at this here. Kinsey says she's never seen anything like this in her life."

Ann gave her mother a look. "Could you just wait a minute, please."

Ori didn't seem to pick up on the prickliness. "You're going to have to go to the bank first thing in the morning. I paid Maxine out of petty cash and there's hardly anything left."

"What happened to the fifty I gave you yesterday?"

"I just told you. I paid Maxine with that."

"You paid her fifty dollars? How long was she here?"

"Well, you needn't take that tone. She come

at ten and didn't leave till four and she never set down once except to eat her lunch."

"I bet she ate everything in sight."

Ori seemed offended. "I hope you don't begrudge the poor woman a little bite of lunch."

"Mother, she worked six hours. What are you paying her?"

Ori, uneasy on this point, began to pluck at the covers. "You know her son has been sick, and she says she doesn't see how she can keep cleaning for six dollars an hour. I told her we could go to seven."

"You gave her a raise?"

"Well, I couldn't very well tell her no."

"Why not? That's ridiculous. She's slow as molasses and she does shitty work."

"Well, pardon *me*, I'm sure. What's wrong with you?"

"Nothing's wrong! I've got problems enough. The rooms upstairs were a mess, and I had to do two of them again—"

Ori cut in. "That's no reason to snap at me. I told you not to hire the girl. She looked like some kind of foreigner with that black hair braided down the back."

"Why do you do this? The minute I walk in the door, you're all over me. I've asked you and asked you to give me time to catch my breath! But oh no . . . whatever you want is the most important thing in the world."

Ori shot me a look. This was the kind of treatment a sick old woman was subjected to. "I was just trying to help," she said, her voice quavering.

"Oh stop that!" Ann said. She left the room in exasperation. A moment later, we could hear her in the kitchen banging drawers and cabinet doors. Ori wiped at her eyes, making certain I noticed how upset she was.

"I have to make a phone call," I murmured, and eased out of the room before she could enlist my support.

I went upstairs, feeling out of sorts. I had never worked for such unpleasant people in my life. I locked myself in my room and lay down on the bed, too exhausted to move and too unsettled to sleep. The tensions of the day were piling up, and I could feel my head begin to pound from the lack of sleep. Belatedly, I realized I'd never eaten lunch. I was starving.

"God," I said aloud.

I got out of bed, stripped, and headed for the shower. Fifteen minutes later, I was dressed in fresh clothes and on my way out. Maybe a decent dinner would help get me back on track. It was absurdly early, but I never eat at a fashionable hour anyway, and in this town the concept would be wasted.

Floral Beach has a choice of restaurants. There's the pizza parlor on Palm Street, and on Ocean, there's the Breakwater, the Galleon, and the Ocean Street Café, which is open for breakfast only. A line was already forming outside the Galleon. I gathered the Early Bird Special drew crowds from as far away as two blocks. The sign indicated "Family-Style Dining," which means no booze is served and there are shrieking kids on booster seats banging spoons.

I pushed into the Breakwater, heartened by the notion of a full bar. The interior was a mix of nautical and Early American: maple captain's chairs, blue-and-white-checked cloths on the tables, candles in fat red jars encased in the kind of plastic webbing it's fun to fiddle with while you talk. Above the bar, fishing nets were draped across the wooden spokes of a ship's wheel. The hostess was dressed in a mock pilgrim's costume, which consisted of a long skirt and a tight bodice with a low-cut neckline. She had apparently donned an Early American push-up bra because her perky little breasts were forced together like two patty-pan squash. If she leaned over too far, one was going to pop right out. A couple of guys at the bar kept an eye on her, hoping against hope.

Aside from those two, the place was nearly deserted and she seemed relieved to have some business. She seated me in the no-smoking section, which is to say between the kitchen and the pay phone. The menu she handed me was over-sized, bound with a tasseled cord, and featured steak and beef. Everything else was deep-fried. I was wrestling with the choice of 'plump shrimp, litely battered & served with our chef's own secret sause,' or 'tender sea scallops, batter-coated, litely sauteed and served with a zesty sweet 'n' sour dip,' when Dwight Shales materialized at my table. He looked as if he'd showered and changed clothes, too, in preparation for a big, hot night on the town.

"I thought that was you," he said. "Mind if I sit down?"

"Be my guest," I said, indicating the empty seat. "What's the story here? Should I have eaten at the Galleon?"

He pulled out a chair and sat down. "The same people own both."

"Well, then, how come the line's so long over there, and this place is empty?"

"Because it's Thursday and the Galleon offers free barbecued ribs as an appetizer. The service is always lousy, so you're not missing anything."

I surveyed the menu again. "What's good here?"

"Not much. All the seafood is frozen and the chowder comes out of cans. The steak is passable. I order the same thing every time I come. Filet mignon, medium rare, with a baked potato, tossed salad with bleu cheese, and apple pie for dessert. If you have two martinis up front, you'll think it's the fourth best meal you ever ate. Up from that is any quarter pounder with cheese."

I smiled. He was flirting, a hitherto unsuspected aspect of his personality. "You're joining me, I hope."

"Thanks. I'd like that. I hate to eat alone."

"Me, too."

The waitress appeared and we ordered drinks. I confess I was curing my fatigue with a martini on the rocks, but it was quick and efficient and I enjoyed every minute of it. While we talked, I did a covert assessment of him. It interests me how people's looks change as you get to know them. The first flash is probably the most accurate, but there are occasions when a face undergoes a transformation that seems almost magical. With Dwight Shales, there seemed to be a more youthful persona submerged in a fifty-five-year-old shell. His hidden self was becoming more visible to me as he talked.

I listened with both eyes and one ear, trying to discern what was really going on. Ostensibly, we were discussing how we spent our leisure time. He gravitated toward backpacking, while I tended to amuse myself with the abridged California Penal Code and textbooks on auto theft. While his mouth made noises about an assault of ticks on a recent day hike, his eyes said something else. I disconnected my brain and fine-tuned my receiver, picking up his code. This man was emotionally available. That was the subliminal message.

A chunk of lettuce dropped off my fork and my mouth closed on the bare tines. Ever the sophisticate. I tried to act as though I preferred to eat my salad that way.

Midway through the meal, I changed the tenor of the conversation, curious what would happen if we talked about something personal. "What happened to your wife? I take it she died."

"Multiple sclerosis. She went into remission numerous times, but it always caught up with her.

Twenty years of that shit. Toward the end, she couldn't do anything for herself. She was luckier than most, if you want to look at it that way. Some patients are rapidly incapacitated, but Karen wasn't in a wheelchair until the last sixteen months or so."

"I'm sorry. It sounds grim."

He shrugged. "It was. Sometimes it looked like she had it licked. Long periods symptom-free. The hell of it was she was misdiagnosed early on. She'd been plagued by minor health problems, so she started seeing a local chiropractor for what she thought was gout. Of course, once he got hold of her, he mapped out a whole bullshit program that only postponed her getting real help. Class three subluxation. That's what he said it was. I should have sued his ass off, but what's the point?"

"She wasn't a patient of Dr. Dunne's, by any chance?"

He shook his head. "I finally forced her to see an internist in town and he referred her to UCLA for a workup. I guess it didn't matter in the final analysis. Things probably would have come out the same, either way. She handled it much better than I did, that's for sure."

I couldn't think of a thing to say to him. He talked about her for a while and then went on to something else.

"May I ask you about your relationship with Shana Timberlake?"

He seemed to debate briefly. "Sure, why not? She's become a good friend. Since my wife died,

I've spent a lot of time with her. I'm not having an affair with the woman, but I do enjoy her company. I know tongues in town are wagging, but to hell with it. I'm too old to worry about that sort of thing anymore."

"Have you seen her today? I've been trying to track her down."

"No, I don't think so."

I looked over to see Ann Fowler coming in the door. "Oh, there's Ann," I said.

Dwight turned and caught her eye, motioning to her with pleasure. As she approached, he got up and borrowed a chair from a nearby table and moved it over to ours. The dark mood was still with her. She radiated tension, her mouth looking pinched. If Dwight was aware of it, he gave no sign.

He held her chair. "Would you like a drink?"

"Yes, sherry." She signaled for the waitress before he had a chance. He sat down again. I noticed she was avoiding eye contact with me. And drinking? That seemed odd.

"Have you eaten?" I asked.

"You could have told me you wouldn't be with us for dinner tonight."

I felt my cheeks heat at her tone. "I'm sorry. It didn't even occur to me. I was going to take a nap when it dawned on me I hadn't eaten all day. I took a quick shower and came straight over here. I hope I didn't put you out."

She didn't bother to reply to that. I could see that unconsciously she'd adopted her mother's strategy, hanging on to her martyrdom and milking it. I'm not crazy about this as a mode of interaction.

The waitress arrived and asked Ann what she wanted. Before she disappeared, Dwight snagged the woman's attention. "Hi, Dorothy. Has Shana Timberlake been in today?"

"Nope. Not that I've seen. She's usually here for lunch, but she may have gone in to San Luis. Thursday's her day to shop."

"Well, if you see her, tell her to give me a buzz if you would."

"Will do." Dorothy moved away from the table, and he turned back to us.

"How are you, Dwight?" Ann said, with forced pleasantness. It was clear she was cutting me right out of the loop.

I was too tired to play games. I finished my coffee, tossed a twenty on the table, and excused myself.

"You're leaving us?" Dwight said, with a quick look at his watch. "It's not even nine-thirty."

"It's been a long day and I'm beat."

We went through our good-night maneuvers, Ann being only minimally more polite than she had been. Her sherry arrived as I left the table and headed for the door. I thought Dwight seemed slightly disappointed at my departure, but I might have been kidding myself. Martinis bring out the latent romantic in me. Also headaches, if anybody's interested.

# 19

The night was clear. The moon was a pale gold, with gray patches forming patterns across the face of it like bruises on a peach. The door to Pearl's Pool Hall was standing open as I passed, but there were no pool players in evidence and just a handful of people at the bar. The jukebox was playing a country-western tune of some haunting melodic sort. There was one couple on the dance floor, the woman stony-faced as she looked over the man's shoulder. He was doing a hip-swaying two-step, moving her in a circle while she pivoted in place. I slowed, recognizing them from the arraignment. Pearl's son and daughter-in-law. On an impulse, I went in.

I perched on a barstool and turned so I could watch them. He seemed self-absorbed. She was bored. They reminded me of one of those middle-aged couples I see in restaurants whose interest in one another has long ago expired. He was wearing a tight, white T-shirt that bowed slightly at the waist where his love handles bulged out. His jeans were low-slung, too short for the heel on his cowboy boots. His hair was a curly blond, damp from all the styling mousse, which I had to guess was going to smell as pungent as buffalo musk. His face was smooth and full, with a pug nose, a sulky mouth, and an expression that suggested he was very smitten with himself. This guy spent a lot of time in front of bathroom mirrors, combing his hair while he decided which side of his mouth to hang his cigarette from. Daisy approached, her gaze following mine.

"That's Pearl's son and daughter-in-law?"

"Yep. Rick and Cherie."

"Happy-looking pair. What's he do?"

"A welder at a company makes storage tanks. He's an old friend of Tap's. She works for the telephone company, or at least she did. She quit a couple weeks back and they been squabbling ever since. Want a beer?"

"Sure, why not?"

Pearl was on the far end of the room in a conversation with a couple of guys in bowling shirts. He nodded when he saw me, and I gave him a wave. Daisy brought my beer in a frosty Mason jar.

The dance number ended. Cherie left the dance floor, with Rick close behind. I put a couple of bucks on the bar and crossed to their table just as they sat down. Close up, her features were delicate, her blue eyes set off by dark lashes and brows. She might have been pretty if she'd had the resources. As it was, she was thin in a way that spoke of poor nutrition: bony shoulders, bad coloring, lifeless hair pulled back with a couple of plastic barrettes. Her fingernails were bitten right down to the quick. The wrinkles in her sweater suggested that she'd snatched it, in passing, from a pile on the bedroom floor. Both Rick and Cherie smoked.

I introduced myself. "I'd like to talk to you, if you don't mind."

Rick lounged in his seat, hooking his arm over the back of his chair while he checked me out. His legs were now extended insolently into my path. The pose was probably meant to look macho, but I suspected his waistband had jammed his stomach right up against his spleen and he was affording himself some relief. "I heard about you. You're that private detective old man Fowler hired." His tone was knowing. Nobody was going to put one over on him.

"Could I sit down?"

Rick motioned me to a chair, which he kicked out with his foot—his notion of etiquette. I sat down. Cherie didn't seem thrilled with my company, but at least it saved her being alone with him. "So what's the deal?" he said.

"The deal?"

"Yeah. What do you want with me?"

"Information about the murder. I understand you saw Bailey and Jean together the night she was killed."

"What of it?"

"Can you tell me what happened? I'm trying to get a feel for what was going on."

From the far side of the room, I saw Pearl's attention focus on our table. He extracted himself from his conversation and ambled over. He was a big man, so that even the exertion of crossing the room left him breathing heavily. "I see you've met my boy and his wife."

I rose halfway from my seat and shook his hand. "How are you, Pearl? Are you joining us?"

"Could." He pulled out a chair and took a seat, signaling to Daisy to bring him a beer. "You fellas want anything?"

Cherie shook her head. Rick ordered another beer.

"How about you?" Pearl said to me.

"I'm fine."

He held up two fingers and Daisy began to fill a jar from the dispenser hose at the bar. Pearl turned back to me. "They catch Bailey yet?"

"Not as far as I know."

"Heard Royce had him a heart attack."

"An attack of some kind. I'm not sure what it was. He's in the hospital now, but I haven't really talked to him."

"Fella's not long for this world."

"Which is why I hope to wrap this thing up," I said. "I was just asking Rick about the night he saw Jean Timberlake."

"Sorry to interrupt. You go right ahead."

"Not much to tell," Rick said uncomfortably. "I drove by and spotted the two of 'em getting out of Bailey's truck. They looked drunk to me."

"They were staggering?"

"Well, not that, but hanging on to each other."

"And that was midnight?"

Rick made a visual reference to his father, who had turned at Daisy's approach. "Could have been a little after that, but right around there." Daisy put the two beers on the table and went back to the bar.

"You see any cars passing? Anybody else on the street?"

"Nuh-unh."

"Bailey says it was ten o'clock. I'm puzzled by the discrepancy."

Pearl intervened. "Coroner put the time of death close to midnight. Naturally, Bailey'd like everybody to believe he was home in bed by then."

I glanced at Rick. He should have been home in bed himself. "You were how old, seventeen at the time?"

"Who, me? I'se a junior in high school."

"You'd been out on a date?"

"I'd been at my grammaw's and I was on my way home. She'd had a stroke and Dad wanted me to stay with her till the visiting nurse got there." Rick lit another cigarette.

Cherie's face was expressionless, except for an occasional flicker of the mouth—meaning what? She checked her nails and decided to give herself a manicure with her teeth.

"Which was when?"

"Ten after twelve. Something like that."

Pearl spoke up again. "Nurse on the early shift called in sick so I had Rick sit in till the other one got there."

"I take it your grandmother lived in the neighborhood."

"Why all the questions?" Rick asked.

"Because you're the only witness who can actually put him at the scene."

"Of course he was there. He admits that himself. I saw the two of 'em get out of his truck."

"It couldn't have been somebody else?"

"I know Bailey. I've known him all my life. He wasn't any farther away than here to there. The two of 'em drove down to the beach and he parked and they got out and went down the steps." Rick's eyes strayed back to his father's face. He was lying through his teeth.

"Excuse me," Cherie said. "Does anybody mind if I bug out? I got a headache."

"You go on home, baby," Pearl said. "We'll be there in a bit."

"Nice meeting you," she said to me briefly, as she got up. She didn't bother to say anything to Rick. Pearl watched her departure, clearly fond of her.

I caught Rick's eye again. "Did you see anybody coming in or out of the motel?" I knew I was being persistent, but I figured this might be the only chance I'd get to question him. His father's presence probably didn't help, but what was I going to do?

"No."

"Nothing out of the ordinary?"

"I already told you that. It was just regular. Normal."

Pearl spoke up. "You've about exhausted the subject, haven't you?"

"Looks like it," I said. "I keep hoping I'll pick up a lead."

"It'd be nothin' more than damn luck after all this time."

"Sometimes I can make luck," I said.

Pearl leaned forward, thrusting his double chins at me. "I'll tell you something. You're never going to get anywhere with this. It's no point. Bailey's confessed and, by God, it's gonna stick. Royce don't want to believe he's guilty and I can understand that. He's near dead and he doesn't want to go to his grave with a cloud hanging over him. I feel sorry for the old fool, but that doesn't change the facts."

"How do we even know what the facts are at this point?" I said. "She died seventeen years ago. Bailey disappeared the year after that."

"My point exactly," Pearl said. "This is old news. A dead horse. Bailey admitted he was guilty. He could've been out by now instead of starting all over. Look at him. He's taken off again. Who knows where, doing who knows what. We might any of us be in danger. We don't know what's going through his head."

"Pearl, I don't want to argue with you, but I won't give up."

"Then you're a bigger fool than he is."

I'd just about had my fill of argumentative old men. Who asked him? "I appreciate your assessment. I'll keep that in mind." I glanced at my watch. "I better get back."

Neither Rick nor Pearl seemed sorry to see me go. I could feel their eyes on me as I left the place, giving me the kind of look that makes you want to step up your pace a bit.

I walked the two blocks to the motel. It was just after ten, and two black-and-whites were parked side by side across the street. Two young cops were leaning on the fenders, coffee cups in hand while their radio kept up a running account of what was going on in town. I kept thinking about Rick. I knew he was lying, but I had no idea why. Unless he killed her himself. Maybe he'd made sexual advances and she'd laughed him off. Or maybe he'd just been trying to look important at the time, the last man who'd seen Jean Timberlake alive. It was bound to lend him status in a community the size of Floral Beach.

I took my keys out as I went up the outside stairs. It was dark on the second-floor landing, but I caught a whisper of cigarette smoke. I stopped.

There was someone standing in the shadow of the vending machine across from my room. I reached for the penlight in my handbag and flicked it on.

Cherie.

"What are you doing here?"

She stepped out of the dark, the dim glow of the flashlight washing her face with white. "I'm sick of Rick's b.s."

I moved to my door and unlocked it, glancing back at her. "You want to come in and talk?"

"I better not. If he gets home and I'm out, he'll want to know where I've been."

"He's been lying, hasn't he?"

"It wasn't midnight when he saw them. It was closer to ten. He was on his way to see me. He knew if his Daddy found out he'd left his granny by herself, he'd get the crap beat outta him."

"So what happened then, he left and went back?"

"Right. He got back by the time the visiting nurse showed up for her shift. Later, when it turned out Jean Timberlake had been murdered, he said he saw her and Bailey. He just blurted it out before he realized how much trouble he'd be in. So then he had to make the time different so he wouldn't get his ass whipped."

"And Pearl still doesn't know?"

"I'm not sure about that. He's real protective of Rick, so maybe he suspects. It didn't seem like it mattered, once Bailey pleaded guilty. He said he killed her, so nobody really cared what time it was."

"Did Rick tell you what really happened?"

"Well, he did see 'em get out of the truck and go down to the beach. He told me that at the time, but Bailey really could have gone back to his room and passed out like he claimed."

"Why are you telling me?"

"It's no skin off my butt. I'm leaving him anyway, first chance I get."

"You never told anyone else?"

"With Bailey gone all those years, who was I going to tell? Rick made me swear I'd keep my mouth shut and I've done it, but I can't stand listening to any more bull. I want my conscience clear and then I'm heading out."

"Where will you go if you leave Floral Beach?"

She shrugged. "Los Angeles. San Francisco. I got a hundred bucks for the bus and I'll just see how far it goes."

"Is there any chance Rick could have been involved with her?"

"I don't think he killed her, if that's what you mean. I wouldn't stick with him if I thought he did that. Anyway, the cops know he lied about the time and they never cared."

"The cops knew?"

"Sure, I'd assume so. They probably saw her themselves. Ten o'clock, they're always down at the beach. That's where they have their coffee break."

"Jesus, people in this town have sure been content to make Bailey the scapegoat."

Cherie stirred restlessly. "I have to get home."

"If you think of anything else, will you let me know?"

"If I'm still around, I will, but don't count on it."

"I appreciate that. Take care."

But she was gone.

# 20

It was eleven o'clock when I finally eased into bed. Exhaustion was making my whole body ache. I lay there, acutely aware of my heartbeat as it pulsed in my throbbing forearm. This would never do. I hauled myself into the bathroom and washed down some Tylenol with codeine. I didn't even want to think about the day's events. I didn't care what had happened seventeen years ago or what would happen seventeen years hence. I wanted healing sleep in excessive doses, and I finally gave myself up to a formless oblivion, undisturbed by dreams.

It was 2:00 A.M. when the ringing telephone woke me from the dead. I picked up the receiver automatically and laid it on my ear. I said, "What."

The voice was labored and slow, low-pitched, gravelly, and mechanically slurred. "You bitch, I'm going to tear you apart. I'm going to make you wish you'd never come to Floral Beach. . . ."

I slammed the phone down and snatched my

hand back before the guy got out another word. I sat straight up, heart thudding. I'd been sleeping so soundly that I didn't know where I was or what was going on. I searched the shadows, disoriented, tuning in belatedly to the sound of the ocean thundering not fifty yards away, discerning in the tawny reflection of the streetlights that I was in a motel room. Ah yes, Floral Beach. Already, I was wishing I'd never come. I pushed the covers back and padded, in my underpants and tank top, across the room, peering out through the sheers.

The moon was down, the night black, surf tumbling its pewter beads along the sand. The street below was deserted. A comforting oblong of yellow light to my left suggested that someone else was awake—reading, perhaps, or watching late-night TV. As I watched, the light was flicked off, leaving the balcony dark.

The phone shrilled again, causing me to jump. I crossed to the bed table and lifted the receiver cautiously, placing it against my ear. Again, I heard the muffled, dragging speech. It had to be the same voice Daisy had heard at Pearl's when someone called to ask for Tap. I pressed a hand to my free ear, trying to pick up any background sounds from the caller's end of the line. The threat was standard fare, real ho-hum stuff. I kept my mouth shut and let the voice ramble on. What kind of person made crank calls like this? The real hostility lay in the disruption of sleep, a diabolical form of harassment.

The repeat call was a tactical error. The first

time, I'd been too groggy to make sense of it, but I was wide awake now. I squinted in the dark, blanking out the message so I could concentrate on the mode. Lots of white noise. I heard a click, but the line was still alive. I said, "Listen, asshole. I know what you're up to. I'll figure out who you are and it won't take me long, so enjoy." The phone went dead. I left mine off the hook.

I kept the lights off while I pulled my clothes on in haste and gave my teeth a quick brushing. I knew the trick. In my handbag I carry a little voice-activated tape recorder with a variable speed. If you record at 2.4 centimeters per second and play back at 1.2, you can produce the same effect: that sullen, distorted, growling tone that seems to come from a talking gorilla with a speech impediment. There was no way to guess, of course, how the voice would sound if it were played back at the proper speed. It could be male or female, young or old, but it almost had to be a voice I would recognize. Else, why the disguise?

I unlocked my briefcase and took out my little .32, loving the smooth, cold weight of it against my palm. I'd only fired the Davis at the practice range, but I could hit damn near anything. I tucked my room key in my jeans pocket and eased the door open a crack. The corridor was dark, but it had an empty feel to it. I didn't really believe anyone would be there. People who intend to kill you don't usually give fair warning first. Murderers are notoriously poor sports, refusing to play by the rules that govern the rest of us. These were

scare tactics, meant to generate paranoia. I didn't
take the death-and-dismemberment talk very seriously. Where could you rent a chain saw at this
time of night? I pulled the door shut behind me
and slipped down the stairs.

The light was on in the office, but the door
leading into the Fowlers' living quarters was closed.
Bert was asleep. He sat behind the counter in a
wooden chair, his head angled to one side. The
snores flapping through his lips sounded like a
whoopee cushion, flat and wet. His suitcoat was
neatly arranged on a wire hanger on the wall.
He'd pulled on a cardigan, with cuffs of paper
toweling secured by rubber bands to protect his
sleeves. From what, I wasn't sure. He didn't seem
to have any work to do aside from manning the
desk for late-night arrivals.

"Bert," I said. No response. "Bert?"

He roused himself, giving his face a dry scrub
with one hand. He looked at me blearily and then
blinked himself awake.

"I take it the calls I just got didn't come
through the switchboard," I said. I watched while
the electrical circuits in his brain reconnected.

"Excuse me?"

"I just received two calls. I need to know
where they came from."

"Switchboard's closed," he said. "We don't
put calls through after ten o'clock." His voice was
hoarse from sleep and he had to cough to clear his
throat.

"News to me," I said. "Bailey called me

the other night at two A.M. How'd he manage that?"

"I connected him. He insisted on that or I wouldn't have done. I hope you understand about my contacting the sheriff. He's a fugitive from—"

"I know what he is, Bert. Could we talk about the calls that just came in?"

"Can't help you there. I don't know anything about that."

"Could someone ring my room without coming through the switchboard?"

He scratched at his chin. "Isn't any way I know of. You can phone out, but you can't phone in. Ask me, the whole business is a pain in the neck. Over at the Tides, they don't even have phones in the rooms. System costs more than it's worth anyhow. We had this one installed a few years back, and then half the time it's down. What's the point?"

"Can I see the board?"

"You're welcome to take a look, but I can tell you right now no calls came through. I been on duty since nine o'clock and there hasn't been a one. I've been doing accounts payable. Phone hasn't made a peep."

I could see a pile of envelopes tucked in the box for outgoing mail. I ducked under the counter. The telephone console was on one end, eighteen inches wide, with a numbered button for every room. The only light showing was my room, 24, because I'd left my phone off the hook. "You can tell when a phone's in use by the light?"

"By the light," he said, "that's correct."

"What about room-to-room? Couldn't a motel guest bypass the switchboard and dial direct?"

"Only if they knew your room number."

I thought back to all the times I'd given out my business card in the last couple of days, the telephone number at the Ocean Street neatly jotted on the back—my room number too, in some cases . . . but which? "If a phone's in use, you can't tell from the light whether a call is to the outside, room-to-room, or off the hook, right?"

"That's right. I could flip that switch and listen in, but of course that'd be against the rules."

I studied the console. "How many rooms are occupied?"

"I'm not at liberty to say."

"What, we have national security at stake here?"

He stared at me for a moment and then indicated with a put-upon air that I could check the registration cards in the upright file. While I flipped through, he hovered, wanting to be certain I didn't pocket anything. Fifteen rooms out of forty were occupied, but the names meant nothing. I don't know what I'd expected.

"I hope you're not fixing to change rooms again," he said. "We'd have to charge extra."

"Oh, really. Why is that?"

"Motel policy," he said, giving his pants a hitch.

Why was I egging him on? He looked as if he was about to launch into a discourse on management strategies over at the Tides. I said good night and went back upstairs.

There was no possibility of sleep. The phone began to make plaintive little sounds as though it were sick, so I replaced the receiver and disconnected the instrument at the jack. I left my clothes on as I had the night before, pulling the spread over me for warmth. I lay awake, staring at the ceiling while I listened to muffled noises through the wall: a cough, a toilet flushing. The pipes clanked and groaned like a clan of ghosts. Gradually, sunlight replaced the streetlights and I became aware that I was drifting in and out of consciousness. At seven I gave it up, dragged myself into the shower, and used up my allotment of hot water.

I tried the Ocean Street Café for breakfast, downing cups of black coffee with the local paper propped up in front of me so I could eavesdrop on the regulars. Faces were beginning to look familiar. The woman who ran the Laundromat was sitting at the counter, next to Ace, who was getting ragged again about his ex-wife, Betty, seated on his other side. There were two other men I recognized from Pearl's.

I was in a booth near the front, facing the plate-glass windows, with a view of the beach. Joggers were trotting along the wet-packed sand. I was too tired to do a run myself, though it might have perked me up. Behind me, the customers were chatting together as they probably had every day for years.

"Where you think he's at?"

"Lord only knows. I hope he's left the state. He's dangerous."

"They better catch him quick is all I can say. I'll shoot his ass if I see him anywheres around here."

"I bet he's got you peekin' under your bed at night."

"I peek every night. 'At's the only thrill I get. I keep hopin' to find somebody peekin' back at me." The laughter was shrill, underscored with anxiety.

"I'll come over there and help you out."

"Big help you'd be."

"I would. I got me a pistol," Ace said.

" 'At's not what Betty says."

"Yeah, he's loaded half the time, but that don't mean his pistol works."

"Bailey Fowler shows his face, you'll see different," Ace said.

"Not if I get him first," one of the other men said.

The front page of the local newspaper was a rehash of the case to date, but the tone of the coverage was picking up heat. Photographs of Bailey. Photographs of Jean. An old news photo of the crime scene, townspeople standing in the background. The faces in the crowd were blurred and indistinct, seventeen years younger than they looked today. Jean's body, barely visible, was covered with a blanket. Trampled sand. Concrete steps going up on the right. There was a quote from

Quintana, who sounded pompous even then. Probably bucking for sheriff since he joined the department. He seemed like the type.

I wolfed down my breakfast and went back to the motel.

As I went up the outside stairs, I saw one of the maids knocking on the door of room 20. Her cart was parked nearby, loaded with fresh linens, vacuum cleaner mounted on the back.

"Maid service," she called. No answer.

She was short, heavyset, a gold-capped tooth showing when she smiled. Her passkey didn't turn in the lock so she moved on to the room I'd been in before Bert had so graciously consented to the change. I let myself into room 24 and closed the door.

My bed was a tumble of covers that beckoned invitingly. I was buzzing from coffee, but under the silver shimmer of caffeine my body was leaden from weariness. The maid knocked at my door. I abandoned all hope of sleep and let her in. She moved into the bathroom, a plastic bucket in hand, filled with rags and supplies. Nothing feels so useless as hanging around while someone else cleans. I went down to the office.

Ori was behind the counter, clinging shakily to her walker while she sorted through the bills Bert had left in the box for outgoing mail. She was wearing a cotton duster over her hospital gown.

Ann called from the other room. "Mother! Where are you? God . . ."

"I'm right here!"

Ann appeared in the doorway. "What are you doing? I told you I want to do your blood test before I go up to see Pop." She caught sight of me and smiled, her dark mood gone. "Good morning."

"Good morning, Ann."

Ori was leaning heavily on Ann's supporting arm as she began to shuffle into the living room.

"You need some help?" I asked.

"Would you please?"

I slipped under the counter, supporting Ori on the other side. Ann moved the walker out of her mother's path and together we walked her back to the bed.

"Do you have to go to the bathroom while you're up?"

"I guess I best," she said.

We did a slow walk to the bathroom. Ann got her settled on the commode and then stepped into the hall, closing the door.

I glanced at Ann. "Could I ask you a couple of questions about Jean while I've got you here?"

"All right," she said.

"I took a look at her school records yesterday and I noticed that you were one of the counselors who worked with her. Can you tell me what those sessions were about?"

"Her attendance, primarily. The four of us did academic counseling—college prep requirements, dropping or adding classes. If a kid didn't get along with a teacher or wasn't performing up to snuff, we'd step in and test sometimes, or settle disputes, but that was the extent of it. Jean was obviously in trouble scholastically and we talked about the fact that it was probably connected to her home life, but I don't think any of us actually felt qualified to play shrink. We might have recommended she see a psychologist, but I know I didn't try to function with her in that capacity."

"What about her relationship to the family? She hung out here quite a bit, didn't she?"

"Well, yes. During the time she and Bailey dated."

"I get the impression both your parents were fond of her."

"Absolutely. Which only made it awkward when I tried to approach her professionally at school. In some ways, the ties were too close to permit any objectivity."

"Did she ever confide in you as a friend?"

Ann frowned. "I didn't encourage it. Sometimes she complained about Bailey—if the two of them weren't getting along—but after all, he was my brother. I was hardly going to jump in and take her side. I don't know. Maybe I should have made more of an effort with her. I've often asked myself that."

"What about other faculty or staff? Anybody else she might have confided in?"

She shook her head. "Not that I ever knew."

We heard the toilet flush. Ann stepped back into the bathroom while I waited in the hall. When Ori emerged, we maneuvered her back into the living room.

She shrugged off her duster and then we struggled to get her into bed. She must have weighed two hundred eighty pounds, all ropey fat, her skin paper white. She smelled fusty and I had to make a conscious effort not to register my distaste.

Ann began to assemble alcohol, cotton wipe, and lancet. If I had to watch this procedure again, I'd pass out.

"Mind if I use the phone?"

Ori spoke up. "I need to keep this line free for business."

"Try the one in the kitchen," Ann said. "Dial nine first."

I left the room.

# 21

From the kitchen, I tried Shana Timberlake's number, but got no answer. Maybe I'd stop by her place again in a bit. I intended to press her for information when I caught up with her. She held a big piece of the puzzle, and I couldn't let her off the hook. The telephone book was on the kitchen counter. I looked up Dr. Dunne's office number and tried that next. A nursey-sounding woman picked up on the other end. "Family practice," she said.

"Oh, hi. Is Dr. Dunne in the office yet?" I'd been told he was out until Monday. My business was with her.

"No, I'm sorry. This is Doctor's day at the clinic in Los Angeles. Can I be of help?"

"I hope so," I said. "I was a patient of his some years ago and I need records of the illness I was seeing him for. Can you tell me how I'd go about getting those?"

Ann came into the kitchen and moved to the

refrigerator, where she removed the glass vial of insulin and stood rolling it in her palms to warm it.

"When would this have been?"

"Uhm, oh gee, 1966 actually."

"I'm sorry, but we don't keep records that far back. We consider a file inactive if you haven't seen Doctor in five years. After seven years, records are destroyed."

Ann left the room. I'd miss the injection altogether if I strung this out long enough.

"And that's true even if a patient is deceased?" I asked.

"Deceased? I thought it was your medical records we were talking about," she said. "Could I have your name please?"

I hung up. So much for Jean Timberlake's old medical chart. Frustrating. I hate dead ends. I returned to the living room.

I hadn't stalled long enough.

Ann was peering at the syringe, holding it needle up, while she tapped to make sure there were no bubbles in the pale, milky insulin. I eased toward the door, trying to be casual about it. She looked up as I passed. "I forgot to ask, did you see Pop yesterday?"

"I stopped by late afternoon, but he was asleep. Did he ask for me again?" I tried to look every place, but at her.

"They called this morning," she said irritably. "He's raising all kinds of hell. Knowing him, he wants out." She swiped alcohol on the bald flesh on her mother's thigh.

I fumbled in my handbag for a Kleenex as she plunged the needle home. Ori visibly jumped. My hands were clammy and my head was already feeling light.

"He's probably making everybody's life miserable." She was blabbing on, but the sound was beginning to fade. Out of the corner of my eye, I saw her break the needle off the disposable syringe, dropping it in the wastebasket. She began to clean up cotton wads, the paper from the lancet. I sat down on the couch.

She paused, a look of concern crossing her face. "Are you all right?"

"I'm fine. I just feel like sitting down," I murmured. I'm sure death creeps up on you just this way, but what was I going to say? I'm a bad-ass private eye who swoons in the same room with a needle? I smiled at her pleasantly to show I was okay. Darkness was crowding my peripheral vision.

She went on about her business, heading toward the kitchen to return the insulin. The minute she left the room, I hung my head down between my knees. They say it's impossible to faint while you're doing this, but I've managed it more than once. I glanced at Ori, apologetically. She was moving her legs restlessly, unwilling, as usual, to concede that anybody might feel worse than she did. I was trying not to hyperventilate. The creeping darkness receded. I sat up and fanned myself as if this was just something I did every day.

"I don't feel good," she said. She scratched at her arm, her manner agitated. What a pair we made. Apparently her mythical rash was acting up again and I was going to have to make a medical evaluation. I sent her a wan smile, which I could feel turning to perplexity. She was wheezing now, a little mewing sound coming from her throat as she clawed at her arm. She looked at me with alarm through thick glasses that magnified the fear in her eyes.

"Oh Lord," she rasped. "It couldn't . . ." Her face was ashen, swelling visibly, hot pink welts forming on her neck.

"What is it, Ori? Can I get you anything?"

Her distress was accelerating so quickly I couldn't take it in. I crossed to the bed and then yelled toward the kitchen. "Ann, could you come in here? Something's wrong."

"Be right there," she called. I could tell from her tone I hadn't conveyed any sense of urgency.

"Ann! For God's sake, get in here!"

Suddenly I knew where I'd seen this before. When I was eight and went to Donnie Dixon's birthday party next door. He was stung by a yellow jacket and was dead before his mother reached the backyard.

Ori's hands went to her throat, her eyes rolling wildly, sweat popping out. It was clear she wasn't getting air. I tried to help, but there was nothing I could do. She grabbed for me like a drowning woman, clutching my arm with such force that I thought she'd tear off a hunk of flesh.

"Now what?" Ann said.

She appeared in the doorway, wearing an expression that was a mix of indulgence and irritation at her mother's latest bid for attention. She paused, blinking as she tried to assimilate the sight before her. "What in the world? Mother, what's wrong? Oh my God!"

I don't think more than two minutes had passed since the attack began. Ori was convulsing, and I could see a flood of urine spread along the bedding under her. The sounds she made were none that I had ever heard from a human being.

Ann's panic was a singing note that rose from low in her throat. She snatched up the phone, fumbling in her haste. By the time she had dialed 911, Ori's body was bucking as if someone were administering electric shock treatments.

It was clear the 911 dispatcher had picked up the call. I could hear a tiny female voice buzz across the room like a fly. Ann tried to respond, but the words turned into a scream as she caught sight of her mother's face. I was frantically trying CPR techniques, but I knew there wasn't any point.

Ori was still, her eyes wide and blank. She was already beyond medical help. I looked at the clock automatically for time of death. It was 9:06. I took the phone out of Ann's hand and asked for the police.

About 20 percent of all people die under circumstances that would warrant an official inquiry into the cause of death. The burden of determining cause and manner of death usually falls to the first police officer to appear on the scene. In this case, Quintana must have been alerted to the call because within thirty minutes the Fowlers' living quarters had been taken over by sheriff's department personnel: Detective Quintana and his partner, whose name I still didn't know, the coroner, a photographer, two evidence techs, a fingerprint tech, three deputies securing the area, and an ambulance crew waiting patiently until the body could be removed. Any matter related to Bailey Fowler was going to be subject to official scrutiny.

Ann and I had been separated shortly after the first county sheriff's car arrived. Clearly, no one wanted us to confer. They were taking no chances. For all they knew, we'd just conspired in the murder of Ori Fowler. Of course, if we'd been brash enough to kill her, you'd think we'd also have been smart enough to get our stories straight before we called the cops. Maybe it was only a question of making sure we didn't contaminate each other's account of events.

Ann, wan and shaken, sat in the dining room. She had wept briefly and without conviction while the coroner went through the motions of listening for Ori's heart. Now she was subdued, answering in low tones as Quintana questioned her. She seemed numbed by circumstance. I'd seen the reaction countless times when death is too sudden to be convincing to those most affected by it. Later, when the finality of the event sinks in, grief breaks through in a noisy torrent of rage and tears.

Quintana flicked a look in my direction as I passed the door. I was on my way to the kitchen, escorted by a female deputy whose law-enforcement paraphernalia must have added ten inches to her waist measurement; heavy belt, portable two-way radio, nightstick, handcuffs, keys, flashlight, ammunition, gun and holster. I was reminded uncomfortably of my own days in uniform. It's hard to feel feminine in a pair of pants that make you look like a camel from the rear.

I took a seat at the kitchen table. I kept my face neutral, trying to act as if I wasn't sucking in every detail of the crime scene activity. I was frankly relieved to be out of sight of Ori, who was beached in death like an old sea lion washed up on the sand. She couldn't even be cold yet, but her skin was already suffused with the bleached, mottled look of decay. In the absence of life, the body seems to deteriorate before your very eyes. An illusion, of course—perhaps the same optical trickery that makes the dead appear to breathe.

Ann must have told them about injecting the insulin, because an evidence technician came into the kitchen within minutes and removed the vial of insulin, which he bagged and labeled. Unless the local labs were a lot more sophisticated than usual in a town this size, the insulin, plus all the samples of Ori's blood, urine, gastric content, bile, and viscera would probably be shipped off to the state crime lab in Sacramento for analysis. Cause of death was almost certainly anaphylactic shock. The question was, what had triggered it? Surely not the insulin after all these years—unless somebody'd tampered with the vial, a not unreasonable guess. Death might have been accidental, but I doubted it.

I looked over to the back door, where the thumb latch on the lock had been turned to the open position. From what I'd seen, the motel office was seldom secured. Windows were left open, doors unlocked. When I thought back to all the people who'd been trooping through the place, it seemed clear that anybody could have sauntered over to the refrigerator for a peek. Ori's diabetes was common knowledge, and her insulin dependency was the perfect means of delivering a fatal dose of who-knew-what. Ann's administering the injection would only add guilt to her grief, a cruel postscript. I was curious as to what Detective Quintana was going to make of it.

As if on cue, he ambled into the kitchen and took a seat at the table across from me. I wasn't looking forward to a chat with him. Like many cops, he took up more than his share of psychological space. Being with him was like being in a crowded elevator, stuck between floors. Not an experience you seek out.

"Let's hear how you tell it," he said.

To give him credit, he seemed more compassionate than he had before, perhaps in deference to Ann. I launched into my account with all the candor I could muster. I had nothing to hide, and there wasn't any point in playing games with the man. I started with the telephone harassment in

the dead of night and proceeded to the moment
when I'd taken the receiver from Ann and asked
for the police. He took careful notes, printing
rapidly in a style that mimicked an italic typeface.
By the time he finished quizzing me, I found
myself trusting his thoroughness and his attention
to detail. He flipped his notebook closed and tucked
it in his coat pocket.

"I'm going to need a list of the people who've
been in and out of here the last couple of days. I'd
appreciate your help with that. Also, Miss Fowler
says the family doctor isn't in the office on Fri-
days. So, you might keep an eye on her. She looks
like she's one step away from collapse. Frankly,
you don't look all that hot yourself," he said.

"Nothing that a month of sleep won't cure."

"Give me a call if anything comes up."

He gave instructions to the deputy in charge.
By the time he left, much of the dusting, bagging,
tagging, and picture-taking was finished and the
CSI team was packing up. I found Ann still seated
at the dining room table. Her gaze traveled to my
face when I entered the room, but she registered
no response.

"Are you all right?" I asked.

No reply.

I sat down next to her. I would have taken
her hand, but she didn't seem like the type you
could touch without asking permission first. "I
know Quintana must have asked you this, but did
your mother have allergies?"

"Penicillin," she said dully. "I remember she
had a very bad reaction to penicillin once."

"What other medications was she taking?"

Ann shook her head. "Just what's on the bed table, and her insulin, of course. I don't understand what happened."

"Who knew about the allergy?"

Ann started to speak and then shook her head.

"Did Bailey know?"

"He would never do such a thing. He couldn't have . . ."

"Who else?"

"Pop. The doctor . . ."

"Dunne?"

"Yes. She was in his office when she had the first bad reaction."

"What about John Clemson? Is his the pharmacy she uses?"

She nodded.

"People from the church?"

"I suppose. She didn't make a secret of it, and you know her. Always talking about her illnesses . . ." She blinked and I saw her face suffuse with pink. Her mouth tightened, turning downward as the tears welled in her eyes.

"I'm going to call someone to come sit with you. I've got things to do. You have a preference? Mrs. Emma? Mrs. Maude?"

She curled in on herself and laid her cheek against the tabletop as if she might go to sleep. Instead she wept, tears splashing onto the polished wood surface like hot wax. "Oh God, Kinsey. I did it. I can't believe it. I actually stood there and injected the stuff. How am I going to live with that?"

I didn't know what to say to her.

I went back into the living room, avoiding the sight of the bed, which was empty now, linens stripped off and carted away with the rest of the physical evidence. Who knew what they might find in the bedding? An asp, a poisonous spider, a suicide note shoved down among the dirty sheets.

I called Mrs. Maude and told her what had happened. After we went through the obligatory expressions of shock and dismay, she said she'd be right over. She'd probably make a few quick telephone calls first, rounding up the usual members of the Family Crisis Squad. I could practically hear them crushing up potato chips for the onslaught of tuna casseroles.

As soon as she'd arrived and taken over responsibility for the office, I went upstairs to my room, locked the door, and sat down on the bed. Ori's death was confusing. I couldn't figure out what it meant or how it could possibly fit in. Fatigue was pressing down on me like an anvil, nearly crushing me with its weight. I knew I couldn't afford to go to sleep, but I wasn't sure how much longer I could go on.

The phone shrilled beside me. I hoped to God it wasn't going to be another threat. "Hello?"

"Kinsey, it's me. What the hell is going on?"

"Bailey, where are you?"

"Tell me what happened to my mother."

I told him what I knew, which didn't sound like much. He was silent for so long I thought he'd hung up. "Are you there?"

"Yes, I'm here."

"I'm sorry. Really. You never even got to see her."

"Yeah."

"Bailey, do me a favor. You have to turn yourself in."

"I'm not going to do that till I know what's going on."

"Listen to me—"

"Forget it!"

"Goddamn it, just hear me out. Then you can do anything you want. As long as you're on the street, you're going to take the blame for whatever happens. Can't you see that? Tap gets blown to hell and you take off like a shot. Next thing you know, your mother's dead, too."

"You know I didn't do it."

"Then turn yourself in. If you're in custody, at least you can't be blamed if something else goes wrong."

Silence. Finally he said, "Maybe. I don't know. I don't like this shit."

"I don't either. I hate it. Look, just do this. Call Clemson and see what he has to say."

"I know what he'll say."

"Then take his advice and do the smart thing for once!" I banged the phone down.

# 22

I had to get some air. I locked the door behind me and left the motel. I crossed the street and sat down on the sea wall, staring down at the stretch of beach where Jean Timberlake had died. Behind me, Floral Beach was laid out in miniature, six streets long, three streets wide. It bothered me somehow that the town was so small. It had all happened right here in the space of these eighteen blocks. The very sidewalks, the buildings, the local businesses—it all must have been much the same back then. The townspeople were no different. Some had moved away, a few had died. In the time I'd been here, I'd probably talked to the killer myself at least once. It was an affront somehow. I turned and looked back at the section of town that I could see. I wondered if someone in one of the little pastel cottages across the street had seen anything that night. How desperate could I get? I was actually contemplating a door-to-door canvass of the citizens of Floral Beach.

But I had to do something. I glanced at my watch.
It was after one o'clock. Tap Granger's funeral
service was scheduled for two. He'd have a good
turnout. The locals had talked of little else since
he was gunned down. Who was going to miss this
climactic event?

I crossed back to the motel, where I picked
up my car and drove a block and a half to Shana
Timberlake's. She'd been out when I'd called this
morning, but she'd have to be home now and
dressing for Tap's funeral if she intended to go. I
pulled in across the street. The little wood-frame
cottages in her courtyard had all the charm of
army barracks. Still no Plymouth in the driveway.
Her front curtains were still as they had been
before. Two days' worth of newspapers were now
piled near the porch. I knocked at her door, and
when I got no response, I slyly tried the knob.
Still locked.

An old woman stood on the porchlet of the
cottage next door. She watched me with the baggy
eyes of a beagle hound.

"Do you know where Shana went?"

"What?"

"Is Shana here?"

She gestured impatiently, turned away, and
banged back into her place. I couldn't tell if she
was mad because she couldn't hear me or because
she didn't give a damn what Shana did. I shrugged
and left the front porch, walking between the two
cottages to the rear.

Everything looked the same, except that some

animal—a dog, or maybe a raccoon—had tipped over her garbage cans and spread her trash around. Very classy stuff. I climbed the porch steps and peered in the kitchen window as I had before. It seemed clear that Shana hadn't been home for days. I tried the back door, wondering if there was any reason to break in. I couldn't think of one. It is, after all, against the law, and I don't like to do it unless I can anticipate some benefit.

As I went down the steps, I noticed a square white envelope among the papers littering the yard. The same one I'd been sniffing at the other day when I talked to her? I picked it up. Empty. Shoot. Gingerly, I began to sort through the garbage. And there it was. The card was a reproduction of a still life, an oil painting of opulent roses in a vase. There was no printed message, but inside, somebody had penned "Sanctuary. 2:00. Wed." Whom could she have met with? Bob Haws? June? I tucked the card in my handbag and drove over to the church.

The Floral Beach Baptist Church (Floral Beach's only church, if you want to get technical) was located at the corner of Kaye and Palm streets—a modest-sized white frame structure with various outbuildings attached. A concrete porch ran the width of the main building, with white columns supporting the composition roof. One thing about the Baptists, they're not going to waste the congregation's money on some worthless architect. I'd seen this particular church design several times before, and I pictured ecclesiastical blueprints making the rounds for the price of the postage. A florist's truck was parked out on the street, probably delivering arrangements for the funeral.

The double doors were standing open and I went inside. There were several paint-by-the-numbers-style stained-glass windows, depicting Jesus in an ankle-length nightgown that would get him stoned to death in this town. The apostles had arranged themselves at his feet, looking up at him like curly haired women with simpering expressions. Did guys really shave back then? As a child, I never could get anybody to answer questions like that.

The interior walls were white, the floor covered in beige linoleum tile. The pews were decorated with black satin bows. Tap Granger's coffin had been placed down near the front. I could tell Joleen had been talked into paying more than she could afford, but that's a tough pitch to resist when you're in the throes of grief. The cheapest coffin in the showroom is inevitably a peculiar shade of mauve and looks as if it's been sprayed with the same stuff they use on acoustic ceilings to cut the sound.

A woman in a white smock was placing a heart-shaped wreath on a stand. The wide lavender ribbon had "Resting In The Arms Of Jesus" written on it in a lavish gold script. I could see June Haws in the choir loft, rocking back and forth as she played the pipe organ with much working of the feet. She was playing a hymn that sounded like a tender moment in a vintage daytime soap, singing to herself in a voice with more tweeter than woofer. The bandages on her hands made her look like something newly risen from the dead. She stopped playing as I approached, and turned to look at me.

"Sorry to interrupt," I said.

She put her hands in her lap. "That's all right," she said. There was something placid about her, despite the fact that the tincture of iodine was working its way up her arms. Was it spreading, this plague, this poison ivy of the soul?

"I didn't know you doubled as the organist."

"Ordinarily, I don't, but Mrs. Emma's sitting with Ann. Haws went over to the hospital to counsel Royce. I guess the doctors told him about Oribelle. Poor soul. A reaction to her medication, was it? That's what we were told."

"Looks that way. They'll have to wait for the lab reports to be sure."

"God love her heart," she murmured, picking at the gauze wound around her right arm. She'd taken her gloves off so she could play. Her fingers were visible, sturdy and plain, the nails blunt-cut.

I took the card out of my bag. "Did you talk to Shana Timberlake here a couple of days ago?"

Her eyes flicked to the card and she shook her head.

"Could your husband have met with her?"

"You'll have to ask him about that."

"We haven't had a chance to talk about Jean Timberlake," I remarked.

"She was a very misguided girl. Pretty little thing, but I don't believe she was saved."

"Probably not," I said. "Did you know her well?"

She shook her head. Some sort of misery had clouded her eyes and I waited to see if she would speak of it. Apparently not.

"She was a member of the youth group here, wasn't she?"

Silence.

"Mrs. Haws?"

"Well, Miss Millhone. You're a mite early for the service, and I'm afraid you're not dressed properly for church," Bob Haws said from behind me.

I turned. He was in the process of shrugging himself into a black robe. He wasn't looking at his wife, but she seemed to shrink away from him. His face was bland, his eyes cold. I had a vivid flash of him stretched out across his desktop, Jean performing her volunteer work.

"I guess I'll have to miss the funeral," I said. "How's Royce?"

"As well as can be expected. Would you like to step into the office? I'm sure I can help you with any information you might be pressing Mrs. Haws for."

Why not? I thought. This man gave me the creeps, but we were in a church in broad daylight with other people nearby. I followed him to his office. He closed the door. Reverend Haws's ordinarily benevolent expression had already been replaced by something less compassionate. He stayed on his feet, moving around to the far side of his desk.

I surveyed the place, taking my time about it. The walls were pine-paneled, the drapes a dusty-looking green. There was a dark green plastic couch, the big oak desk, a swivel chair, bookcases, various framed degrees, certificates, and biblical-looking parchments on the walls.

"Royce asked me to deliver a message. He's been trying to get in touch. He won't be needing your services. If you'll give me an itemized statement, I'll see that you're paid for the time you've put in."

"Thanks, but I think I'll wait and hear it from him."

"He's a sick man. Distraught. As his pastor, I'm authorized to dismiss you on the spot."

"Royce and I have a signed contract. You want to take a peek?"

"I dislike sarcasm and I resent your attitude."

"I'm skeptical by nature. Sorry if that offends."

"Why don't you state your case and leave the premises."

"I don't have a 'case' to state at this point. I thought maybe your wife might be of help."

"She has nothing to do with this. Any help you get will have to come from me."

"Fair enough," I said. "You want to tell me about your meeting with Shana Timberlake?"

"Sorry. I never met with Mrs. Timberlake."

"What do you think this means, then?" I said. I held the card up, making sure the penned message was visible.

"I assure you I have no idea." He busied

himself, needlessly straightening some papers on his desk. "Will there be anything else?"

"I did hear a rumor about you and Jean Timberlake. Maybe we should discuss that as long as I'm here."

"Any rumor you may have heard would be difficult to substantiate after all this time, don't you think?"

"I like difficulty. It's what makes my job fun. Don't you want to know what the rumor is?"

"I have no interest whatever."

"Ah well," I said. "Perhaps another time. Most people are curious when gossip like this circulates. I'm glad to hear it doesn't trouble you."

"I don't take gossip seriously. I'm surprised you do." He gave me a chilly smile, adjusting his shirt cuffs under the wide sleeves of the robe. "Now, I think you've taken up enough of my time. I have a funeral to conduct and I'd like to have time alone to pray."

I moved to the door and opened it, turning casually. "There was a witness, of course."

"A witness?"

"You know, somebody who sees somebody else do something naughty."

"I'm afraid I don't follow. A witness to what?"

I fanned the air with a loose fist, using a hand gesture he seemed to grasp right away.

His smile was losing wattage as I closed the door behind me.

Outside, the air seemed mercifully warm. I got in my car and sat for a few minutes. I leafed through my notes, looking for unturned stones. I don't even know what I was hoping to find. I reviewed the information I'd jotted down when I went through Jean Timberlake's school records. She'd lived on Palm then, just around the corner from where I sat. I craned around in the seat, wondering if it was worth it to go have a look. Oh hell, why not? In lieu of hard facts, I might as well hope for a psychic flash.

I started the VW and headed for the old Timberlake address. It was only one block down, so I could have left the car where it was, but I thought I'd better free up a parking space for the hearse. The building was on the left, two stories of shabby, pale green stucco jammed up against a steep embankment.

As I approached, I realized there was nothing much to see. The building was abandoned, the windows boarded up. On the left, a wooden staircase angled up to the second floor, where a balcony circled the perimeter. I climbed the stairs. The Timberlakes had lived in number 6, in the shadow of the hill. The whole place looked dreary. The front door of their apartment had a perfect round hole where the knob should have been. I pushed the door open. The veneer had been splintered, leaving stalagmites of lighter wood showing along the bottom edge.

The windows here were still intact, but so grimy that they might as well have been boarded up. The incoming light was filtered by dust. Soot had settled on the linoleum floors. The kitchen counters were warped, the cabinet doors hanging by their hinges. Mouse pellets suggested recent occupancy. There was only one bedroom. The back door opened off this bedroom onto the rear of the building, where the balcony connected to a clumsy stairway anchored to the side of the hill. I looked up. The sheer sides of the dirt embankment were eroded. Dense vines spilled over the lip of the hill maybe thirty feet above. Up there, at the top, I caught a glimpse of a private residence that boasted a spectacular view of the town, with the ocean stretching off to the left and a gentle hill on the right.

I returned to the apartment, trying to roll back the years in my mind. Once this place had been furnished, not grandly perhaps, but with an eye to modest comfort. From gouges in the floor, I could guess where the couch had been. I suspected they'd used the dining ell as a sleeping alcove, and I wondered which of them had slept there. Shana had mentioned Jean's sneaking out at night.

I passed through the bedroom to the back door and studied the rear stairs, letting my eye follow the line of ascent. She might have used these, climbing up to the street above, where her various boyfriends could have picked her up and dropped her off again. I tested the crude wooden handrail, which was flimsily constructed and loose after years of disuse. The risers were unnaturally steep and it made climbing hazardous. Many of the balusters were gone.

I trudged upward, huffing and puffing my way to the top. A chain-link fence ran along the crest of the embankment. There was no gate now, but there might have been at one time. Carefully I turned my head, looking back over the neighborhood from above the rooftops. The view was heady—treetops at my feet, the town spread out below—creating a mild vertigo. A parked car was about the size of a bar of soap.

I studied the house in front of me, a two-story frame-and-glass structure with a weathered exterior. The yard was immaculate and beautifully landscaped, complete with a swimming pool, decking, a hot tub, a Brown-Jordan glass-topped table and chairs. Situated anyplace else in town, the property would have required shielding shrubs for privacy. Up here, the owners could enjoy an unobstructed 180-degree view.

I struck off to the right, clinging to the fence as I made my way along the narrow path that skirted the property. When I reached the lot line on the right, I followed the fence, which defined the vacant lot next door. The street beyond was the last stretch of a cul-de-sac, with only one other house in sight. As far as I'd seen, this was Floral Beach's only classy neighborhood.

I approached the house from the front and rang the bell. I turned and stared out at the street. Up here on the hill, the sun beat down unmercifully on the chaparral. There were very few trees and there was very little to cut the wind. The ocean was visible perhaps a quarter of a mile away.

I wondered if the fog stretched this far; could be desolate in its way. I rang the bell again, but there was apparently no one home. Now what?

The word "Sanctuary" was nagging at me. I'd assumed it meant the church, but there was another possibility. The hot tubs up at the mineral springs all had names like that. Maybe it was time for another visit with the Dunnes.

# 23

The parking lot at the mineral springs was empty except for two service trucks, one from a pool company and the other a high-sided pickup with gardening tools visible in the bed. I could hear the whine of a wood chipper somewhere on the property, and I assumed brush was being cleared. I approached the spa from the rear, as I had on my first visit to the place.

The reception area was quiet and there was no one at the desk. Maybe everyone was off at Tap's funeral. I checked the bulletin board. The schedule of classes showed nothing for Friday afternoons. I was not above nosing around on my own as long as I was there, but I had an uneasy feeling I might run into Elva Dunne.

I poked my head out into the corridor, hoping to spot a stairway that would lead to the hotel lobby above. There didn't seem to be anyone around at all. Well, gee whiz, folks, what was I supposed to do? Casually, I eased behind the desk. Taped to

the counter on the right was a plot map of all the
hot tubs on the hill. Curling lines represented the
winding paths between the spas. A band across
the top of the map was marked as a fire lane. I let
my fingers do the walking, past "Peace," "Serenity," "Tranquillity," and "Composure." A real snore,
this place. "Sanctuary" was a little two-person tub
located way up on the far corner of the hill. According to the schedule lying open on the desk, no
one was booked into "Sanctuary" on Wednesday
afternoon, or on any day after that. I flipped back
a week. Nothing. My guess was that Shana's rendezvous was 2:00 A.M. instead of P.M. and probably
not officially listed anyplace. I did a quick search
of the drawers, which yielded nothing of signifi-
cance. A cardboard box on the counter, labeled
"Lost & Found," contained a silver bracelet, a
plastic hairbrush, a set of car keys, and a fountain
pen. I checked the pigeonholes to the left and
then felt myself do a double take. The car keys in
the lost-and-found box had a big metal T attached
to the key ring. Shana's.

I heard footsteps in the corridor. I did a quick
tippy-toe out from behind the desk. I grabbed the
door open and turned, timing my entrance so it
looked like I was just arriving as Elva and Joe
Dunne walked into the reception area. Elva's face
went blank when she caught sight of me. I pulled
the card out of my handbag. Dr. Dunne seemed
to know what it was right away. He patted her arm
and murmured something, probably letting her
know he'd take care of any dealings either of them

might have to have with me. She continued on into the little side office. Dr. Dunne took me by the elbow and steered me out the door. I hadn't really wanted to go in that direction.

"This is not a good idea," he was murmuring in my left ear. He still held my arm, trotting me toward the parking lot.

"I thought this was your day at the clinic down in Los Angeles."

"I had to do a great deal of talking to persuade Mrs. Dunne not to file assault charges against you," he said, apropos of nothing. Or was it meant to be a threat?

"Let her go for it," I said. "Make sure she does it before my knuckle heals. And while we're at it, let's have the cops take a look at this." I pulled my sleeve up far enough for him to see the pattern of bruises left by Madame's tennis serve. I jerked my arm out of his grasp and held the card up. "Want to talk about this?"

"What is it?"

"Oh, come on. It's the card you sent Shana Timberlake."

He shook his head. "I never saw that in my life."

"Excuse my language, Doctor, but that's a fuckin' fib. You wrote her last week when you were down in L.A. You must have heard about Bailey's arrest and thought the two of you better have a chat. What's the deal? Can't you just pick the phone up and call your lady love?"

"Please lower your voice."

When we reached the parking lot, he glanced back at the building. I followed his gaze, catching sight of his wife peering at us through the office window. She realized we'd spotted her, and withdrew. Dr. Dunne opened my car door on the driver's side as though to usher me in. His manner was uneasy and his eyes kept shifting to the building behind us. I pictured Mrs. Dunne belly-crawling through the bushes with a knife between her teeth.

"My wife is a paranoid schizophrenic. She's violent."

"I'll say! So what?"

"She handles all the books. If she found I'd put a call through to Shana, she'd . . . well, I don't know what she'd do."

"I'll bet I could guess. Maybe she was jealous of Jean and wrapped a belt around her neck."

His ruddy complexion glowed pinker from within, as if a bulb had gone on behind his face. Perspiration was collecting in the crevices in his neck. "She would never do such a thing," he said. He took a handkerchief from his hip pocket and mopped at his forehead.

"What *would* she do?"

"This has nothing to do with her."

"What's the story, then? Where's Shana?"

"She was supposed to meet me here Wednesday night. I was late getting up there. She never showed, or she might have left early. I haven't spoken to her, so I don't know where she was."

"You'd meet her here on the *premises*?" My voice fairly squeaked with incredulity.

"Elva takes a sleeping pill every night. She never wakes."

"As far as you know," I said tartly. "I take it your affair is ongoing?"

I saw him hesitate. "It's not an affair in that sense of the word. We haven't been sexual with one another for years. Shana's a dear woman. I enjoy her company. I'm entitled to friendship."

"Oh, right. I conduct all my friendships in the dead of night."

"Please. I'm begging you. Get in your car and go. Elva will want to know every word we said."

"Tell her we were talking about Ori Fowler's death."

He stared at me. "Ori's dead?"

"Oh yeah. This morning she got what was probably a penicillin shot. She went to heaven right after that."

For a moment he didn't say a word. The look on his face was more convincing than denial. "What was the circumstance?"

I did a quick verbal sketch of the morning's events. "Does Elva have access to penicillin?"

He turned abruptly and started walking toward the building.

I wasn't going to let him off the hook that easily. "You were Jean Timberlake's father, weren't you?"

"It's over. She's dead. You'll never prove it anyway, so what difference does it make?"

"My question exactly. Did she know who you were when she asked for the abortion?"

He shook his head, walking on.

I scooted after him. "You didn't tell her the truth? You didn't even offer to help?"

"I don't want to discuss it," he said, biting off the words.

"But you do know who she was involved with, I bet."

"Why ruin a promising career?" he said.

"Some guy's career meant more than her *life*?"

He reached the door to the reception area and went in. I debated going in, but I couldn't see any purpose in pursuing the point. I needed corroboration first. I reversed myself, heading for my car. I glanced back over my shoulder. Mrs. Dunne was standing at the window again, her expression inscrutable. I wasn't sure if my voice had carried that far or not, and I didn't care. Let them sort it out. I wasn't worried about him. He knew how to look out for himself. It was Shana I was worried about. If she hadn't showed up at all Wednesday night, then where had her car keys come from? And if she'd arrived for their meeting as planned, then where the hell had she gone?

I drove back to the motel. Bert was handling the desk. Mrs. Emma and Mrs. Maude had taken charge of the Fowlers' living room. They stood side by side, plump women in their seventies, one in purple jersey, the other in mauve. Ann was resting, they said. They'd taken the liberty of having Ori's bed moved into Royce's room. The living room had been restored to some former arrangement of furniture and geegaws. It seemed enormous somehow after the overbearing presence of the hospital bed with its cranks and side rails. The bed table was gone. The tray of medications had been removed by the police. Nothing could have eradicated Ori more effectively.

Maxine had arrived, and she seemed faintly mystified to be there with no responsibility to clean. "I'll make some tea," she murmured the minute I arrived.

We were all using our library voices. I found myself mimicking that tone they all used—saccharine, solicitous, patently maternal. Actually, I was discovering that it was useful for situations like this. Mrs. Maude was all set to bring me a little lunch, but I demurred.

"I have something to take care of. I may be gone for a while."

"Well now, that's just fine," Mrs. Emma said, patting my hand. "We'll take care of everything here, so don't you worry about that. And if you want a bite to eat later, we can fix you a tray."

"Thanks." We all exchanged sorrowful smiles of a long-suffering sort. Theirs were more sincere than mine, but I must say Ori's death had generated a nagging sensation down in my gut. Why had she been murdered? What could she possibly have known? On the face of it, I couldn't see how her death bore any relation to Jean Timberlake's.

Bert appeared in the doorway and gave me a look. "Call for you," he said. "It's that lawyer fella."

"Clemson? Great. I'll take it in the kitchen. Can I pick it up in there?"

"Suit yourself," he said.

I moved into the kitchen and picked up the phone. "Hi, it's me," I said. "Hang on." I paused decently and then said, "Thanks, Bert. I've got it." There was a little click. "Go ahead."

"What was that about?" Clemson asked.

"It's not worth going into. How are things with you?"

"Interesting development. I just got a call from June Haws at the church. You never heard this from me, but apparently she's been hiding Bailey all along."

"He's with her?"

"That's the problem. He was. The sheriff's department is starting a house-to-house search. I guess a deputy came to her door and next thing she knew, Bailey'd bolted. She doesn't know where he's gone. Have you heard from him?"

"Not a word."

"Well, stick around. If he gets in touch, you gotta talk him into turning himself in. With word out on his mom's death, the town's going nuts. I'm worried about his safety."

"Me too, but what am I supposed to do?"

"Just stay by the phone. This is critical."

"Jack, I can't. Shana Timberlake's missing. I saw her car keys at the hot springs and I'm going up after dark to take a look."

"Screw Shana. This is more important."

"Then why don't you come over here yourself? If Bailey calls, you can talk to him."

"Bailey doesn't trust me!"

"Why is that, Jack?"

"Damned if I know. If he heard me on the phone, he'd be gone again in a flash, convinced the line was tapped. June says aside from her, you're the only one he trusts."

"Look, this may not take me long. I'll be back as soon as possible and touch base with you then. If I hear from Bailey, I'll talk him in. I swear."

"He *has* to surrender."

"Jack, I know that!" I felt a flash of irritation as I hung up the phone. Why was the guy suddenly on my case? I knew the kind of jeopardy Bailey Fowler was in.

I turned to leave the kitchen. Bert was standing in the hall. He moved into the kitchen as if he'd been in motion all along. "Miss Ann wants some water," he mumbled.

Bullshit, I thought. You little snoop.

I went upstairs to my room and changed into my jogging shoes. I tucked my penlight, my picks, and my room key in my jeans pocket. I wasn't sure I'd need the picks, but I thought I should be prepared. I debated about my little .32. When I bought the Davis, I got myself a custom-fitted Alessi shoulder rig, adjusted so that the holster and weapon would lie snugly against my left side, just under the breast. I yanked my shirt off and strapped the rig into place. I pulled a black turtleneck over it and studied the effect in the bathroom mirror. It would do.

I tried Shana's first, just to be sure she hadn't come back in the meantime. Still no one home

and no sign she'd been there. I took one of the
side streets that arched up over the hill, intersecting Floral Beach Road on the far side of town. The
funeral cortege for Tap Granger had probably taken
this same route and I was anxious to be off the
road before they returned. I did a slow trot north,
toward 101. The two-lane road smelled of eucalyptus, hot sun, and sage. A pale brown grasshopper
kept pace with me for a bit, darting from one
weed top to the next. On my right was a narrow,
rocky ditch, a low wire fence, and then the grassy
hillside, strewn with boulders. Live oaks provided
an occasional patch of shade. The stillness was
broken only by the shrill peeping of the birds.

I heard a vehicle approaching from around a
bend up ahead. A Ford pickup barreled into view,
slowing when the driver caught sight of me. It was
Pearl, with his son, Rick, beside him in the pas-
senger seat. I slowed to a walk and then halted for
him. The old man's big, beefy arm hung out the
open window. He was wearing a short-sleeved
blue dress shirt and a tie that he'd pulled loose so
he could unbutton his collar.

"Hello, Pearl. How are you?" I said, giving
Rick a nod.

"You missed the funeral," Pearl said.

"I didn't know Tap that well and I felt like the
service should be reserved for his friends. You're
just coming back?"

"Everybody else is still at the grave site, I
guess. Me and Rick ducked out early so's we can
open the pool hall for the wake. Joleen says it's

what he'd want. What are you up to? Out for some exercise?"

"That's right," I said. I had to leap right over the image of the wake itself—french fries and a pony keg. I mean, was that class or what? Rick murmured something to his father.

"Oh yeah. Rick wants to know if you've seen Cherie."

"Cherie? I don't think so." I figured she was on a bus to Los Angeles, but I didn't say that.

"She was supposed to go with us, but she went off to the store and hadn't come back by the time we left. You see her, tell her we're at the pool hall." He checked the rearview mirror. "I better get out of the way here before somebody plows into me. Why don't you stop by for a beer when you get done with your jog?"

"I'll do that. Thanks."

Pearl pulled away and I began to trot. As soon as the truck was out of sight, I crossed the ditch and hopped over the wire fence. I climbed straight up, heading for the cover of the trees. In two more minutes I had reached the crest and was peering down the slope toward the mineral springs hotel, half obscured in the eucalyptus grove.

The tennis courts were empty. From where I crouched, I couldn't see the swimming pool, but I was very much aware of the work crew: three men and a wood chipper just off to my right. I found a natural hideaway in the shadow of some rocks and settled in to wait. In the absence of people, reading matter, and ringing telephones, exhaustion crept over me and I sank into sleep.

The sun began to drop in the sky about four. It was technically winter, which, in California, means the perfect days are cut from fourteen hours to ten. In past years, February usually brought the rains, but that was changing of late. The hillside was quiet now, the work crew apparently gone. I scrambled out of my hiding place, reassured myself of some privacy, and peed in some bushes, taking care not to wet my good jogging shoes. My only objection to being female is that I can't pee standing up.

I took up a position where I could watch the hotel. An unmarked police car pulled into the parking lot at one point: Quintana and his partner on the move again. Or maybe Elva had filed a complaint. That'd be rich. Fifteen minutes later, they came out again and took off. As darkness gathered in the trees, a few lights came on. Finally, at seven, I began to traverse the hill, heading for the fire lane that cut across the top of the property. From there I could angle down to the hotel from the rear. I used my penlight sparingly, picking my way with care through heavy brush, twigs snapping underfoot. I was hoping the work crew had cleared a nice path for me, but they'd apparently been laboring farther down on the hill.

I stumbled onto the fire lane, a packed dirt road just wide enough to admit one vehicle. I moved to the left, trying to calculate where the hotel was in relation to me. The whole backside of the building was apparently dark, and it was tricky to calculate my exact location. I risked the pen-

light. The shallow beam picked up an object loom-
ing in my path. I stopped dead. Ahead of me,
nearly obscured by overhanging branches, was
Shana's battered Plymouth.

# 24

I circled the car, which looked vaguely sinister on the path, like the hulking carcass of some inexplicable beast. All four tires were flat. Someone hadn't wanted Shana to go anywhere. I would almost have been willing to bet she was dead, that she'd arrived for her rendezvous with Dunne and had somehow never left. I lifted my head. The woods were chilly, smelling of leaf mold, damp mosses, and sulfur. The dark was intense, the night sounds eradicated, as if my very presence were a warning to the cicadas and tree frogs whose songs had been stilled. I didn't want to find her. I didn't want to look. Every bone in me was aching with the certainty that her body was here somewhere.

I could feel my stomach churn as I flashed the narrow beam from the penlight across the front seat of Shana's car. Nothing. I checked the backseat. Empty. I stared at the trunk lid. I didn't think my lock picks would work, so if the trunk was locked, I was going to have to go down to the office, break in, lift Shana's car keys from the lost-and-found box, and come back. I pressed the catch and the trunk swung open. Empty. I let out the breath I'd been holding unconsciously. I left the lid up, not wanting to risk the noise I'd make slamming it shut. "Sanctuary" had to be somewhere close.

I tried to picture the plot map for the spas in this area. I flashed the penlight across the close-growing shrubs, looking for a path. Foliage that appeared to be a vivid green by day now had the matte, washed-out look of construction paper. A set of packed dirt steps, shored up by railroad ties, descended through a gap in the bushes.

I went down. A rustic wood arrow indicated that "Aerie" was just off to my left. I passed "Haven" and "Tip Top." "Sanctuary" was the fourth hot tub from the summit. I remembered then that it was located at the end of a long, twisted path, with two smaller paths branching off it. The leaves underfoot were soggy and made scarcely any sound, but I noticed I was leaving marshy prints in my wake. When I reached "Sanctuary," I played the penlight across the ground. There were three cigarette butts trampled among the leaves. I hunkered down, bending close. Camel unfiltered. Shana's brand.

The silence was undercut by the intermittent high whining of a siren out on the highway. An erratic breeze, as moist as the inside of an ice chest, rattled among the tree branches. With the strong odor from the mineral springs in the air, it was difficult to discern any other scent. I've been known to find bodies with my nose, but not in this case.

The spa had a bi-fold insulated cover pulled over it with a plastic handhold along the rim. I hesitated for a moment and then lifted it. A dense sulfurous cloud wafted into my face. The water in the redwood tub was pitch black, as still as glass. Mist hovered on the surface. I could feel my mouth purse. I wasn't going to put my hand in there, folks. I wasn't going to plunge my arm in up to the elbow, feeling around to determine if Shana's body was submerged in the depths. I experienced a nearly physical sensation of undulating hair, soft and feathery, at my fingertips. At the back of my mind, it did occur to me that if Shana'd been killed and then dumped in here, she'd be floating by now, buoyed by accumulating gases . . . sort of like a pool toy. I could feel my eyes cross. Sometimes I sicken myself with my own thoughts.

At knee height, there was a wooden door that apparently opened onto the heater and pump works tucked away out of sight. I pulled the door open. The body had been jammed in feet first. She unfolded from the waist, her bloody head coming to rest against my foot, sightless eyes staring up at me. A sound came up in my throat like bile.

"Don't move!"

I jumped, whipping around, a hand against my lurching heart.

Elva Dunne was standing there, flashlight in her left hand.

"Jesus, Elva. You scared the shit out of me," I snapped.

She glanced briefly at Shana, not nearly as startled by the sight as I had been. Belatedly, I noticed that she had a little .22 semiautomatic pointed at my gut. Gun buffs are dismissive of a .22, apparently convinced that a weapon doesn't count unless it's capable of blowing a fist-sized hole through a board. Unfortunately, Elva hadn't heard about this and she looked as if she was ready to drill me a second belly button right above the first. Let a little .22 slug rip around in your gut and see how good you feel. It'll bounce off bone like a tiny bumper car, tearing up every organ in its path.

"I got a phone call from some guy who said Bailey Fowler was up here," she said. "Just stay where you are and don't move or I'll shoot."

I raised my hands like they do in the movies, thinking to reassure her. "Hey, no Bailey. It's just me and I'm cool," I said. I gestured at Shana's body. "I hope you don't think I did that."

"Bullshit. Of course you did. Why else would you be here?"

I could hear the siren now in its winding approach on the road down below. Somebody must have called the cops as well. Mention Bailey's name and you got service real quick. "Look, put the gun down. Honest to God, I saw Shana's keys in the lost-and-found box this afternoon. I figured she must have been here at some point, so I thought I'd check it out."

"Where's the weapon? What'd you do, hit her with a baseball bat?"

"Elva, she's been dead for days. She was probably killed Wednesday night. If I'd just done it,
the blood would be bright red and, uh, you know
. . . spurting." I hate it when people can't com-
prehend the elementary stuff.

Elva's gaze jumped around and she shifted
nervously. Dr. Dunne had said she was a paranoid
schizophrenic, but what does that mean? I thought
all those people were tripping out on Thorazine
these days, as placid as rocks. This woman was
big, one of those ham-shouldered Nordic types. I
already knew she was as weird as they come. If
she'd whacked at me with a Wilson, what was she
going to do with a gun in her hand? Two deputies,
with flashlights, were zigzagging up the path from
below. Things were not looking good.

I let my eyes drift toward her pants, and
lifted my eyebrows a bit. "Oh wow. I wouldn't
worry about it, but there's a spider the size of a
meatball crawling down your leg."

She had to look. How could she not?

I kicked upward, my running shoe lifting the
gun right out of her hand. I saw the .22 do a high,
tumbling somersault and disappear into the dark. I
rammed into her, knocking her ass-over-teakettle
right after it. She yelped as she tumbled backward, crashing down the hill.

The first of the deputies had apparently reached
the midpoint of the hill. I shoved my penlight in
my pocket and ran like hell. I wasn't sure where I
was going, but I hoped to get there quick. I angled up through the trees, headed for the fire

lane, figuring I could run for a while unimpeded. Shana's Plymouth was blocking the overgrown lane, so even if they managed to get a sheriff's car up here, they'd have trouble getting through. I was making too much noise to hear if anyone was behind me, but it seemed smarter to assume the cops were close on my heels. I quickened my pace, sailing over the trunk of a tree in my path.

The fire lane began to climb steeply, dead-ending in a gate with a wire fence that stretched away on either side. I took a flying leap, put a hand on the gatepost and arched my back, catching my foot as I tried to clear the top. I smacked down with an "Oof!" rolled, and got up again, suppressing a moan. The fall had rammed the Davis right into my ribs. Much pain.

I plugged on, heading upward. The hill leveled out in a rugged pasture dotted with scrub oak and manzanita. The moon wasn't full, but there was enough of it to illuminate the choppy field through which I ran. I must have been a quarter of a mile from the road, in an area inaccessible to vehicles. I was desperately in need of rest. I looked over my shoulder. There was no sign of pursuit. I slowed to a jog and searched out a depression in the grass.

I sank down, winded, blotting my sweaty brow on the sleeve of my turtleneck. Some winged creature swooped down close to me and then cruised away, temporarily mistaking me for something edible. I hate nature. I really do. Nature is composed entirely of sticks, dirt, fall-down places, biting and stinging things, and savageries too numerous to list. And I'm not the only one who feels this way. Man has been building cities since the year oughty-ought, just to get away from this stuff. Now we're on our way to the moon and other barren spots where nothing grows and you can pick up a rock without having something jump out at you. The quicker we get there, the better, as far as I'm concerned.

Time to move. I staggered to my feet again and began to trot, wishing I had a plan. I couldn't go back to the motel—the sheriff's department was going to be there in ten minutes flat—but without my car keys and some bucks, what was I going to do? It occurred to me I might have been better off hanging out with Elva until the deputies arrived, taking my chances with the law. Now *I* was a fugitive, and I didn't like it much.

A flash of Shana's face popped into my head. She'd been bludgeoned to death, from the look of her, shoved into the narrow space under the hot tub until someone could dispose of her—if that was the intent. Maybe that's what Elva had trudged up there in the dark to do. I couldn't decide if I should believe her claim about the phone call. Had *she* killed Shana Timberlake? Killed her daughter seventeen years before that? Why the lag time? And why Ori Fowler? Given Elva as the killer, I couldn't come up with a scenario in which Ori's death made any sense. Could the phone call have been meant to trap me up there? As far as I knew, the only two people who were aware of where I'd be were Jack Clemson and Bert.

I halted again. The ground was beginning to slant downward, and I found myself squinting through the dark at a sharp drop-off. Below, a gray ribbon of road curled along the base of the hill. I had no idea where it led, but if the cops were smart, they'd be calling for backup cars, which might be cruising by any minute, hoping to cut me off. I scrambled down the rocky incline as fast as I could, half-humping, half-sliding on my backside, preceded by a tiny landslide of loose stones and dirt. I could hear approaching sirens as I skidded the last few feet. I was panting from exhaustion, but I didn't dare stop. I hightailed it across the road, reaching the far side just as the first black-and-white rounded the bend maybe six hundred yards away.

I plunged into the brush, hugging the ground as I belly-crawled my way through the weeds. Once I was safely in the cover of the trees, I paused to reorient myself, rolling over on my back. Against the encroaching fog bank I could see the reflection of the vapor lights that lined Ocean Street. Floral Beach wasn't far. Unfortunately, what lay between me and the town was the posted property belonging to the oil refinery. I studied the eight-foot chain-link fence. Strands of barbed wire were strung along the top. No crossing that. Big oil storage tanks loomed up on the far side, painted in pastel shades, like a series of cakes.

I was still close enough to the road that I could hear the squawking of the sheriff's cars in position along the berm. Lights raked the hillside.

I hoped the suckers hadn't brought dogs. That was all I'd need. I crawled to the base of the fence, clinging to it doggedly as I pushed on. In the dark, it served not only as a guide, but as a needed support. More warning signs. This was a hard hat area . . . and me with no hard hat. I was winded and sweating, my hands torn, nose beginning to run. The smell of the ocean was getting stronger and I took comfort from that.

Abruptly, the fence took a hard cut left. What opened up in front of me was a dirt path strewn with trash, a lovers' lane perhaps. I didn't dare use my penlight. I was still in the hills above Floral Beach, but I was getting closer to the town. In less than a quarter of a mile, I found myself at the tag end of the lane that spilled into a cul-de-sac. Oh glory, now I knew where I was. This was the bluff above Jean Timberlake's old apartment building. Once I reached the wooden stairway, I could climb down to the rear door of her place and hide. To my right, I spotted the glass-and-frame house where I'd knocked earlier. Lights were on inside.

I skirted the house, groping my way along the property line, marked by waist-high shrubs. As I passed the kitchen window, I caught sight of the occupant looking straight out at me. I dropped, realizing belatedly that the guy must be standing at the kitchen sink. The window would be throwing his own reflection back at him, effectively blocking out the sight of me, I hoped. Cautiously I rose and peered closer. Dwight Shales.

I blinked, debating with myself. Could I trust him? Was I safer up here with him or hiding in the abandoned building below? Oh hell, this was no time to be shy. I needed help.

I doubled back to the front porch and rang the bell. I kept an eye on the street, worried a patrol car would cruise into sight. At some point they were going to realize I'd slipped through the net. Given the impenetrability of the oil company property, this was probably the logical place to end up. The porch light came on. The front door opened. I turned to look at him. "Kinsey, my God. What happened to you?"

"Hello, Dwight. Can I come in?"

He held the door open, stepping back. "Are you in some kind of trouble?"

"That would cover it," I said. My explanation was worthy of a box top, twenty-five words or less, tendered while I followed him through the foyer— all raw woods and modern art. We went down a step into the living room, which was dead ahead: two stories of glass looking out toward the view. The roof of Jean's apartment building wasn't visible, but I could see the lights of Floral Beach stretching almost as far as the big hotel on the hillside half a mile away.

"Let me get you a drink," he said.

"Thanks. Do you mind if I clean up?"

He nodded to his left. "Straight down the hall."

I found the bathroom and ran some water, scrubbing my hands and face. I blotted my face dry, staring at myself in the bathroom mirror. I had a big scratch on my cheek. My hair was matted with dirt. I found a comb in his medicine cabinet and ran it through my mop. I peed, brushed myself off, washed my hands and face again, and returned to the living room where Dwight handed me some brandy in a softball-sized snifter.

I took it neat and he poured me a second.

"Thanks," I said. I could feel the liquor defining my insides as it eased through. I had to breathe with my mouth open for a bit. "Whew! Great."

"Sit down. You look beat."

"I am," I said. I glanced anxiously toward the front door. "Are we visible from the street?"

The narrow panels on either side of the front door were frosted glass. It was the exposed living room that bothered me. I felt as if I were onstage. He crossed the room and closed the drapes. The room was suddenly much cozier and I relaxed a bit.

He sat down in the chair across from me. "Tell me again."

I went back through the story, filling in the details. "I probably should have just waited for the cops."

"You want to go ahead and call them and turn yourself in? The phone's right there."

"Not yet," I said. "That's what I kept telling Bailey, but now I know how he felt. They'd just keep me up all night, hounding me with questions I don't have the answers for."

"What are you going to do?"

"Don't know. Get my head together and see if I can figure this out. You know, I was up here earlier and knocked on the door, but you weren't home. I wanted to ask if anybody up here ever saw Jean using the stairs."

"The stairs?"

"Up from the Timberlakes' apartment. It was right down there." I found myself pointing to the floor to indicate the base of the bluff.

"Oh, that's right. I'd forgotten about that. Talk about small towns. I guess none of us are that far from anybody else."

"That's for sure," I said. At the back of my mind, uneasiness was beginning to stir. Something about his response wasn't quite ringing true. Maybe it was his manner, which was suddenly too studiously casual to be believable. Pretending to be "normal" is a lot harder than you'd think. Did it mean anything, his having lived this close? "You forgot Jean Timberlake lived thirty feet away?"

"No big deal," he said. "I think they only lived there a few months before she died." He set his brandy snifter on the coffee table. "You hungry? I'd be happy to fix you something to eat."

I shook my head, easing him back toward the subject that interested me. "I realized this afternoon that the back door of the Timberlake apartment opened right onto the stairs. I figure she could easily have used the road up here as a rendezvous point for the guys she screwed around with. You never saw her up here?"

He considered the possibility, searching his

memory. "No, I don't believe so. Is it that important?"

"Well, it could be. If somebody saw Jean, they might have also seen the guy she was having the affair with."

"Come to think of it, I did see cars up here at night on occasion. I guess it never occurred to me it might be somebody waiting to pick her up."

I love bad liars. They work so hard at it and the effort is so transparent. I happen to lie well myself, but only after years of practice. Even then, I can't pull it off every time. This guy didn't even come close. I sat and looked at him, giving him time to reconsider his position.

He frowned with concern. "By the way, what's the story on Ann's mother? Mrs. Emma called about an hour ago and told me Bailey switched the medication. I couldn't believe it . . ."

"Excuse me, could we get back to Jean Timberlake first?"

"Oh, sorry. I thought we were done, and I've been awfully worried about Ann. It's unbelievable what she's been through. Anyway, go ahead."

"Were you fucking Jean Timberlake yourself?"

The word was just right, crude and to the point. He let out a little laugh of disbelief, like he must not have heard me right. "What?"

"Come on. 'Fess up. Just tell me the truth. I'd really like to know."

He laughed again, shaking his head as though to clear it. "My God, Kinsey. I'm a high school principal."

"I know what you are, Dwight. I'm asking you what you did."

He stared at me, apparently annoyed that I'd persist. "This is ridiculous. The girl was seventeen."

I said nothing. I returned a look of such skepticism that his smile began to fade. He got up and poured himself another drink. He held the brandy bottle toward me, mutely asking me if I wanted more. I shook my head.

He sat down again. "I think we should move on to something more productive. I'm willing to help, but I'm not going to play any games with you." He was all business now. The meeting was called to order and we were going to get serious. No more silly bullshit. "I'd have to be crazy to get involved with a student," he went on. "Jesus. What an idea." He rolled his shoulders. I could hear the joint pop. I knew he wanted to convince me, but the words carried no conviction.

I dropped my gaze to the tabletop, pushing my empty snifter an inch. "We're all capable of astonishing ourselves when it comes to sex."

He was silent.

I focused on him intently.

He recrossed his legs. Now it was him, not looking at me.

"Dwight?"

He said, "I thought I was in love with her."

Careful, I thought. Take care. The moment is fragile and his trust is tenuous. "It must have been a tough time. Karen was diagnosed with MS right about then, wasn't she?"

He set the glass down again and his gaze met mine. "You have a good memory."

I kept silent.

He finally took up the narrative thread. "She was actually in the process of being evaluated, but I think we knew. It's staggering how something like that affects you. She was bitter at first. Withdrawn. In the end, she was better about it than I was. God, I couldn't believe it was happening, and then I turned around and Jean was there. Young, lusty, outrageous."

He was quiet for a moment.

I said nothing, letting him tell it his way. He didn't need any prompting from me. This was a story he knew by heart.

"I didn't think Karen would survive anyway because the first round was acute. She seemed to go downhill overnight. Hell, I didn't think she'd live till spring. In a situation like that, your mind leaps ahead. You get into survival mode. I remember thinking, 'Hey, I can make it. The marriage isn't that great, anyway.' I was only what, thirty-nine? Forty? I had a lot of years ahead of me. I figured I'd marry again. Why not? We weren't perfect, the two of us. I'm not sure we were even very well suited to each other. The MS changed all that. When she died, I was more in love with her than I'd ever been."

"And Jean?"

"Ah, but Jean. Early on"—he paused to shake his head—"I was crazy. I must have been. If that relationship had ever become public knowledge

. . . well, it would have ruined my life. Karen's, too . . . what was left of it."

"Was the baby yours?"

"I don't know. Probably. I wish I could say no, but what could I do? I only found out about it after Jean died. I can't imagine what the consequences would have been . . . you know . . . if the pregnancy had come to light."

"Yeah, unlawful sexual intercourse being what it is."

"Oh God, don't say that. Even now the phrase is enough to make me sick."

"You kill her?"

"No. I swear. I was capable of a lot of craziness back then, but not that."

I watched him, sensing that he was telling the truth. This wasn't a killer I was listening to. He might have been desperate or despairing. He might have realized after the fact how perilous his situation was, but I didn't hear the kind of rationalization killers get into. "Who else knew about the pregnancy?"

"I don't know. What difference would it make?"

"I'm not sure. You can't really be certain the baby was yours. Maybe there was somebody else."

"Bailey knew about it."

"Aside from him. Couldn't someone else have heard?"

"Well, sure, but so what? I know she showed up at the school very upset and went straight to the counselor's office."

"I thought the guidance counselors only handled academic matters—college prep requirements and stuff like that."

"There were exceptions. Sometimes we had to screen personal problems and refer kids out for professional counseling."

"What would have been done then, if Jean had asked for help?"

"We'd have done what we could. San Luis has social agencies set up for things like that."

"Jean never talked to you herself?"

He shook his head. "I wish she had. Maybe I could have done something for her, I don't know. She had her crazy side. We're not talking about a girl who'd agree to an abortion. She never would have given that baby up and she wouldn't have kept quiet. She'd have insisted on marriage, regardless of the price. I have to tell you—I know it sounds horrible, but I have to say this—I was relieved when she died. Enormously. When I understood the risk I'd taken . . . when I saw what I had at stake. It was a gift. I cleaned up my act right then. I never screwed around on Karen again."

"I believe you," I said. But what was bothering me? I could feel an idea churning, but I couldn't quite sense what it was.

Dwight was going on. "It was a bit of a rude awakening when I heard the stories going around after she'd been killed. I was naïve enough to think we had something special between us, but that turned out not to be the case."

I kept picking at it like a bone. "So if she

didn't turn to you for help, she could have turned to somebody else."

"Well, yes, but she didn't have much time for that, as I understand. She had the test done in Lompoc and got the results that afternoon. By midnight she was dead."

"How long does it take to make a phone call?" I said. "She had hours. She could have called half the guys in Floral Beach and some in San Luis, too. Suppose it was someone else? Suppose you were just a cover for another relationship? There must have been other guys with just as much to lose."

"I'm sure it's possible," he said, but he sounded dubious.

The phone rang, a harsh sound in the stillness of the big house. Dwight leaned back, reaching over to pick up the receiver from the end table by the couch. "Hello? Oh, hi."

His face had brightened with recognition and I saw his eyes stray to my face as the person on the other end of the line went on. He was making "unh-hunh" noises while someone rattled on. "No, no, no. Don't worry. Hang on. She's right here." He held the phone out and I took it. "It's Ann," he said.

"Hi, Ann. What's happening?"

Her voice was cold and she was clearly upset. "Well. At long last. Where the hell have *you* been? I've been looking for you for hours."

I found myself squinting at the phone, trying to determine the reason for the tone she had taken.

What was wrong with her? "Is there a deputy with you?" I asked.

"I think we could say that."

"You want to wait and call me back when he goes?"

"No, I don't, dear. Here's what I want. I want you to get your ass down here right away! Daddy checked himself out of the hospital and he's been bugging me ever since. WHERE HAVE YOU BEEN?" she shrieked. "Do you have any idea . . . do you have any IDEA what's been going on? DO YOU? Goddamn it! . . ."

I held the phone away from my ear. She was really building up a head of steam here. "Ann, stop that. Calm down. It's too complicated to go into right now."

"Don't give me that. Don't you dare ever, ever give me that."

"Don't give you what? What are you so upset about?"

"You know perfectly well," she snapped. "What are you doing over there? You listen to me, Kinsey. And you listen good . . ."

I started to interrupt, but she'd just put a palm across the mouthpiece, talking to someone in the background. The deputy? Oh hell, was she telling him where I was?

I replaced the receiver in the cradle.

Dwight was looking at me with perplexity. "You okay? What was that about?"

"I have to go to San Luis Obispo," I said carefully. It was a lie, of course, but it was the first thing that occurred to me. Ann had told them where I was. Within minutes this whole cul-de-sac would be blocked off, the neighborhood swarming with deputies. I had to get out of there, and I didn't think it was wise to let him know where I was headed.

"San Luis?" he said. "What for?"

I moved toward the front door. "Don't worry about it. I'll be back in a bit."

"Don't you need a car?"

"I'll get one."

I closed the door behind me, leaped off the porch, and ran.

# 25

The Ocean Street Motel was only four blocks away. It wasn't going to take the cops long. I kept to the pavement until I caught the sound of a vehicle accelerating up the hill. I took a dive into the bushes as a black-and-white sped into view, heading straight for Dwight's place. Lights flashing, no siren. A second black-and-white gunned up the hill after the first. Hotdoggers. The deputy in the second car was probably twenty-two. Big career ahead of him, careening through Floral Beach legally. He must have been having the time of his life.

The solution to so many problems seems obvious once you know where to look. My conversation with Dwight had generated a shift in my mind-set and the questions that had troubled me before now seemed to have answers that made perfect sense. Some of them, at any rate. I needed confirmation, but at least now I had a working premise. Jean Timberlake had been murdered to protect Dwight Shales. Ori Fowler had died because she was meant to die . . . to get her out of the way. And Shana? I thought I understood why she had died, too. Bailey was supposed to take the rap for all of it, and he'd fallen for it like a chump. If he'd had sense enough not to run—if he'd just stayed put—he couldn't have been blamed for everything that'd happened since.

I approached the motel from the rear, through a vacant lot filled with weeds and broken glass. Many of the motel windows were ablaze with lights. I could imagine all the uproar caused by the presence of sheriffs' cars. I suspected there was still a deputy posted somewhere close, probably just outside my room. I reached the Fowlers' back door. The kitchen light was on, and I could see the shadow of someone moving around in the back part of the apartment. A little black-and-white television now sat on the counter, a taped newscast flickering across the empty room. Quintana was making mouth noises on the courthouse steps. Must have been this afternoon. A picture of Bailey Fowler followed. He was being led, in handcuffs, to a waiting vehicle. On came the announcer, turning to the weather map. I tried the kitchen door. Locked. I didn't want to stand out there trying to pick the lock.

I circled the building, hugging the outside wall, checking darkened windows for one left ajar. What I found instead was a side door that was located just across from the stairway inside the back hall. The knob turned in my hand and I pushed the door open cautiously. I peered in. Royce, in a ratty bathrobe, was shuffling down the hall toward me, slump-shouldered, eyes on his slippers. I could hear the hum of his weeping, broken by intermittent sighs. He was walking his grief like a baby, back and forth. He reached the door to his room and turned, shuffling back toward the kitchen. Now and then he murmured Ori's name, voice breaking off. Lucky is the spouse who dies first, who never has to know what survivors endure. Royce must have signed himself out of the hospital after Reverend Haws paid his call. Ori's death had pushed him past struggling. What did he care if he sped death along?

The lights from the living room gave the uncomfortable sense of other people very near. I could hear two women in the dining room, talking in low tones. Was Mrs. Emma still with Ann? Royce was reaching the kitchen, where I knew he'd turn again, coming back.

I closed the door behind me, crossed to the stairs, and took them two at a time, moving silently. I should have put two and two together when I saw that the maid's master key wouldn't open room 20. That room had probably been sealed off, part of the Fowlers' apartment upstairs.

The second floor was dark, except for a window on the landing through which a soft yellow light now spilled. I was disoriented. Somehow this didn't look the way I'd expected it to. There was a short corridor to my left, ending in a door. I crossed to it, stopped, and listened carefully. Silence. I tried the knob and pushed the door open a crack. Cold air wafted in. I was facing the exterior corridor that ran right by my room. I could see the vending machine and the outside stairs. To my immediate left was room 20, next to that room 22, where I'd spent my first night. There was no sign of a deputy on duty. Did I dare simply mosey down, use my key, and go in? What if the deputy was waiting inside?

I reached around and tried the knob from the outside. Ah, locked. Once I went out this door, I couldn't get back in unless I jammed it open. I stayed where I was, easing the door shut. The door to my left was unlocked. I slipped inside, taking out my penlight. Like the rest of the Fowlers' living quarters, this had once been a regular motel room, converted now to office space.

Sliding glass doors along the front opened onto a second-floor balcony overlooking Ocean Street. The drapes were open and I could make out a desk, a swivel chair, bookcases, a reading lamp. I swept the room with the narrow beam of the penlight, getting my bearings. The book titles were half fiction, half college textbooks in psychology. Ann's.

On the desk was a photo of Ori in her youth. She really had been beautiful, with large luminous eyes. I searched the desk drawers. Nothing of interest. Checked the closet alcove, which was filled with summer clothing. The bathroom held nothing. The door that connected this room to room 20 was locked. Locked doors are always more

interesting than the other kind. This time I got out
my set of key picks and set to work. In TV shows,
people pick locks with remarkable ease. Not so in
real life, where you have to have the patience of a
saint. I was working in the dark, clamping the
penlight in my mouth like a cigar while I used the
rocker pick in my left hand and the wire in my
right. Sometimes I do this efficiently, but that's
usually when the light is good. This time it took
forever, and I was sweating from the tension when
the lock finally gave.

Room 20 was a duplicate of the one I'd occupied. This was Ann's bedroom, the one Maxine
was not to clean. I could see why. On the closet
floor, dead ahead, was a Ponsness-Warren shot
shell reloader with a built-in wad guide, an adjust-
able crimp die, and two powder reservoirs filled
with rock salt. I crossed to the closet and hunkered down, inspecting the device, which looks
like a cross between a bird feeder and a cappuc-
cino machine, and is designed to pack a shell with
anything you like. A blast of rock salt, at close
range, usually ends up buried under your skin
where it stings like a son of a bitch, but doesn't
do much else. Tap had found out just how inef-
fectual salt can be in staving off the sheriff's
deputies.

I had really hit the jackpot. On the floor
beside the reloader was a microcassette recorder
with a tape in it. I pressed the rewind button and
then pressed play, listening to a familiar voice
slowed down to a series of quite nasty gravel-

throated threats. I rewound, switched the tape speed, and tried it again. The voice was clearly Ann's, spelling out her intentions with an ax and a chain saw. The whole thing sounded stupid, but she must have had a ball. "I am going to get you. . . ." We used to do shit like this as kids. "I am going to cut your head off. . . ." I smiled grimly, remembering the night those calls had come through. I'd taken comfort from the fact that someone two doors away was wide awake like me. The square of light had looked so cozy at that hour. All the time she'd been in here, dialing room-to-room, part of her campaign of psychological abuse. At this point I couldn't even remember when I'd had an uninterrupted night's sleep. I was being carried on adrenaline and nerve, the momentum of events sweeping me willy-nilly down the path. The night my room was broken into, all she'd had to do was use her passkey and jimmy up the sliding glass door afterward so it would look like the point of entry. I got to my feet and checked the shelf above. In a shoebox, I found a windowed envelope addressed to "Erica Dahl" containing quarterly dividends and year-end tax summaries for IBM stock. There must have been more than a hundred such envelopes neatly packed into the box, along with a social security card, driver's license, and passport—with Ann Fowler's photograph affixed. The statements from Merrill Lynch showed a $42,000 investment in shares of IBM back in 1967. With stock splits in the intervening years, the shares had more than doubled in value. I noticed that "Erica" had dutifully paid taxes on the interest that accrued from year to year. Ann Fowler was too shrewd to get tripped up by the IRS.

I flashed the penlight through her living room and kitchenette, doing a one-eighty turn. When the narrow beam crossed the bedstead, I caught an oval of white and flashed the light back over it again. Ann was propped up in bed watching me. Her face was dead pale, her eyes enormous, so filled with lunacy and hate that my skin crawled. I felt as if I'd been pierced with an icy arrow, the chill spreading from the core of my body to my fingertips. In her lap she held a double-barreled shotgun, which she raised and pointed right at my chest. Probably not rock salt. I didn't think the spider story was going to work with her.

"Finding everything you need?" she asked.

I raised my hands just to show I knew how to behave. "Hey, you're pretty good. You almost got away with it."

Her smile was thin. "Now that you're 'wanted,' I can do it, don't you think?" she said conversationally. "All I have to do is pull the trigger and claim trespass."

"And then what?"

"You tell me."

I hadn't quite worked the whole story out, but I knew enough to make a flying guess. Why you have chats with killers in circumstances like these is because you hope against hope you can (1) talk them out of it, (2) stall until help arrives, or (3) enjoy a few more moments of this precious commodity we call life, which consists (in large part) of breathing in and out. Hard to do with your lungs blown out your back.

"Well," said I, hoping to make a short story long, "I figure once your daddy dies and you unload this place, you'll take the proceeds, add them to the profits from the forty-two thou you stole, and sail off into the sunset. Possibly with Dwight Shales, or so you hope."

"And why not?"

"Why not, indeed? Sounds like a great plan. Does he know about it yet?"

"He will," she said.

"What makes you think he'll agree?"

"Why wouldn't he? He's free now. And I will be, too, as soon as Pop dies."

"And you think that constitutes a relationship?" I said, astonished.

"What do *you* know about relationships?"

"Hey, I've been married twice. That's more than you can say."

"You're divorced. You don't know dick."

I had to shrug at that.

"I bet Jean was sorry she confided in you."

"Very. At the end, she put up quite a fight."

"But you won."

"I had to. I couldn't have her ruining Dwight's life."

"Assuming it was his," I said.

"The babe? Of course it was."

"Oh great. No problem, then. You're completely justified," I said. "Does he know how much you've done for him?"

"That's our little secret. Yours and mine."

"How did you know where Shana would be Wednesday night?"

"Simple. I followed her."

"But why kill the woman?"

"Same reason I'm going to kill you. For screwing Dwight."

"She was going up there to meet Joe Dunne," I said. "Neither one of us screwed Dwight."

"Bullshit!"

"It's not bullshit. He's a nice enough guy, but he's not my type. He told me himself he and Shana were just friends. It was strictly platonic. They hadn't even screwed *once!*"

"You liar. You think I don't know what's been going on? You sashay into town and start coming on to him, riding around in his car, having cozy dinners . . ."

"Ann, we were talking. That's all it was."

"Nobody's going to get in my way, Kinsey. Not after all I've been through. I've worked too hard and waited too long. I've sacrificed my entire adult life, and you're not going to spoil things now that I'm almost free."

"Well, listen, Ann . . . if I may say so, you're as crazy as a bug. No offense, but you are looney-tunes, completely cuckoo-nuts." I was just making mouth noises while I thought about my gun. My little Davis was still in the holster tucked up against my left breast. What I wanted to do was take it out

and plug her right between the eyes—or someplace fatal. But here's the way I figured it. By the
time I reached up under my turtleneck, snatched
the gun out, pointed it, and fired, that shotgun of
hers would have taken off my face. And how was I
going to get the gun, feign a heart attack? I didn't
think she'd fall for it. My eyes had adjusted to the
dark, and since I could see her perfectly, I had to
guess she could see me just as well.

"Mind if I turn off the penlight? I hate to use
up the batteries," I said. The beam was pointed at
the ceiling, and my arms were getting tired. Probably hers, too. A shotgun like that weighs a good
seven pounds—not easy to hold steady, even if
you're used to lifting weights.

"Just stay where you are and don't move."

"Wow, that's just what Elva said."

Ann reached over and turned on the bedside
lamp. She looked worse in the light. She had a
mean face, I could see that now. The slightly
receding chin made her look like a rat. The shotgun was a twelve-gauge, over-and-under, and she
seemed to know which end did the hurt.

Dimly, I became aware of a shuffling sound in
the hall. Royce. When had he come upstairs? "Ann?
Aw, Annie, I found some pictures of your mother
I thought you'd like. Can I come in?"

I saw her eyes flick toward the door. "I'll be
down in a minute, Pop. We can look at them
then."

Too late. He had pushed the door open, peering in. He had a photograph album in his arms,

and his face held such innocence. His eyes seemed very blue. His lashes were sparse, still wet from his tears, his nose red. Gone was the gruffness, the arrogance, the dominance. His illness had made him frail, and Ori's death had knocked him to his knees, but here he came again, an old man full of hope. "Mrs. Maude and Mrs. Emma are looking for you to say good night."

"I'm busy right now. Will you take care of it?"

He caught sight of me. He must have wondered what I was doing with my hands in the air. His attention strayed to the shotgun Ann held at shoulder height. I thought he was going to turn and shuffle out again. He hesitated, uncertain what to do next.

I said, "Hello, Royce. Guess who killed Jean Timberlake?"

He glanced at me and then looked away. "Well." His gaze slid over to Ann as if she might deny the accusation. She got up from the bed and reached behind him for the door.

"Go on downstairs, Pop. I have something to do and then I'll be down."

He seemed confused. "You're not going to hurt her."

"No, of course not," she said.

"She's going to shoot my ass!" I said.

His gaze strayed back to hers, looking for reassurance.

"What do you think she's doing with that

shotgun? She's going to kill me dead and then claim trespass. She told me so."

"Pop, I caught her going through my closet. The cops are after her. She's in cahoots with Bailey, trying to help him get away."

"Oh, don't be a silly. Why would I do that?"

"Bailey?" Royce said. It was the first time tonight I'd seen comprehension in his eyes.

"Royce, I've got proof he's innocent. Ann's the one who killed Jean—"

"You *liar!*" Ann cut in. "The two of you are trying to take Pop for everything he's worth."

God, I couldn't believe this. Ann and I were squabbling like little kids, each of us trying to persuade Royce to be on our side. "Did too." "Did not." "Did too."

Royce put a trembling finger to his lips. "If she's got proof, maybe we should hear what it is," he said, talking almost to himself. "Don't you think so, Annie? If she can prove Bailey's innocent?"

I could see the rage begin to stir at the mention of his name. I was worried she would shoot and argue with her daddy afterward. The same thought apparently occurred to him. He reached for the shotgun. "Put it down, baby."

Abruptly, she backed away. "DON'T TOUCH ME!"

I could feel my heart start to thud, afraid he'd yield. Instead, he seemed to focus, gathering his strength.

"What are you doing, Ann? You can't do that."

"Go on. Get out of here."

"I want to hear what Kinsey has to say."

"Just do what I tell you and get the hell out!"

He clamped a hand on the barrel. "Give me that before you hurt someone."

"No!" Ann snatched it out of his reach.

Royce lunged, grabbing it. The two of them struggled for possession of the shotgun. I was immobilized, my attention fixed on the big black 8 of the two barrels that pointed first at me, then the floor, ceiling, weaving through the air. Royce should have been the stronger, but illness had sapped him and Ann's rage gave her the edge. Royce jerked the gun by the stock.

Fire spurted from the barrel, and the blast filled the room with powder smell. The shotgun thumped to the floor as Ann screamed.

She was looking down in disbelief. Most of her right foot had been blown away. All that was left was a torn stump of raw meat. I could feel heat rip through me as though the sensation were mine. I turned away, repelled.

The pain must have been excruciating, blood pumping out. What color she had left drained from her face. She sank to the floor, speechless, her body rocking as she clutched herself. Her cries dropped to a low, relentless pitch.

Royce backed away from her, his voice feeble with regret. "I'm sorry. I didn't mean to do that. I tried to help."

I could hear people pounding up the stairs: Bert, Mrs. Maude, a young deputy I'd never seen. Another kid. Wait until he got a load of this.

"Get an ambulance!" I yelled. I was pulling a pillowcase off the bed, wadding it against her mangled foot, trying to stanch the blood spewing everywhere. The deputy fumbled with his walkie-talkie while Mrs. Maude babbled, wringing her hands. Mrs. Emma had pushed into the room behind her, and she began to shriek when she saw what was going on. Maxine and Bert were both white-faced, holding on to each other. Belatedly, the deputy herded all of them into the corridor and closed the door again. Even through the wall I could hear Mrs. Emma's shrill cries.

Ann was lying on her back by then, one arm flung across her face. Royce clung to her right hand, rocking back and forth. She was weeping like a five-year-old. "You were never there for me . . . you were never there. . . ."

I thought about my papa. I was five when he left me . . . five when he went away. An image came to me, a memory repressed for years. In the car, just after the wreck, when I was trapped in the backseat, wedged in tight, with the sound of my mother's weeping going on and on and on, I had reached around the edge of the front seat, where I found my father's hand, unresisting, passive, and soft. I tucked my fingers around his, not understanding he was dead, simply thinking everything would be all right as long as I had him. When had it dawned on me that he was gone for good? When had it dawned on Ann that Royce was

never going to come through? And what of Jean
Timberlake? None of us had survived the wounds
our fathers inflicted all those years ago. Did he
love us? How would we ever know? He was gone
and he'd never again be what he was to us in all
his haunting perfection. If love is what injures us,
how can we heal?

# Epilogue

The case against Bailey Fowler has been dismissed. He turned himself in when he heard news of Ann's arrest. She was charged with two counts of first-degree murder in the deaths of Ori Fowler and Shana Timberlake. The DA's office may never be able to assemble sufficient evidence to prosecute her for the death of Jean Timberlake.

Two weeks have passed. I'm now back in my office in Santa Teresa, where I've itemized expenses. With the hours I put in, my mileage, and meals, I'm billing Royce Fowler for $1,832 against the two grand he advanced. We chatted about it by phone and he's told me to keep the change. He's still hanging on to life with all the stubbornness he can muster and at least Bailey will be with him during his last weeks.

I find that I'm looking at Henry Pitts differently these days. He may be the closest thing to a father I'll ever have. Instead of viewing him with suspicion, I think I'll enjoy him for the time we have left, whatever that may be. He's only eighty-two, and God knows, my life is more hazardous than his.

Respectfully submitted,
*Kinsey Millhone*

# SUE GRAFTON'S KINSEY MILLHONE

**"A" IS FOR ALIBI** . . . Laurence Fife was a slick divorce lawyer and slippery ladies' man. Until someone killed him. The jury believed his pretty young wife was guilty, but after eight years in prison she still denies it and hires Kinsey Millhone to discover who the real killer is. But the trail's eight years cold . . . and at its end is a second eight-year-old murder and a brand-new corpse.

**"B" IS FOR BURGLAR** . . . Finding wealthy Elaine Boldt seems like a quickie case to Kinsey Millhone. But somewhere in between her Santa Teresa home and her condo in Boca Raton, the rich widow disappears. Soon Kinsey's clues begin to form a capital *M*—not for missing, but for murder.

**"C" IS FOR CORPSE** . . . Bobby Callahan is a scarred young man struggling back to life after a car forced his Porsche over the edge of a canyon, battering his body and destroying his memory. All he knows is that someone, for some reason, tried to kill him. Kinsey can't resist the brave kid—and neither can the killers.

**"D" IS FOR DEADBEAT** . . . The client came to Kinsey with an easy job: just deliver $25,000 to a fifteen-year-old kid. A little too easy, but she took his retainer check, anyway. It turned out to be as phony as he was. By the time Kinsey caught up with him, he was a dead body. How do you make a stiff pay up what he owes you?

**"E" IS FOR EVIDENCE** . . . Evidence planted, evidence lost. E is for everything Kinsey stands to lose if she can't exonerate herself: her license, her livelihood, her good name. So she takes on a new client . . . namely, herself.

# "A" Is for Alibi

My name is Kinsey Millhone. I'm a private investigator, licensed by the state of California. I'm thirty-two years old, twice divorced, no kids. The day before yesterday I killed someone and the fact weighs heavily on my mind. I'm a nice person and I have a lot of friends. My apartment is small but I like living in a cramped space. I've lived in trailors most of my life, but lately they've been getting too elaborate for my taste, so now I live in one room, a "bachelorette." I don't have pets. I don't have houseplants. I spend a lot of time on the road and I don't like leaving things behind. Aside from the hazards of my profession, my life has always been ordinary, uneventful, and good. Killing someone feels odd to me and I haven't quite sorted it through. I've already given a statement to the police, which I initialed page by page and then signed. I filled out a similar report for the office files. The language in both documents is neutral, the terminology oblique, and neither says quite enough.

Nikki Fife first came to my office three weeks ago. I occupy one small corner of a large suite of offices that house the California Fidelity Insurance Company, for whom I once worked. Our connection now is rather loose. I do a certain number of investigations for them in exchange for two rooms with a separate entrance and a small balcony overlooking the main street of Santa Teresa. I have an answering service to pick up calls when I'm out and I keep my own books. I don't earn a lot of money but I make ends meet.

I'd been out for most of the morning, only stopping by the office to pick up my camera. Nikki Fife was standing in the corridor outside my office door. I'd never really met her but I'd been present at her trial eight years before when she was convicted of murdering her husband, Laurence, a prominent divorce attorney here in town. Nikki was in her late twenties then, with striking white-blonde hair, dark eyes, and flawless skin. Her lean face had filled out some, probably the result of prison food with its high starch content, but she still had the ethereal look that had made the accusation of murder seem so incongruous at the time. Her hair had grown out now to its natural shade, a brown so pale that it appeared nearly colorless. She was maybe thirty-five, thirty-six, and the years at the California Institute for Women had left no visible lines.

I didn't say anything at first; just opened the door and let her in.

"You know who I am," she said.

"I worked for your husband a couple of times."

She studied me carefully. "Was that the extent of it?"

I knew what she meant. "I was also there in court when you were being tried," I said. "But if you're asking if I was involved with him personally, the answer is no. He wasn't my type. No offense. Would you like coffee?"

She nodded, relaxing almost imperceptibly. I pulled the coffeepot from the bottom of the file cabinet and filled it from the Sparkletts water bottle behind the door. I liked it that she didn't protest the trouble I was going to. I put in a filter paper and ground coffee and plugged in the pot. The gurgling sound was comforting, like the pump in an aquarium.

Nikki sat very still, almost as though her emotional gears had been disengaged. She had no nervous mannerisms, didn't smoke or twist her hair. I sat down in my swivel chair.

"When were you released?"

"A week ago."

"What's freedom feel like?"

She shrugged. "It feels good, I guess, but I can survive the other way too. Better than you'd think."

I took a small carton of half-and-half out of the little refrigerator to my right. I keep clean mugs on top and I turned one over for each of us, filling them when the coffee was done. Nikki took hers with a murmured thanks.

"Maybe you've heard this one before," she went on, "but I didn't kill Laurence and I want you to find out who did."

"Why wait this long? You could have initiated an investigation from prison and maybe saved yourself some time."

She smiled faintly. "I've been claiming I was innocent for years. Who'd believe me? The minute I was indicted, I lost my credibility. I want that back. And I want to know who did me in."

I had thought her eyes were dark but I could see now that they were a metallic gray. Her look was level, flattened-out, as though some interior light were growing dim. She seemed to be a lady without much hope. I had never believed she was guilty myself but I couldn't remember what had made me so sure. She seemed passionless and I couldn't imagine her caring enough about anything to kill.

"You want to fill me in?"

She took a sip of coffee and then set the mug on the edge of my desk.

"I was married to Laurence for four years, a little more than that. He was unfaithful after the first six months. I don't know why it came as such a shock. Actually, that's how I got involved with him . . . when he was with his first wife, being unfaithful to her with me. There's a sort of egotism attached to being a mistress, I suppose. Anyway, I never expected to be in her shoes and I didn't like it much."

"According to the prosecutor, that's why you killed him."

"Look, they needed a conviction. I was it," she said with the first sign of energy. "I've just spent the last eight years with killers of one kind or another and believe me, the motive isn't apathy. You kill people you hate or you kill in rage or you kill to get even, but you don't kill someone you're indifferent to. By the time Laurence died, I didn't give a damn about him. I fell out of love with him the first time I found out about the other women. It took me a while to get it all out of my system . . ."

"And that's what the diary was all about?" I asked.

"Sure I kept track at first. I detailed every infidelity. I listened in on phone calls. I followed him around town. Then he started being more cautious about the whole thing and I started losing interest. I just didn't give a shit."

A flush had crept up to her cheeks and I gave her a moment to compose herself. "I know it looked like I killed him out of jealousy or rage, but I didn't care about that stuff. By the time he died, I just wanted to get on with my own life. I was going back to school, minding my own business. He went his way and I went mine . . ." Her voice trailed off.

"Who do you think killed him?"

"I think a lot of people wanted to. Whether they did or not is another matter. I mean, I could make a couple of educated guesses but I don't have proof of anything. Which is why I'm here."

I studied her for a moment. She was forthright and what she said made sense. Laurence Fife had been a difficult man. I hadn't been all that fond of him myself. If she was guilty, I couldn't see why she would stir it all up again. Her ordeal was over now and her so-called debt to society had been taken off the books except for whatever remaining parole she had to serve.

"Let me think about it some," I said. "I can get in touch with you later today and let you know."

"I'd appreciate that. I do have money. Whatever it takes."

"I don't want to be paid to rehash old business, Mrs. Fife. Even if we find out who did it, we have to make it stick and that could be tough after all this time. I'd like to check back through the files and see how it looks."

She took a manila folder out of her big leather bag. "I have some newspaper clippings. I can leave those with you if you like. That's the number where I can be reached."

We shook hands. Hers was cool and slight but her grip was strong. "Call me Nikki. Please."

"I'll be in touch," I said.

# "B" Is for Burglar

I'd been in the office no more than twenty minutes that morning. I'd opened the French doors out onto the second-floor balcony to let in some fresh air and I'd put on the coffee pot. It was June in Santa Teresa, which means chill morning fog and hazy afternoons. It wasn't nine o'clock yet. I was just sorting through the mail from the day before when I heard a tap at the door and a woman breezed in.

"Oh good. You're here," she said. "You must be Kinsey Millhone. I'm Beverly Danziger."

We shook hands and she promptly sat down and started rooting through her bag. She found a pack of filter-tipped cigarettes and shook one out.

"I hope you don't mind if I smoke," she said, lighting up without waiting for a response. She inhaled and then extinguished the match with a mouthful of smoke, idly searching about for an ashtray. I took one from the top of my file cabinet, dusted it off, and passed it over to her, offering her coffee at the same time.

"Oh sure, why not?" she said with a laugh, "I'm already hyper this morning so I might as well. I just drove up from Los Angeles, right through the rush-hour traffic. Gawd!"

I poured her a mug of coffee, doing a quick visual survey. She was in her late thirties by my guess; petite, energetic, well groomed. Her hair was a glossy black and quite straight. The cut was angular and perfectly layered so that it framed her small face like a bathing cap. She had bright blue eyes, black lashes, a clear complexion with just a hint of blusher high on each cheekbone. She wore a boat-necked sweater in a pale blue cotton knit, and a pale blue poplin skirt. The bag she carried was quality leather, soft and supple, with a number of zippered compartments containing God knows what. Her nails were long and tapered, painted a rosy pink and she wore a wedding ring studded with rubies. She projected self-confidence and a certain careless attention to style, conservatively packaged like the complimentary gift wrap in a classy department store.

She shook her head to the offer of cream and sugar so I added half-and-half to my own mug and got down to business.

"What can I help you with?"

"I'm hoping you can locate my sister for me," she said.

She was searching through her handbag again. She took out her address book, a rosewood pen-and-pencil set, and a long white envelope, which she placed on the edge of my desk.

"You'll want to make a note of the address and telephone number," she said. "Her name is Elaine Boldt. She has a condo on Via Madrina and that second one is her address in Florida. She spends several months a year down in Boca."

I was feeling somewhat puzzled, but I noted the addresses while she took a legal-looking document out of the long white envelope. She studied it briefly, as though the contents might have changed since she'd last seen it.

"How long has she been missing?" I asked.

Beverly Danziger gave me an uncomfortable look. "Well, I don't know if she's 'missing' exactly. I just don't know where she is and I've got to get these papers signed. I know it sounds dumb. She's only entitled to a ninth interest and it probably won't come to more than two or three thousand dollars, but the money can't be distributed until we have her notarized signature. Here, you can see for yourself."

I took the document and read through the contents. It had been drawn up by a firm of attorneys in Columbus, Ohio, and it was full of whereases, adjudgeds, ordereds, and whatnots, which added up to the fact that a man named Sidney Rowan had died and the various people listed were entitled to portions of his estate. Beverly Danziger was the third party listed, with a Los Angeles address, and Elaine Boldt was fourth, with an address here in Santa Teresa.

"Sidney Rowan was some kind of cousin," she went on garrulously. "I don't believe I ever met the man, but I got this notice and I assume Elaine got one too. I signed the form and got it notarized and sent it off and then didn't think any more about it. You can see from the cover letter that this all took place six months ago. Then, lo and behold I got a call last week from the attorney . . . what's his name again?"

I glanced at the document. "Wender," I said.

"Oh, that's right. I don't know why I keep blocking that. Anyway, Mr. Wender's office called to say they'd never heard from Elaine. Naturally, I assumed she'd gone off to Florida as usual and just hadn't bothered to have her mail sent, so I got in touch with the manager of her condominium here. She hasn't heard from Elaine in months. Well, she did at first, but not recently."

"Have you tried calling the Florida number?"

"From what I understand, the attorney tried several times. Apparently, she had a friend staying with her and Mr. Wender left his name and number, but

Elaine never called back. Tillie had about the same luck."

"Tillie?"

"The woman who managed the building here where Elaine has her permanent residence.

I was still taking notes, but I suppose the skepticism was showing in my face.

"What's the matter? Isn't this the sort of work you do?"

"Sure, but I charge thirty dollars an hour, plus expenses. If there's only two or three thousand dollars involved, I wonder if it's going to be worth it to you."

Beverly gave me a smile then, but it had a hard edge to it and I realized, at long last, that she was used to getting her way. Her eyes had widened to a china glaze, as blue and unyielding as glass. The black lashes blinked mechanically.

"Elaine and I are not on the best of terms," she said smoothly. "I feel I've already devoted quite enough time to this, but I promised Mr. Wender I'd find her so the estate can be settled. He's under pressure from the other heirs and he's putting pressure on me. I can give you an advance if you like."

She was back in her bag again, coming up with a checkbook this time. She uncapped the rosewood pen and stared at me.

"Will seven hundred and fifty dollars suffice?"

I reached into my bottom drawer. "I'll draw up a contract."

The neighborhood Elaine Boldt lived in was composed of modest 1930s bungalows mixed with occasional apartment complexes. There's a lot of money in Santa Teresa and much of it is devoted to maintaining a certain "look" to the town. There are no flashing neon signs, no slums, no fume-spewing manufacturing complexes to blight the landscape. Everything is stucco, red tile roofs, bougainvillea, distressed beams, adobe brick walls, arched windows, palm trees, balconies, ferns, fountains, paseos, and flowers in bloom. Historical restorations abound. It's all oddly unsettling—so lush and refined that it ruins you for anyplace else.

I passed through the courtyard and found myself in a glass-enclosed lobby with a row of mailboxes and door buzzers on the right. I gave "E. Boldt" a buzz first. For all I knew, she'd answer on the intercom and then my job would be done. Stranger things had happened and I didn't want to make a fool of myself looking high and low for a lady who might well by now be at home. There was no response so I tried Tillie Ahlberg.

After ten seconds, her voice crackled into the intercom as though the sound were being transmitted from outer space.

"Yes?"

I placed my mouth near the box, raising my voice slightly.

"Mrs. Ahlberg, my name is Kinsey Millhone. I'm a private detective here in town. Elaine Boldt's sister asked me to see if I could locate her and I wondered if I might talk to you."

There was a moment of white noise and then a reluctant reply.

"Well. I suppose. I was on my way out, but I guess ten minutes won't hurt. I'm on the ground floor. Come through the door to the right of the elevator and it's down at the end of the hall to the left." The buzzer sounded and I pushed through the glass doors.

Tillie Ahlberg was probably in her sixties, with apricot-tinted hair in a permanent wave that looked as if it had just been done. The curl must have been a little frizzier than she liked because she was pulling on a crocheted cotton cap. An unruly fringe of apricot hair was still peeking out, like Ronald McDonald's, and she was in the process of tucking it away. Her eyes were hazel and there was a powdery patina of pale ginger freckles on her face. She wore a shapeless skirt, hose, and running shoes, and she looked like she was capable of covering ground when she wanted to.

"I hope I didn't seem unsociable," she said comfortably. "But if I don't get to the market first thing in the morning, I lose heart."

"It shouldn't take long anyway," I said. "Can you tell me when you last heard from Mrs. Boldt? Is she Miss or Mrs.?"

"Mrs. She's a widow, though she's only forty-three years old. She was married to a man who had a string of manufacturing plants down south. As I understand it, he dropped dead of a heart attack three years ago and left her a bundle. That's when she bought this place. Here, have a seat if you like."

Tillie moved off to the right, leading the way into a living room furnished with antique reproductions. A gauzy golden light came through the pale yellow sheers and I could still smell the remnants of breakfast: bacon and coffee and something laced with cinnamon.

Having established that she was in a hurry, she seemed ready to give me as much time as I wanted. She sat down on an ottoman and I took a wooden rocking chair.

"I understand she's usually in Florida this time of year," I said.

"Well, yes. She's got another condominium down there. In Boca Raton, wherever that is. Near Fort Lauderdale, I guess. I've never been to Florida myself, so these towns are all just names to me. Anyhow, she usually goes down around the first of February and comes back to California late July or early August. She likes the heat, she says."

"She didn't mention taking a side trip or anything like that?"

"Not a word. Of course, it's none of my business in the first place."

"Did she seem distressed?"

Tillie smiled ruefully. "Well, it's hard to seem upset on the message side of a postcard, you know. There isn't but that much room. She sounded fine to me."

"Do you have any guesses about where she might be?"

"Not a one. All I know is it's not like her not to write. I tried calling four or five times. Once some woman friend of hers answered but she was real abrupt and after that, there wasn't anything at all."

"Who was the friend? Anyone you knew?"

"No, but now I don't know who she knows in Boca. It could have been anyone. I didn't make a note of the name and wouldn't know it if you said it to me right this minute."

"What about the mail she's been getting? Are her bills still coming in?"

She shrugged at that. "It looks that way to me. I haven't paid much attention. I just shipped on whatever came in. I do have a few I was about to forward if you'd like to see them." She got up and crossed to an oak secretary, opening one of the glass doors by turning the key in the lock. She took out a short stack of envelopes and sorted through them, then handed them to me. "This is the kind of thing she usually gets."

I did the same quick sorting job. Visa, MasterCard, Saks Fifth Avenue. A furrier named Jacques with an address in Boca Raton. A bill from a John Pickett, D.D.S., Inc., right around the corner on Arbol. No personal letters at all.

"Does she pay utility bills from here too?" I asked.

"I already sent those this month."

"Could she have been arrested?"

That sparked a laugh. "Oh no. Not her. She wasn't anything like that. She didn't drive a car, you know, but she wasn't the type to get so much as a jaywalking ticket."

"But there are lots of explanations for where she might be," I said. "She's an adult. Apparently she's got money and no pressing business. She really doesn't have to notify anybody of her whereabouts if she doesn't want to. She might be on a cruise. Or maybe she's taken a lover and absconded with him. Maybe she and this girl friend of hers took off on a toot. It might never occur to her that anyone was trying to get in touch."

"That's why I haven't really done anything so far, but it doesn't sit well with me. I don't think she'd leave without a word to anyone."

"Well, let me look into it. I don't want to hold you up right now, but I'll want to see her apartment at some point," I said. I got up and Tillie rose automatically. I shook her hand and thanked her for her help.

"Hang on to the mail for the time being, if you would," I said. "I'm going to chase down some other possibilities, but I'll get back to you in a day or two and let you know what I've come up with. I don't think there's any reason to worry."

"I hope not," Tillie said. "She's a wonderful person."

I gave Tillie my card before we parted company. I wasn't worried yet myself, but my curiosity had been aroused and I was eager to get on with it.


## "C" Is for Corpse


I met Bobby Callahan on Monday of that week. By Thursday, he was dead. He was convinced someone was trying to kill him and it turned out to be true, but none of us figured it out in time to save him. I've never worked for a dead man before and I hope I won't have to do it again. This report is for him, for whatever it's worth.

It was August and I'd been working out at Santa Teresa Fitness, trying to remedy the residual effects of a broken left arm. The days were hot, filled with relentless sunshine and clear skies. I was feeling cranky and bored, doing push-downs and curls and wrist rolls. I'd just worked two cases back-to-back and I'd sustained more damage than a fractured humerus. I was feeling emotionally battered and I needed a rest. Fortunately, my bank account was fat and I knew I could afford to take two months off. At the same time, the idleness was making me restless and the physical-therapy regimen was driving me nuts.

Santa Teresa Fitness is a real no-nonsense place: the brand X of health clubs. No Jacuzzi, no sauna, no music piped in. Just mirrored walls, body-building equipment, and industrial-grade carpeting the color of asphalt. The whole twenty-eight-hundred square feet of space smells like men's jockstraps.

Bobby Callahan came in at the same time I did. I wasn't sure what had happened to him, but whatever it was, it had hurt. He was probably just short of six feet tall, with a football player's physique: big head, thick neck, brawny shoulders, heavy legs. Now the shaggy blond head was held to one side, the left half of his face pulled down in a permanent grimace. His mouth leaked saliva as though he'd just been shot up with Novocain and couldn't quite feel his own lips. He tended to hold his left arm up against his waist and he usually carried a folded white handkerchief that he used to mop up his chin. There was a terrible welt of dark red across the bridge of his nose, a second across his chest, and his knees were crisscrossed with scars as though a swordsman had slashed at him. He walked with a lilting gait, his left Achilles tendon apparently shortened, pulling his left heel up. Working out must have cost him everything he had, yet he never failed to appear. There was a doggedness about him that I admired. I watched him with interest, ashamed of my own interior complaints. Clearly, I could recover from my injuries while he could not. I didn't feel sorry for him, but I did feel curious.

That Monday morning was the first time we'd been alone together in the gym. He was doing leg curls, facedown on the bench next to mine, his attention turned inward. I watched him do a set of twelve repetitions and then start all over again.

"I hear you're a private detective," he said without missing a beat. "That true?" There was a slight drag to his voice, but he covered it pretty well.

"Yes. Are you in the market for one?"

"Matter of fact, I am. Somebody tried to kill me."

"Looks like they didn't miss by much. When was this?"

"Nine months ago."

"Why you?"

"Don't know."

"How'd it happen?"

"I was driving up the pass with a buddy of mine late at night. Some car came up and started ramming us from behind. When we got to the bridge just over the crest of the hill, I lost it and we went off. Rick was killed. He bailed out and the car rolled over on him. I should have been killed too. Longest ten seconds of my life, you know?"

"I bet." The bridge he's soared off spanned a rocky, scrub-choked canyon, four hundred feet deep, a favorite jumping-off spot for suicide attempts. Actually, I'd never heard of anyone surviving that drop. "You're doing great," I said. "You've been working your butt off."

"I was out at Rehab for eight months and now I'm doing this. What happened to you?"

"Some asshole shot me in the arm."

Bobby laughed. It was a wonderful snuffling sound. He finished the last rep and propped himself up on his elbows.

He said, "I got four machines to go and then let's bug out. By the way, I'm Bobby Callahan."

"Kinsey Millhone."

He held his hand out and we shook, sealing an unspoken bargain. I knew even then I'd work for him whatever the circumstances.

We ate lunch in a health-food café, one of those places specializing in cunning imitation meat patties that never fool anyone. Eating, for Bobby, was the same laborious process as working out, but his single-minded attention to the task allowed me to study him at close range. His hair was sunbleached and coarse, his eyes brown with the kind of lashes most women have to buy in a box. The left half of his face was inanimate, but he had a strong chin, accentuated by a scar like a rising moon. My guess was that his teeth had been driven through his lower lip at some point during the punishing descent into that ravine. How he'd lived through it all was anybody's guess.

He glanced up. He knew I'd been staring, but he didn't object.

"You're lucky to be alive," I said.

"I'll tell you the worst of it. Big hunks of my brain are gone, you know?" The drag in his speech was back, as though the very subject affected his voice. "I was in a coma for two weeks, and when I came out, I didn't know what the fuck was going on. I still don't. But I can remember how I used to be and that's what hurts. I was smart, Kinsey. I knew a lot. I could concentrate and I used to have ideas. My mind would make these magic little leaps. You know what I mean?"

I nodded. I know about minds making magic little leaps.

He went on. "Now I got gaps and spaces. Holes. I've lost big pieces of my past. They don't exist anymore." He paused to dab impatiently at his chin, then shot a bitter glance at the handkerchief.

"You're convinced it was a murder attempt? Why couldn't it have been some prankster or a drunk?"

He thought for a moment. "I knew the car. At least I think I did. Obviously, I don't anymore, but it seems like . . . at the time, I recognized the vehicle."

"How do you know Rick wasn't meant to be the victim instead of you?"

He pushed his plate away and signaled for coffee. He was struggling. "I knew something. Something had happened and I figured it out. I remember that much. I can even remember knowing I was in trouble. I was scared. I just don't remember why."

Bobby glanced up. The waitress was standing at his elbow with a coffeepot. He waited until she'd poured coffee for both of us. She departed and he smiled uneasily. "I don't know who my enemies are, you know? I don't know if people around me know this 'thing' I've forgotten about. I don't want anyone to overhear what I say . . . just in case. I know I'm paranoid, but I can't help it."

I sat and stared at him for a while, trying to get a fix on the situation. I stirred what was probably raw milk into my coffee. Health-food enthusiasts like eating microbes and things like that. "Do you have any sense at all of how long you'd known this thing? Because I'm wondering . . . if it was potentially so dangerous . . . why you didn't spill the beans right away."

He was looking at me with interest. "Like what? To the cops or something like that?"

"Sure. If you stumbled across a theft of some kind, or you found out someone was a Russian spy . . ." I was rattling off possibilities as they occurred to me. "Or you uncovered a plot to assassinate the President . . ."

"Why wouldn't I have picked up the first telephone I came to and called for help?"

"Right."

He was quiet. "Maybe I did that. Maybe . . . shit, Kinsey, I don't know. You don't know how frustrated I get. Early on, those first two, three months in the hospital, all I could think about was the pain. It took everything I had to stay alive. I didn't think about the accident at all. But little by little, as I got better, I started going back to it, trying to remember what happened. Especially when they told me Rick was dead. I didn't find out about that for weeks. I guess they were worried I'd blame myself and it would slow my recovery. I did feel sick about it once I heard. What if I was drunk and just ran off the road? I had to find out what went on or I knew I'd go crazy on top of everything else. Anyway, that's when I began to piece together this other stuff."

"Maybe the rest of it will come back to you if you've remembered this much."

"But that's just it," he said. "What if it does come back? I figure the only thing keeping me alive right now is the fact that I can't remember any more of it."

"Have you tried the cops?"

"Sure, I've tried. As far as they're concerned, it was an accident. They have no evidence a crime was committed.

"Maybe you should hire a bodyguard—"

"Screw that! It's you I want."

"Bobby, I'm not saying I won't help you. Of course I will. I'm just talking about your options. It sounds like you need more than me."

He leaned forward, his manner intense. "Just get to the bottom of this. Tell me what's going on. I want to know why somebody's after me and I want them stopped. Then I won't need the cops or a bodyguard or anything else." He clamped his mouth shut, agitated. He rocked back.

"Fuck it," he said. He shifted restlessly and got up. He pulled a twenty out of his wallet and tossed it on the table. He started for the door with that lilting gait, his limp more pronounced than I'd seen it. I grabbed my handbag and caught up with him.

"God, slow down. Let's go back to my office and we'll type up a contract."

He held the door open for me and I went out.

"I hope you can afford my services," I said back over my shoulder.

He smiled faintly. "Don't sweat it."

We turned left, moving toward the parking lot.

"Sorry I lost my temper," he murmured.

"Quit that. I don't give a shit."

"I wasn't sure you'd take me seriously," he said.

"Why wouldn't I?"

"My family thinks I've got a screw loose."

"Yeah, well, that's why you hired me instead of them."

"Thanks," he whispered. He tucked his hand through my arm and I glanced over at him. His face was suffused with pink and there were tears in his eyes. He dashed at them carelessly, not looking at me. For the first time, I realized how young he was. God, he was just a kid, banged up, bewildered, scared to death.

We walked back to my car slowly and I was conscious of the stares of the curious, faces averted with pity and uneasiness. It made me want to punch somebody out.

## "D" Is for Deadbeat

Later, I found out his name was John Daggett, but that's not how he introduced himself the day he walked into my office. Even at the time, I sensed that something was off, but I couldn't figure out what it was. The job he hired me to do seemed simple enough, but then the bum tried to stiff me for my fee. When you're self-employed, you can't afford to let these things slide. Word gets out and first thing you know, everybody thinks you can be had. I went after him for the money and the next thing I knew, I was caught up in events I still haven't quite recovered from.

It was late October, the day before Halloween, and the weather was mimicking autumn in the Midwest—clear and sunny and cool. Driving into town, I could have sworn I smelled woodsmoke in the air and I half expected the leaves to be turning yellow and rust. All I actually saw were the same old palm trees, the same relentless green everywhere. The fires of summer had been contained and the rains hadn't started yet. It was a typical California *un*season, but it *felt* like fall and I was responnding with inordinate good cheer, thinking maybe I'd drive up the pass in the afternoon to the pistol range, which is what I do for laughs.

I'd come into the office that Saturday morning to take care of some bookkeeping chores—paying personal bills, getting out my statements for the month. I had my calculator out, a Redi-Receipt form in the type-writer, and four completed statements lined up, addressed and stamped, on the desk, to my left. I was so intent on the task at hand that I didn't realize anyone was standing in the doorway until the man cleared his throat. I reacted with one of those little jumps you do when you open the evening paper and a spider runs out. He apparently found this amusing, but I was having to pat myself on the chest to get my heart rate down again.

"I'm Alvin Limardo," he said. "Sorry if I startled you."

"That's all right," I said, "I just had no idea you were standing there. Are you looking for me?"

"If you're Kinsey Millhone, I am."

I got up and shook hands with him across the desk and then suggested that he take a seat. My first fleeting second glance, I couldn't find anything in particular to support the idea.

He was in his fifties, too gaunt for good health. His face was long and narrow, his chin pronounced. His hair was an ash gray, clipped short, and he smelled of citrus cologne. His eyes were hazel, his gaze remote. The suit he wore was an odd shade of green. His hands seemed huge, fingers long and bony, the knuckles enlarged. The two inches of narrow wrist extending, cuffless, from his coat sleeves suggested shabbiness though his clothing didn't really look worn. He held a slip of paper which he'd folded twice, and he fiddled with that self-consciously.

"What can I do for you?" I asked.

"I'd like for you to deliver this." He smoothed out the piece of paper then and placed it on my desk. It was a cashier's check drawn on a Los Angeles bank, dated October 29, and made out to someone named Tony Gahan for twenty-five thousand dollars.

I tried not to appear as surprised as I felt. He didn't look like a man with money to spare. Maybe he'd borrowed the sum from Gahan and was paying it back. "You want to tell me what this is about?"

"He did me a favor. I want to say thanks. That's all it is."

"It must have been quite a favor," I said. "Do you mind if I ask what he did?"

"He showed me a kindness when I was down on my luck."

"What do you need me for?"

He smiled briefly. "An attorney would charge me a hundred and twenty dollars an hour to handle it. I'm assuming you'd charge considerably less."

"So would a messenger service," I said. "It's cheaper still if you do it yourself." I wasn't being a smart-mouth about it. I really didn't understand why he needed a private detective.

He cleared his throat. "I tried that, but I'm not entirely certain of Mr. Gahan's current address. At one time, he lived on Stanley Place, but he's not there now. I went by this morning and the house is empty. It looks like it hasn't been lived in for a while. I want someone to track him down and make sure he gets the money. If you can estimate what that might run me, I'll pay you in advance."

"I'd be happier if you'd tell me what's going on."

This was where he hooked me, because what he said was just offbeat enough to be convincing. Liar that I am, it still didn't occur to me that there could be so much falsehood mixed in with the truth.

"I got into trouble with the law awhile back and served some time. Tony Gahan was helpful to me just before I was arrested. He had no idea of my circumstances so he wasn't an accessory or anything, nor would you be. I feel indebted."

"Why not take care of it yourself?"

He hesitated, almost shyly I thought. "It's sort of like that Charles Dickens book, *Great Expectations*. He might not like having a convicted felon for a benefactor. People have strange ideas about ex-cons."

"What if he won't accept an anonymous donation?"

"You can return the check in that case and keep the fee."

I shifted restlessly in my chair. What's wrong with this picture, I asked myself. "Where'd you get the money if you've been in jail?"

"Santa Anita. I'm still on parole and I shouldn't be playing the ponies at all, but I find it hard to resist. That's why I'd like to pass the money on to you. I'm a gambling man. I can't have that kind of cash around or I'll piss it away, if you'll pardon my French." He closed his mouth then and looked at me, waiting to see what else I might ask. Clearly, he didn't want to volunteer more than was necessary to satisfy my qualms, but he seemed amazingly patient. I realized later, of course, that his tolerance was probably the function of his feeding me so much bullshit. He must have been entertained by the game he was playing. Lying is fun. I can do it all day myself.

"What was the felony?" I asked.

He dropped his gaze, addressing his reply to his oversized hands, which were folded in his lap. "I don't think that pertains. This money is clean and I came by it honestly. There's nothing illegal about the transaction if that's what's worrying you."

Of *course* it worried me, but I wondered if I was being too fastidious. There was nothing wrong with his request on the face of it. I chased the proposition around in my head with caution, wondering what Tony Gahan had done for Limardo that would net him this kind of payoff. None of my business, I supposed, as long as no laws had been broken in the process. Intuition was telling me to turn this guy down, but it happens that the rent on my apartment was due the next day. I had the money in my checking account, but it seemed providential to have a retainer drop in my lap unexpectedly. In any event, I didn't see a reason to refuse. "All right," I said.

He nodded once, pleased. "Good."

He stood up and I did too, moving with him as he walked toward the door. With both of us on our feet, I could see how much taller he was than I . . . maybe six-four to my five-foot-six. He paused with his hand on the knob, gazing down at me with the same remote stare.

"One other thing you might need to know about Tony Gahan," he said.

"What's that?"

"He's fifteen years old."

I stood there and watched Alvin Limardo move off down the hall. I should have called him back, folks. I should have known right then that it wasn't going to turn out well.

## "E" Is for Evidence

The minute I stepped into Mac's office, I knew something was wrong. I've know Maclin Voorhies since I started working for California Fidelity nearly ten years ago. He's in his sixties now, with a lean, dour face. He has sparse gray hair that stands out around his head like dandelion fuzz, big ears with drooping lobes, a bulbous nose, and small black eyes under unruly white brows. His body seems misshapen: long legs, short waist, narrow shoulders, arms too long for the average sleeve length. He's smart, capable, stingy with praise, humorless, and devoutly Catholic, which translates out to a thirty-five-year marriage and eight kids, all grown. I've never seen him smoke a cigar, but he's usually chewing on a stub, the resultant tobacco stains tarnishing his teeth to the color of old toilet bowls.

I took my cue not so much from his expression, which was no darker than usual, but from Andy's, standing just to his left. Andy and I don't get along that well under the best of circumstances. At forty-two, he's an ass-kisser, always trying to maneuver situations so that he can look good. He has a moon-shaped face and his collar looks too tight and everything else about him annoys me, too. Some people just affect me that way. At that moment he seemed both restless and smug, studiously avoiding eye contact.

Mac was leafing through the file. He glanced over at Andy with impatience. "Don't you have some work to do?"

"What? Oh sure. I thought you wanted me in this meeting."

"I'll take care of it. I'm sure you're overloaded as it is."

Andy murmured something that made it sound like leaving was his big idea. Mac shook his head and sighed slightly as the door closed. I watched him roll the cigar stub from one corner of his mouth to the other. He looked up with surprise, as if he'd just realized I was standing there. "You want to fill me in on this?"

I told him what had transpired to date, sidestepping the fact that the file had sat on Darcy's desk for three days before it came to me. I wasn't necessarily protecting her. In business, it's smarter not to bad-mouth the help. I told him I had two rolls of film coming in, that there weren't any estimates yet, but the claim looked routine as far as I could see. I debated mention of my uneasiness, but discarded the idea even as I was speaking. I hadn't identified what was bothering me and I felt it was wiser to stick to the facts.

The frown on Mac's face formed about thirty seconds into my recital, but what alarmed me was the silence that fell when I was done. Mac is a man who fires questions. Mac gives pop quizzes. He seldom sits and stares as he was doing in this case.

"You want to tell me what this is about?" I asked.

"Did you see the note attached to the front of this file?"

"What note? There wasn't any note," I said.

He held out a California Fidelity memo form, maybe three inches by five, covered with Jewel's curlicue script. "Kinsey . . . this one looks like a stinker. Sorry I don't have time to fill you in, but the fire chief's report spells it out. He said to call if he can give you any help. J."

"This wasn't attached to the file when it came to me."

"What about the fire department report? Wasn't that in there?"

"Of course it was. That's the first thing I read."

Mac's expression was aggrieved. He handed me the file, open to the fire-department report. I looked down at the familiar STFD form. The incidental information was just as I remembered. The narrative account I'd never seen before. The fire chief, John Dudley, had summed up his investigation with a no-nonsense statement of suspected arson. The newspaper clipping now attached to the file ended with a line to the same effect.

I could feel my face heat, the icy itch of fear beginning to assert itself. I said, "This isn't the report I saw." My voice had dropped into a range I scarcely recognized. He held his hand out and I returned the file.

"I got a phone call this morning," he said. "Somebody says you're on the take."

I stared. "What?"

"You got anything to say?"

"That's absurd. Who called?"

"Let's not worry about that for the moment."

"Mac, come on. Somebody's accusing me of a criminal act and I want to know who it is."

He said nothing, but his face shut down in that stubborn way of his.

"All right, skip that," I said, yielding the point. I thought it was better to get the story out before I worried about the characters. "What did this unindentified caller say?"

He leaned back in his chair, studying the cold coin of ash on the end of his cigar. "Somebody saw you accept an envelope from Lance Wood's secretary," he said.

"Bullshit. When?"

"Last Friday."

I had a quick flash of Heather calling to me as I left the plant. "Those were inventory sheets. I asked Lance Wood to have them ready for me and he left 'em in his out box."

"What inventory sheets?"

"Right there in the file."

He shook his head, leafing through. From where I stood, I could see there were only two or three loose papers clipped in on one side. There was nothing resembling the inventory sheets I'd punched and inserted. He looked up at me. "What about the interview with Wood?"

"I haven't done that yet. An emergency came up and he disappeared. I'm supposed to set up an appointment with him for today."

"What time?"

"Well, I don't know. I haven't called him yet. I was trying to get the report typed up first." I couldn't seem to avoid the defensiveness in my tone.

"This the envelope?" Mac was holding the familiar envelope with the Wood/Warren logo, only now there was a message jotted on the front. "Hope this will suffice for now. Balance to follow as agreed."

"Goddamn it, Mac. You can't be serious! If I were taking a payoff, why would I leave that in the file?"

No answer. I tried again. "You really think Lance Wood paid me off?"

"I don't think anything except we better look into it. For your sake as well as ours . . ."

"If I took money, where'd it go?"

"I don't know, Kinsey. You tell me. If it was cash, it wouldn't be that hard to conceal."

"I'd have to be a fool! I'd have to be an idiot and so would he. If he's going to bribe me, do you think he'd be stupid enough to put the cash in an envelope and write a note to that effect! Mac, this whole thing has frame-up written all over it!"

"Why would anyone do that?" At this point, his manner wasn't accusatory. He seemed genuinely puzzled at the very idea. "Who would go to such lengths?"

"How do I know? Maybe I just got caught in the loop. Maybe Lance Wood is the target. You know I'd never do such a thing. I'll bring you my bank statements. You can scrutinize my accounts. Check under my mattress, for God's sake. . . ." I broke off in confusion.

I saw his mouth move, but I didn't hear the rest of what he said. I could feel the trap close and something suddenly made sense. In the morning mail, I'd gotten notice about five thousand dollars credited to my account. I think I knew now what that was about.

## ABOUT THE AUTHOR

SUE GRAFTON has written novels, articles, short fiction, a screen-play, and numerous teleplays. She has also lectured on writing at colleges and conferences in Southern California and the Midwest. Her first mystery, *"A" Is for Alibi,* won an award from the Cloak and Clue Society of Wisconsin. *"B" Is for Burglar* won both the Anthony and the Shamus awards for best novel of 1985, and *"C" Is for Corpse* won the Anthony Award for Best Novel in 1986. "The Parker Shotgun" won a Macavity Award from the Mystery Readers of America and an Anthony for Best Short Story of 1986. Grafton, who was born in Louisville, Kentucky, now lives in Southern California with her husband, Steven Humphrey.

# Kinsey Millhone is...

"The best new private eye."  —*The Detroit News*

"A tough-cookie with a soft center."  —*Newsweek*

"A stand-out specimen of the new female operatives."
—*Philadelphia Inquirer*

# Sue Grafton is...

The Shamus and Anthony Award winning creator of Kinsey Millhone and quite simply one of the hottest new mystery writers around.